PRAISE FOR LUCINDA BERRY

OFF THE DEEP END

"As usual, Berry tightens the screws smartly in the opening pages and never lets up, and as usual, her ending is more intent on deepening the nightmare than providing a plausible explanation for it. Warning: the title applies as much to the audience as to the characters."

—*Kirkus Reviews*

"As the suspense mounts, the action drives to a harrowing conclusion. Berry delivers the goods."

—*Publishers Weekly*

"A well-done mystery with a plausible yet surprising ending."

—*Library Journal*

UNDER HER CARE

"The action never wavers, and the surprises are unending. Berry is writing at the top of her game."

—*Publishers Weekly* (starred review)

"[It's] a humdinger . . . Perfect for suspense fans."

—*Publishers Weekly*

"Lucinda delivers every time. Unputdownable."

—Tarryn Fisher, *New York Times* bestselling author

"Lucinda Berry's latest, *Under Her Care*, is her best thriller yet! A dark, riveting read that will keep you up late, racing to the chilling end."
—Kaira Rouda, *USA Today* bestselling author of *The Next Wife* and *Somebody's Home*

"Lucinda Berry's *Under Her Care* is stunning, diabolical, and gripping, with one of the best and most gasp-worthy twists I have read in a very long time. Fast paced, fabulous, and enthralling, the pages practically turn themselves. Absolutely captivating."
—Lisa Regan, *USA Today* and *Wall Street Journal* bestselling author

"Creepy and chilling, *Under Her Care* is a tense page-turner that leaves you questioning everything you ever knew about motherhood and the family bond."
—Tara Laskowski, award-winning author of *The Mother Next Door*

THE SECRETS OF US

"Those looking for an emotional roller-coaster ride will be rewarded."
—*Publishers Weekly*

"Combine Lucinda Berry's deep understanding of the complexities of the human mind with her immense talent for storytelling and you have *The Secrets of Us*, an intense psychological thriller that kept my heart racing until the shocking, jaw-dropping conclusion. Bravo!"
—T. R. Ragan, *New York Times* bestselling author

"*The Secrets of Us* is an unputdownable page-turner with two compelling female protagonists that will keep readers on their toes. Fantastic!"
—Cate Holahan, *USA Today* bestselling author of *One Little Secret*

"Lucinda Berry's *The Secrets of Us* is a tense psychological thriller that explores the dark corners of the mind and turns a mind can take when it harbors secret guilt. The interplay between sisters Krystal and Nichole and their hidden past is gradually revealed, and in the end, the plot twists keep coming. Right and wrong can be ambivalent, and this story explores all shades of gray, from their dysfunctional family to an old childhood friend to a husband who may or may not be too good to be true. Berry's background as a clinical psychologist shines in this novel with a character so disturbed they spend time in seclusion lockdown at a psychiatric ward. Don't miss this one!"
—Debbie Herbert, *USA Today* and Amazon Charts bestselling author

"*The Secrets of Us* is an utterly gripping, raw, and heartbreaking story of two sisters. Berry's flawlessly placed clues and psychological expertise grab you from the first word, not letting go until the last. Compelling, intricate, and shocking, this inventive thriller cleverly weaves from past to present with stunning precision. I was absolutely enthralled."
—Samantha M. Bailey, *USA Today* and #1 national bestselling author
of *Woman on the Edge*

"The past and present collide with explosive consequences in this addictive, twisty thriller from an author at the top of her game. *The Secrets of Us* grips from the first page and doesn't let go until the final shocking twist."
—Lisa Gray, bestselling author of *Dark Highway*

THE BEST OF FRIENDS

"A mother's worst nightmare on the page. For those who dare."
—*Kirkus Reviews*

"*The Best of Friends* gripped me from the stunning opening to the emotional, explosive ending. In this moving novel, Berry creates a beautifully crafted study of secrets and grief among a tight-knit group of friends and of how far a mother will go to discover the truth and protect her children."

—Heather Gudenkauf, *New York Times* bestselling author of *The Weight of Silence* and *This Is How I Lied*

"In *The Best of Friends*, Berry starts with a heart-stopping bang—the dreaded middle-of-the-night phone call—and then delivers a dark and gritty tale that unfolds twist by devastating twist. Intense, terrifying, and at times utterly heartbreaking. Absolutely unputdownable."

—Kimberly Belle, international bestselling author of *Dear Wife* and *Stranger in the Lake*

THE PERFECT CHILD

"I am a compulsive reader of literary novels . . . but there was one book that kept me reading, the sort of novel I can't put down . . . *The Perfect Child*, by Lucinda Berry. It speaks to the fear of every parent: What if your child was a psychopath? This novel takes it a step further. A couple, desperate for a child, has the chance to adopt a beautiful little girl who, they are told, has been abused. They're told it might take a while for her to learn to behave and trust people. She can be sweet and loving, and in public she is adorable. But in private—well, I won't give away what happens. But needless to say, it's chilling."

—Gina Kolata, *New York Times*

KEEP
YOUR
FRIENDS
CLOSE

OTHER TITLES BY LUCINDA BERRY

KEEP YOUR FRIENDS CLOSE

LUCINDA BERRY

THOMAS & MERCER

Published by Thomas & Mercer, Seattle

www.apub.com

Amazon, the Amazon logo, and Thomas & Mercer are trademarks of Amazon.com, Inc., or its affiliates.

ISBN-13: 9781662512605 (paperback)
ISBN-13: 9781662512599 (digital)

Front cover design by Olga Grlic
Back cover design by Faceout Studio, Amanda Kreutzer
Cover image: © agrobacter / Getty

Printed in the United States of America

To the most supportive group of people I've ever met.
This one's for you #BookTok.

Women bond over secrets. That's what female friendships are made of—shared secrets. It doesn't matter if they're yours or somebody else's. You want to know the hidden parts of a woman's life? The things she keeps tucked away from the outside world? Ask her best friend. She knows all her secrets.

CHAPTER ONE

NOW

BROOKE

"How does a woman drown in her own backyard with a house packed full of people?" the police officer asked, peering down at me. I shivered on the edge of the bed and tried to keep my eyes focused on his. Whitney's sobs cut through the walls of the guesthouse. She hadn't stopped wailing since they pulled Kiersten's body out of the pool. Kiersten's vomit stained my lips like someone had thrown up in my face. It didn't matter if I breathed through my nose or my mouth—the putrid smell made its way inside me. I was her last kiss.

The paramedics hadn't put their lips on top of hers. Kiersten's lips were already blue by the time they arrived. They'd thrown me off her and wasted no time jabbing a tube down her throat and pumping air into her lungs.

My wet clothes stuck to me like rot, and I wanted to rip them off, but the police wouldn't let me change. They'd given me a towel, but that was it. They hadn't let anyone out of the guesthouse since they'd herded us in here ten minutes ago. The main house was officially a crime scene, and none of us were allowed to touch it.

Emergency vehicles surrounded the property. Their lights danced and sparkled like Christmas bulbs in the windows. But this wasn't Christmas, and there wasn't an emergency. Not anymore. They were too late.

"Maybe you can help us start figuring this mess out, Mrs. Lyons?" the police officer continued after a few beats had passed and I still hadn't spoken. I stared at the badge on his puffed-out chest: BEVERLY HILLS POLICE DEPARTMENT. My teeth chattered against each other as I finally spoke for the first time since he'd brought me into the bedroom. "None of this makes any sense to me either. None of it."

"Well, we have to start somewhere, and you're a logical starting point since you were the one trying to save her when we arrived." I stiffened at his choice of words. I didn't want that responsibility. Never did. He noticed my reaction and quickly continued. "And also the fact that you're the only one around here not losing their shit at the moment." He smiled and let out a small laugh, trying to lighten the mood, but it wasn't funny.

Suddenly, a woman broke into the room and pushed him aside like she was annoyed with his approach. He was dressed in the standard police uniform, but she was in regular business clothes. Expensive ones. Bitchy-boss vibes emanated from her. She folded her arms across her chest and propped her leg up on the bed frame. Doc Martens peeked out from underneath her pants. "Ethan's right, you know." She motioned over her shoulder at him, and he gave me a knowing nod. "You're the only person keeping it together around here. Do you have a medical background?"

I shook my head and fought the urge to break away from her penetrating eyes. Ten years of Catholic school had trained me well in keeping still and not looking away.

"Humph . . . ," she said like she was genuinely surprised by it, but I wasn't buying her act. Any more than she was probably buying mine.

"It's usually people with a history of working in the medical field that are so calm around dead bodies."

"There was only one," I blurted without thinking.

She cocked her head like she was confused. Her long ponytail flopped to the other side of her head. "Excuse me?"

"You said dead bodies." I blushed, feeling suddenly embarrassed. "That's plural."

"You're right, I did." A smile played at the corner of her lips. I couldn't tell if she was playing with me or genuinely amused. Either way, it made me uncomfortable. "Your response to all this sure is interesting, Mrs. Lyons."

"Maybe I'm just in shock," I said, even though I wasn't, but she didn't know that. She didn't know anything about me. I shrugged. "Everyone responds to stress differently."

Three months ago, I would've been just like everyone else outside this bedroom door—hysterical and sobbing, falling to pieces on the newly remodeled floor. But I was unshockable. After the worst thing happened to you, you weren't afraid of bad things happening anymore. It wasn't like Natasha's bloodcurdling scream hadn't startled me like everyone else. It absolutely did. There was no way that it couldn't. I'd never heard anyone scream like that before, and it came out of nowhere.

I raced outside along with my friends, but Kiersten's body floating facedown in the swimming pool hadn't affected me like it had them. All I could think about was how buoyant she looked. The way she just bobbed in the water like she was doing the dead man's float they'd taught us in swimming lessons when we were kids. What kind of a cruel person thought something like that about her friend? While the others spiraled into panic, that's what I was doing, cut off from my emotions. Completely removed. I never used to be this way, but I didn't know who I was anymore.

That was the scariest part.

CHAPTER TWO

NOW

WHITNEY

The bedroom door opened. An officer led Brooke out. She was still wrapped in a dirty white towel. She lifted her head and scanned the room. Her eyes landed on mine. They were dead inside. Just like her.

She shouldn't even be here. What was she doing here anyway? This was all her fault.

I leaped from the couch and lunged for her, but Jade jumped up and grabbed me before I could reach her, pulling me back. I flailed wildly at Brooke. I just wanted to hurt her. Pummel her calm-looking face with my fists. Somebody had to pay for this.

"Whit, stop, just stop," Jade cried out, struggling to hold me back. I flung her off and went after Brooke again. The officer jumped in front of Brooke, blocking her with his body. He grabbed my shoulders and held me back.

"Young lady," he said sternly even though he was way younger than me, "how about you come with me and take a minute to get settled down?" But it wasn't a question. It was a direct order. I shot Brooke daggers with my eyes over his shoulder. This wasn't over.

He led me like a scolded child into the guest bedroom and shut the door behind us. Kiersten's energy flooded me. This room was all her. She'd spent weeks poring over websites and Pinterest boards with her designer trying to pick the perfect furnishings and colors for the space. Her home was a safe haven for people. That's how she saw it. That's how she wanted it to be. Safe and comfortable. She was so kind. Caring. So nice. Everyone loved her. Such a bright light in a world filled with so much darkness.

And now she was gone. Just like that. Her light snuffed out.

Kiersten.

Heaving sobs surged through me.

But we were just having a party. A moms' night out.

We were in the middle of a party.

Kiersten's party.

Ohmigod. Kiersten.

My legs folded underneath me. The officer caught me and helped me to the bed, setting me down gently like I might break. This couldn't be happening. No way. It was all a bad dream. *Wake up,* I screamed silently to myself. *Wake up, please!*

A woman with a tight ponytail knelt in front of me at eye level. "I'm Detective Perez, and I'm here to find out what happened to your friend tonight, okay?" She motioned to the door behind her, and her partner hurried to shut it. "Does that outburst with your friend just now have something to do with what happened to Kiersten tonight?"

Her question just made me sob harder. There was no part of my life that didn't have something to do with Kiersten. Didn't she know that? I gulped down the sobs, trying to stop crying so I could answer her question, but I couldn't. I took a few ragged breaths, trying to gather myself. It wasn't working.

Detective Perez watched me cry like she was waiting for me to stop before asking any more questions, but she quickly realized there was no way that was happening. I was too big of a wreck. "Maybe you could start with what all of you were doing here tonight?" she asked.

Brooke hadn't told her that already? What were they talking about then? I sat up straighter and pulled the hair off my face. "We were having a party." That's all I could get out before another sob took over my voice.

"Looks like it was a pretty special occasion," she said, motioning to my dress with a slightly turned-up nose. It was a $12,000 Armani, but I wasn't the only one in a designer gown. We all were. Our hair and makeup was done up, too, just like we'd been to the Oscars.

"It was so special," I said through my tears. "We're all part of the West Hollywood Moms' Club. Tonight was supposed to be a celebration for us."

She looked confused. "I'm sorry, but I don't have any kids, so you're going to have to give me a bit more than that. What does that mean that you're all part of a moms' club? And what were you celebrating?"

"We're all moms living on the west side, and our kids are the same age. Most of us are first-time moms, and our kids are still babies." I paused, trying to think straight so I could explain who we were. She needed to understand that about us. "Most moms' clubs are like that, you know—moms in the same area, babies all the same age—but we're not like a typical moms' club. We have rules."

"Rules?" She raised her eyebrows.

"Yes." I nodded. "Basically, we only allow people who meet certain membership criteria to join, and everyone has to sign a nondisclosure agreement. We have to be careful with who we let be around our kids, you know?"

She didn't look impressed. "I'm not following you. What's so special about your group?"

"I'm sorry. I'm doing a terrible job explaining. I just—" I forced down the emotions trying to heave their way to the surface. "How do I say this?" I took another beat to gather myself. "We all have to be careful with who we let around our kids. Our circle includes very influential and successful people. Basically, everyone in the group is wealthy enough to worry about their kids being kidnapped. Not by the sick predators. By greedy people." I gave her a pointed look to make sure she understood the world we lived in, and she did. She knew the zip code, and she'd seen the house on her way in. "So, we meet together every week at the Grove. Right by the fountain. We have coffee and then usually walk around, but sometimes we just sit and chat while the babies roll all over the grass."

"You meet every week? That's it?"

I shook my head. "We do lots of other stuff too. There's a part of it that runs like a business, so we have business meetings where we talk about things like . . . I don't know . . . business stuff."

"For example?"

My thoughts were thick and spinning. "We . . . we . . . uh, vote on new members . . . we talk about and, uh, organize upcoming events." This was so hard. How was I supposed to formulate thoughts? Answer questions. "But then we do other things with the kids too. Like we take them to mommy-and-me classes. We do lots of hikes. Go to the libraries. Have playdates. We're just trying to survive the early-mom stage, you know?"

She shrugged. "Like I said, I don't have kids, but I've heard. Lots of crying and sleepless nights. Diapers. Never having time to do anything for yourself because you're always taking care of everybody else. Tired. Exhausted. Hormones from hell. Am I getting it right?"

"Pretty much." I nodded. "Anyway, last month, Kiersten decided we should have our first moms'-night-out event. Like I was telling you, we've done all kinds of things together. There's something to do every day if you wanted, but everything's centered on our kids or our husbands. Nothing just for us, you know? So, Kiersten decided we should do our first big event without any kids or husbands. Make it a party just for us." The emotions rose back in my chest as I spoke. The memories were too much.

Kiersten had been so excited the day she came up with the idea. She loved parties. She liked having fun, period. That's why I loved her. Everybody did. Nobody brought more energy into a room than her, and she made everyone feel like they were the most important person there.

She'd grabbed my arm where we sat next to each other on a bench at the park after all the other moms had left. "We should have a moms-only party." She said it the same way she'd suggested we build a beer bong from the roof of our sorority house back in sophomore year at UCLA. Fiery eyes. Wide grin. "No husbands. No babies. No nannies. Just us. We deserve time just to hang out and have fun. Not have to worry about anyone but ourselves for the night. Remember when the only person you had to worry about was yourself?" She laughed then. Her huge contagious and infectious laugh. The one that made everyone else laugh too. "And ohmigod," she squealed, bouncing in her seat and grabbing my hand across the picnic table. "I just had the most amazing idea. You know what else we should do?" Her voice grew louder, even more excited and bubbly. "We should make it an award night too. How fun would that be?"

"An award night?"

"Yeah, like we'll give out all kinds of awards for different mothering tasks. Like best bottle maker or best at getting the baby to burp. Fastest diaper changer. Things like that. We'll make them all funny."

She'd taken the idea and run with it. Her entire focus for the last three weeks, and she'd loved every minute because there was nothing she liked more than planning a party or big event. Me? I was a nervous wreck the whole time and always felt like I never got things right, but she was a master.

And tonight wasn't any different. Everything was perfect—the music, the food, the caterers—just like she'd wanted. Everyone was having so much fun. It was exactly what we needed.

Detective Perez cut into my memory, startling me back into the moment. This awful moment. "So, you were having a party?" she asked.

"Yes, we . . ." That was all I could get out before I started crying again. I'd kept it together for as long as I could, but I had to know.

"How did she drown?" I looked up at Detective Perez, searching her eyes. Pleading with them for answers. "Like seriously. How did she? There's no way." I shook my head at her. At this room. This situation. "She was a great swimmer. An absolutely incredible one. She swam all the way through college. You know that, right?" I didn't wait for her to give me any kind of answer, because this was ridiculous. "Kiersten wouldn't just drown. That's pretty much impossible. You know what else? Her mom made her do that whole 'throw your baby in the pool with their clothes on and see if they can float to the other side' thing when she was like a baby. Nine months old, I think it was. Nine months old." I wanted to shake the detective. Get her to see this made no sense. "How could someone like her drown? Tell me how—how?"

"We don't know, and I'm sorry this happened, but what I can tell you is that we're going to do everything in our power to find out." She pulled her phone out of her back pocket. "Mind if I take notes on this?" I sniffled and nodded. "I have to write things down. Absolutely have to or I can't remember anything. Anyway"—she stood up as she talked—"was there drinking at the party?"

"Of course there was drinking. It was a party," I snapped at the detective. I didn't mean to. It just came out that way.

"Had Kiersten been drinking tonight?"

I nodded.

"Any idea how much she'd been drinking?"

I had no clue. I was just glad she did because drunk Kiersten was so much fun. She always watched what she drank when she was in public. She came from a family of politicians spanning three generations, so caring what other people thought about her and maintaining a certain image were ingrained in her DNA. Doing something stupid because she'd been drinking was too big a risk.

That's how you knew you were really in with Kiersten. If she let her guard down with you, and there were very few people she did that with. She rarely ever let anyone see her drunk, and I felt special to be one of the people on her short list. I loved watching all her pretenses fall away. It wasn't just the pretenses—it was the perfectionism. Not that she expected it of others. She was the kindest and most compassionate soul to others. It was the demands she placed on herself. She put impossible standards on herself and punished herself mercilessly when she didn't achieve them.

But drunk?

You got to see who she really was, and that's who I loved the most. She was hilarious. There was nobody that made me laugh harder. And she was happy. She grinned wide and carefree. That's how I remembered her. That's how I'd always remember her.

Not that awful washed-up way.

How would I ever erase those memories? The way she looked splayed out on the concrete. Her face so swollen. Like she'd swallowed so much water, it'd made her bloated. And her face didn't look peaceful. She looked scared. Vulnerable. Terrified. People's eyes were supposed to close when they died, but hers were wide open. Bulging and big. Like fish eyes.

She was gone. She was really gone.

"I don't understand. I just don't understand how this happened." I burst into tears again. Or maybe I never stopped.

Detective Perez leaned over and rested her hand on my arm. "Can you take me through finding her?"

"I can't. I don't know." I shook my head. "I just don't know. She was with us. She was there." I pointed outside like she was right outside this door. Next to me in the living room where I thought she'd been all night except for a few moments. "I told her to go grab another bottle of wine and hurry back. I didn't want her to miss out on anything. We were having so much fun. She was there. She was just there."

And now she was gone. Her hole ripped my heart open. She was my everything. Closer than my husband. She came before all that, but now she was gone.

"Kiersten can't be gone. She can't be." I shook my head. "No." Like saying it out loud would make it so. Bring her back.

"This is hard, and I'm so sorry for your loss. Were the two of you close?"

"She was my best friend in the entire world." I sounded like a little kid. I didn't mean to. Calling her my best friend only made me sob harder. I was never going to stop crying. I didn't know how to live in a world without Kiersten. What about her baby girl?

Who was gonna take care of Rinley?

Ohmigod. Rinley.

A baby couldn't be without a mother.

"That isn't right." I didn't realize I'd spoken it until Detective Perez put her arm around me. She steadied me on the bed, but I still felt like I was falling off the earth. I pinched the inside of my thigh. The familiar sting that could bring me back. It worked every time with my husband, Colin. But this wasn't him. And I couldn't keep it together. I wanted to stab a knife in my guts to make it stop. Tear my skin off my body. Instead, I just wailed.

"It's okay," Detective Perez said, trying to hug me again, but I didn't want her to touch me. I didn't want her anywhere near me. I wanted Kiersten.

"Don't," I cried, pulling away. "Please just don't. I can't do this. Ohmigod, I can't do this. I'm not going to be okay." We used to talk about our husbands dying. What we'd do. Never each other. It'd never been a possibility.

"Do you want me to get one of your friends to come sit with you?"

I didn't want one of my other friends. I wanted Kiersten, but nothing was going to bring her back. And then there was this howling. This awful howling that filled the room. It took a second to realize the sounds were coming from me.

CHAPTER THREE

NOW

JADE

Detective Perez stuck her head out the door, and everybody froze, including all the police officers standing around the room doing nothing. There were enough for each of us to have one. "Can someone come in here and help Whitney?"

All eyes slowly turned to me. I shook my head at them all. That was Kiersten's job. Kiersten helped Whit when she was upset. I couldn't do that. I wasn't second place. But somebody had to do it. She sounded like an animal being wounded in there. Like someone was hitting her with their car over and over again. I wanted to cover my ears. Not go in there with her.

But somebody had to hold her hand through it. Be there until the special paramedics got here. They were bringing something to calm her down. A few of the officers were whispering about it in the corner by the wine bar. It sounded like they were calling in the psych team too.

Psychologists scared me more than police. Whitney needed to calm down.

"Poor little lady can't get a grip on herself," I overheard the chubby guy say to the woman with the crew cut. But he didn't say it like he felt sorry for Whitney. He said it like he was mocking her. He'd rolled his eyes and motioned around himself at the guesthouse and all of us locked inside. The guesthouse was probably bigger than his house.

Yes, Whitney was a spoiled princess living in a palace, but her best friend just died. And not just any best friend—the friends-from-kindergarten kind. How was she supposed to react?

I stood slowly. Was I really the logical second place? The fill-in? Everyone's eyes bore into me, making me sick, and I scanned the room until I found Natasha's. She gave me a brief nod, and I shoved my feelings down. I followed Detective Perez into the room.

Whitney was curled into a tiny ball on the edge of the bed. Her eyes were red and nearly swollen shut. Bright-red blotches covered her face. She was making these low whimpering cries that were suddenly punctuated with painful ones like she'd just been kicked in the side. I took small steps toward her and hovered awkwardly over her. Should I sit down? Stand up? I wanted to touch her, but I didn't want to spook her. She'd tried to scratch the eyes out of the paramedic who'd put us in here earlier. She hadn't wanted to leave Kiersten.

"No!" she'd shrieked, throwing herself on Kiersten's body. "I'm going wherever you take her."

But the only place they were taking Kiersten was the morgue.

"Honey, I'm here. It's Jade," I said softly. My throat was thick with emotions, but I couldn't break down. I had to be strong for her. She needed me.

Whitney just stared straight ahead like she hadn't heard me and I wasn't standing next to her. Her eyes were glazed over, lost somewhere. She looked like a crumpled deer on the side of the road. I hated seeing her like this.

Get up. That's what I wanted to say to her. *You can't just lie there. You have to get up.* She was the strong one. If she fell down, what would the rest of us do? But I couldn't say that.

Instead, I stuck my hand out and slowly rubbed her back. It was damp underneath her V-scoop-back Armani that she'd obsessed over and dropped three pounds to get into like tonight was an actual awards night. And it had been so magical.

"It's gonna be okay," I said, but it wasn't. We both knew that. Nothing was ever going to be okay or the same after tonight. For any of us. She trembled underneath my touch. I turned to the officer left standing in the room. Detective Perez had disappeared somewhere. I hadn't even noticed. She'd snuck out of the room that quick. She was sneaky. I wasn't sure I liked that. Sneaky people made me nervous.

"Can I just take her home?" This place was too confined. The walls closing in on us. The air thick with grief and sweat. So thick it made it hard to breathe.

He shook his head. "It's still going to be a while." He saw my annoyed expression and shrugged. "Sorry. We have to process the scene, and none of you can leave until we're done."

"How long—" Before I could finish, the door opened and two young people made their way inside. They weren't dressed in police uniforms like all the other ones swarming the property like ants. They were in regular clothes. One of them carried a medical kit like the paramedics. He hurried over to Whitney and quickly knelt beside her.

"Hey, honey," he said in the world's most soothing voice. "My name is Carl, and I'm one of the technicians on the crisis-response team. I never get called to anyone's house when it's a good day, so I just want to start off by saying that I'm so sorry you're having such an awful day. I really am." He took a deep breath when he finished. He was so calm. He didn't rush to fill in the space. He just sat there. Perched on his heels.

Just his presence eased my nerves, but Whitney didn't seem affected. She was in the same state. Same position.

One of the other officers leaned over and whispered in his ear, "Be careful. She's fine unless you try to move her. That's when she freaks." Except it wasn't a whisper. It was loud enough for me to hear and Whitney, too, if she cared, but she'd detached. The medic gave him an annoyed look, and I was grateful for it. There was no reason for him to treat Whitney like that.

"I have some medicine I can give you to make you feel better. It's going to help you sleep. Sometimes that's all we can do when something really bad happens to us," Carl said.

Was he going to give that to all of us when we left here tonight? I was going to need some of it too. Whitney wasn't the only one who was going to have trouble sleeping tonight.

I peeled the hair crusted with snot off her face and rubbed her head. "Sweetie, he's going to give you a shot, okay?" I said it to her the same sweet way I said it to my daughter, Lily, when I was coaxing her to get shots at the pediatrician.

Whitney let out a small whimper. But it wouldn't be long until her whimpers worked their way up again. This was how it'd been ever since it happened.

None of this felt real. It hadn't looked real either.

Kiersten's white gown had looked like a huge balloon floating on top of the water. Like she was just standing there in the pool, except she wasn't. Her toes weren't touching the bottom. She was floating. That's what everyone thought she was doing at first. Until she didn't respond.

"KayKay?" That's what Natasha called out when she spotted her in the pool. She'd run into the kitchen to grab the plate of cookies from Crumbl and was bringing it back to the family room when she glanced out the window.

"I don't know what made me look outside. What if I would've looked out earlier? What if I could've saved her?" She kept saying it over and over again to anyone who would listen.

But she couldn't have. She'd only been gone a few seconds. Just long enough to dash to the kitchen to grab the cookies from the counter. Something had made her look. That's when she'd spied Kiersten out back. Bobbing.

"KayKay?" she'd called her pet name again. When she didn't answer a second time, she'd gotten scared and run outside. All the way to the edge of the pool.

She screamed. And then she just froze.

She said it took a second to register before she jumped in. Then she turned into an idiot. Flailing and splashing around Kiersten, attempting to save her but only making it worse. So hysterical you would've thought she was drowning, but that's how some people reacted to trauma. They lost it. Then the rest of us came running.

I didn't know how I responded to trauma. Nothing this bad had ever happened to me before, but I was going to find out.

Carl didn't speak as he opened his medical bag and pulled out the needle kit. "I'm going to need your arm. Can you give it to me for just a second? I promise that's all it will be." He paused, waiting for her consent. She stayed silent. "Just for a teensy second."

Nothing.

"Whit, can he give you some medicine? It's going to make you feel better," I said, hoping she might respond to my voice. This wouldn't take her pain away, but at least it would knock her out. Give her a moment of nothingness. That had to be preferable to this.

She ignored me too.

I put my hand on her shoulder and nudged her a little. "Can you put your arm out for him?"

Still nothing.

"Can I help you do it?" I asked.

A barely perceptible nod. I glanced up and made eye contact with Carl. We exchanged consent with our eyes. I took one of Whitney's arms off her head and placed it flat against the mattress. Carl moved quickly, and it was over in seconds. She didn't even flinch. I tucked her hand in place and rubbed her back until her eyes folded shut. It didn't take long. Every few seconds, her body gave out a violent twitch, but she stayed asleep.

I breathed a sigh of relief as Carl returned things to his bag and stood up. He gave me a nod and a smile as he exited. Right as Detective Perez made her way back into the room. She looked pleased to see Whitney asleep on the end of the bed. I headed for the door, but she motioned for me to stay and closed the door behind us instead.

"Great. I'm so happy she's finally gotten some peace." She pointed to the spot next to Whitney on the bed like she wanted me to sit, but I preferred to stand. "Since I have you, can you tell me what happened here tonight?"

CHAPTER FOUR

THEN

BROOKE

Julian's cries hadn't stopped or gotten any quieter since we'd left the house. Not even the car ride made a difference. When he got this worked up, there was nothing you could do to stop him. He just had to cry it out. I pressed my AirPods hard into my ears and turned the volume up on my phone even though it was already as loud as it could go. I just needed quiet. Just for a minute. Quiet. A moment to breathe before I got out of this car and had to face all those women.

How dare Abby act like this wasn't what she wanted? My blood still boiled. I gripped the steering wheel with both hands to keep them from shaking. Palms sweaty underneath. She'd been desperate to have a baby. It was all we'd talked about for three years—how we'd raise them, where we'd live when they were older so they would go to good schools, her fears about being a parent, how we'd work together as a team so they didn't favor one parent over the other. I mean, she was on board with all of it. Our domestic life had always been more of her idea than mine. She wanted the traditional cookie-cutter family life. I would've been fine with lots of other options.

The car alarm next to me went off, and I jumped. I had to calm down. I needed to calm down.

All this was just because she couldn't carry Julian herself. She couldn't carry any babies. We hadn't known that when we started the journey toward motherhood, though. That's when everything went wrong. Everything would be different, and none of this would be happening right now if things had gone according to her plans—she'd carry the first baby, and I'd carry the second. Back then we'd wanted at least two and each of us to have the experience of being pregnant. And she would never have admitted it, but she was secretly crossing her fingers, hoping we'd get one boy and one girl. Our perfect family complete. That's how she wanted it. That's how she saw it. That's how she designed it.

Now that seemed laughable. In less than half a second, I was crying. I was always on the verge of tears. I didn't bother trying to stop them.

Everything had to go according to her plans. Always had. Control was one of the core issues she'd worked on in treatment, where we met over eight years ago. This divorce was no different.

This divorce. I hated the way the word sounded in my head. I still couldn't say it out loud. That's why I hadn't told anyone yet. They all knew we were having troubles and were split up, but nobody knew the *D* word had been thrown out there. It'd been more than thrown out there.

Abby just walked into the kitchen while I was unloading the dishwasher four nights ago and announced, "I don't want to be married to you anymore."

There was no beating around the bush. It didn't get any clearer than that. This wasn't an *I'm confused and need some time to figure things out* or *I'm not sure I want to do this anymore*. She was out. Just like that. In the blink of an eye.

How could she do this? How could she just walk away?

Getting married had been her idea too. Just like having kids, and I'd let her talk me into both the same way I let her talk me into everything like a stupid dummy. I gave up everything for her. Everything. Every single piece of me. Why? Why was I so stupid?

Because I loved her.

Still did. Even now.

I believed in us. In love. Real true love. The kind very few people ever got but we were one of the lucky ones. We had the stuff romance novels were made of. We were the friends-to-lovers trope destined for happily ever after. How could we not be? Being roommates in an inpatient treatment center meant we'd seen each other at our absolute worst and knew everything about each other before becoming anything more than friends. We'd been best friends throughout our first year of recovery and each other's biggest support. Once we finally got together, it was like this sweet gift, never having to be anyone else but ourselves because that's who we'd always been to each other.

"I can never leave her—she knows all my secrets" used to be Abby's favorite joke at parties, but she wasn't kidding. She loved that she didn't have to hide anything from me. That's what pissed me off the most—this was her story!

And she'd thrown it away like it all meant nothing. Like she didn't want it in the first place.

"I'm sorry. I thought this was what I wanted for my life, but it's just not working out," she'd said as she leaned against the kitchen island explaining herself. Like we were a business transaction or a purchase she'd changed her mind about. But we both knew what this was really about.

Liza.

That's her name. I found out Thursday. Not because Abby told me. She refused to acknowledge there was somebody else. That her unhappiness had anything to do with the fact that she'd fallen in love with somebody else.

I haven't felt this way in a long time. It's been years.

That's what her DMs said to Liza. In her other Instagram account that she thought I didn't know about or have the password to. Hacking into her stuff had never been hard. Quite frankly, she made it too easy. She used the same three passwords over and over again.

Liza Jane.

Like she's really named after a song? Come on. She made that up. It couldn't be her real name. She was probably one of those bright young hopefuls who'd left their small-town roots behind to start a new life as an actress, and you couldn't start a new life in Hollywood without a great Hollywood name.

I'd spent all last night stalking Liza's Instagram and TikTok accounts. Her TikTok was useless for anything personal. She was one of those people that never posted a single video. Her Instagram wasn't much more helpful than that. Up until a few months ago—which was when I was assuming this had started since that's when things really began changing—it was filled with pictures of food and funny memes with her cat. There were barely any photos of her, and none of them were recent.

Then all that changed. Suddenly, she was posting selfies. Taking pics of herself at fancy restaurants and VIP clubs. Splashing inspirational quotes in between all the pictures about how she was living her best life. And I hadn't been wrong. Not only was she from a small town—Iowa born and bred until three years ago—she was also really young. Like in her early twenties young, which felt like an extra-hard slap in my face. She was newly out too. A baby gay and you never fell harder than you did with your first.

How could I compete with all that?

None of parenthood had gone like it was supposed to. Not from the very beginning. It wasn't cute or sexy or fun. Those were the things Abby loved. That's who she was. Abby liked things exciting. She liked things fun. It was why she had so many friends. Everyone wanted to be around her. She was one of those people that commanded a room with her energy. It was what had drawn me to her, too, since the very beginning. The first time I met her in group therapy, I thought she was one of the therapists. I'd been shocked to discover she was one of the patients. A drug addict like the rest of us.

I'd waited up for her last night so that I could talk to her. I had no idea when she was getting home because she'd stopped telling me what was happening in her life or her schedule months ago. She acted like it was a big inconvenience for her. Like I was no longer entitled to know what was happening because it was over between us. What did that matter? She was still the mother of my child, and that came with certain rights and responsibilities. Things she was going to have to talk to me about. Period. Whether she liked it or not. She might be able to leave me, but she couldn't leave Julian.

I'd paced the living room waiting for her. Working as a sports agent for some of LA's elite athletes meant her schedule was packed full of travel and late nights. That's how we spent most of our first year together. We rarely hung out in LA back then. I was still on the East Coast, so I'd fly to whichever city she was in for the weekend and spend it with her. I was like this secret sex prisoner she had waiting in her hotel room to service her between every meeting. Those were back in the days when we couldn't keep our hands off each other.

She never even wanted to touch me now. It'd never occurred to me it was because of someone else. I just thought it was because I'd turned into a saggy blob and still had varicose veins on my vagina left over from delivery.

I'd forced myself to get dressed up nice last night, and hated myself for it, but I couldn't help it. I even put on a regular bra instead of a nursing bra. I couldn't stand that I still had a baby bump. It wasn't fair. I was supposed to celebrate my womanhood and wear the scars of motherhood like a champion fighter, but I wanted to be pretty again. I wanted to look like me again. Not this frumpy, overweight, and pimply-faced-looking teenager that cried at sad ads on my social media feeds.

It was the second night in a row that I'd waited up for her, but the same thing happened last night as it did then. I'd sat down on the couch to wait her out, but as the clock passed ten, I could barely keep my eyes open. I was exhausted. I was always exhausted since Julian was such a poor sleeper, and when those waves of fatigue hit me, I couldn't fight them. My lids had grown heavy, and before I knew it, I'd been out.

I woke up shortly after one. Disoriented and confused on the couch. Still in my clothes. My mouth cotton and sour. I quickly peeked out the window to see if her car was in the driveway. It wasn't, which meant she hadn't gotten home and snuck inside without waking me like she had the night before. On that night, she hadn't even laid a blanket over me on the couch. She'd just left me there.

I sat up and grabbed the coffee mug on the side table and took a big swig. She wasn't getting away with that for a second night.

It wasn't long before I heard the sound of her car in the driveway. It'd taken me by surprise since there weren't any headlights leading up to it, but then I quickly realized she'd turned them off on purpose, and my blood instantly boiled. I peered out the window and watched as she stepped out of the car and shut the door quietly behind herself. She tiptoed up the sidewalk, looking like a teenager coming home after they'd snuck out for the night and trying not to wake their parents. She walked stealthily up to the front door and tried to slide her way inside without making a sound.

I'd been there to greet her with my hands on both my hips.

"Hi," I said, not even trying to pretend like there wasn't something weird about me standing in front of her at 1:00 a.m. like some crazy person.

Her face was a mixture of surprise and disappointment that she didn't even try to erase.

"How was your night?" I asked, attempting to ease into the difficult conversation. Maybe we wouldn't even have any of the tough conversations tonight. Maybe those could wait until later. We could start small. But we had to start. We had to find a way to fix this.

"It was all right," she said, slipping her shoes off, then walking into the kitchen to put her stuff on the island. She kept glancing around the house like she was looking for a way out. Like just being in the room with me was too uncomfortable to bear. She wouldn't even look at me. "I'm really tired. I had a super-busy day, and I just want to go to bed. Can we not do this now?"

"What do you mean, *do this*? I'm not doing anything," I said, trying to sound normal. Trying to keep my voice from rising. From sounding strained. Too confrontational.

"I don't want to fight with you right before I go to bed. I've got an even bigger day tomorrow." She rubbed her neck while she spoke.

"Yeah, well, maybe you shouldn't have gone out with Liza after work then," I spat. It flew out of my mouth without thinking.

"I wasn't with Liza. I was with Rebecca and the crew."

"You don't have to lie to me anymore."

She let out a deep sigh. "I never lied to you, Brooke. I'm not a liar." She let out another huff like this part of her day—this part of me—was too exhausting to deal with.

"Why are you being like this?" I couldn't stand her apathy or her indifference. It made me furious.

"Being like what? I'm not doing anything. I just got home after a long day, and I want to go to bed. I wasn't trying to get jumped by my ex-wife when I—"

Her words stopped us both.

Ex-wife.

There it was. She'd never said it. I'd never let myself think it, but there it was. This horrible word. Unbelievable idea. Just dropped like a bomb in our kitchen.

I'm still your wife! I wanted to scream it at her, but the look on her face made me swallow my words inside. It didn't matter that none of the papers had been signed; it was over for her. She'd labeled me as an ex. That's who I'd become in her mind. I could see it in her eyes.

But she wasn't my ex. There was nothing past about her. She was my present. My life. All I wanted.

I'd rushed toward her. "Please don't do this, Abby. Please don't do this." I couldn't help myself. I grabbed for her arms to pull her close to me, but she stepped back. She put her hands up to keep me away.

"Don't, Brooke. Please, don't."

Tears slid down my cheeks. I didn't want to cry. I'd told myself all day not to cry. *Be strong.* But I couldn't. Not when I was losing the love of my life. And I didn't care what anyone said. There was only one person for me. And I'd found her. Most people didn't. I'd always felt so lucky to find my person. Some people spent their whole life looking for them.

"Please," I said again because I didn't know what else to say. "Just talk to me. We can get through this. You just need to let me know what's going on. We can figure it out together. I know we can."

"I've told you what's going on, Brooke. There's nothing left to talk about," she said. She turned on her heels and started walking down the hallway to the guest bedroom. She'd moved in there at the beginning of the summer. I hurried along beside her.

"You can't keep treating me like I did something wrong. I didn't do anything wrong." I pulled on her arm, trying to stop her. I hated how desperate I sounded and how pathetic I looked, but I was powerless to stop myself. I just kept grabbing at her arm, and she kept jerking away until finally she shoved me off and I stumbled, smacking into the hallway wall to steady myself. The noise sent Julian's cries ripping through the house. Instead of her face filling with concern and care, she looked irritated. She always acted like he was such a huge inconvenience. She looked at him the same way she looked at me—annoyed. And it broke my heart for both of us.

Just like his cries had interrupted our argument last night, they interrupted my thoughts today as he let out a loud shriek from the back seat. It was so loud. A headache had been pounding my temples all morning. The late-night caffeine and lack of sleep had left me feeling strung out. I was frozen in the driver's seat in the parking lot. I didn't want to do this. Get out and try to pretend like everything was normal. I wasn't sure how much longer I could keep going until something broke inside me.

CHAPTER FIVE

THEN

WHITNEY

"Oh god," I said, spotting Brooke hurrying toward us with the stroller and her baby, Julian. He was strapped to her chest while she pushed the empty stroller. Her unzipped diaper bag was thrown over her shoulder with diapers and wipes almost spilling out as she walked. "It's Brooke."

Kiersten glanced up from where she was carefully arranging all the cupcakes she'd picked up from Sprinkles and the Starbucks traveler she'd gotten on her way here even though she said she wasn't going to. "She looks a bit rough."

"You think?" I snorted. She'd been looking rough for months. Ever since her wife, Abby, told her that it was over. Normally, we had a strict no-spouse rule for our moms' club meetings or hangouts, but Abby and Brooke were both Julian's moms, so they were obviously an exception. "Man, I was hoping we'd get Abby today. Brooke's been here for the last three meetings."

"You're terrible!" Kiersten smacked my arm with a pile of napkins.

I laughed and gave her a playful shove back. "I'm sorry, but people break up and get divorced all the time. I'm more shocked when people actually stay together than I am when they split up. You're entitled to a good mental breakdown, but then, come on, get over it," I said underneath my breath just as Brooke reached the table.

"Hi, honey! It's so good to see you," Kiersten gushed, then quickly pointed to the coffee and cupcakes beside her. "I know you're nursing, but there are all these goodies here if you want them." She gave her a huge smile.

Suddenly, Julian lurched in Brooke's arms and milk spurted from his nose, spraying the front of Kiersten's shirt.

"Oh shit!" Brooke quickly grabbed a burp cloth from her diaper bag, which sent the contents spilling out all over the sidewalk. The bag slipped off her shoulder, and she tried to grab it, nearly dropping Julian, which made him wail.

"Here. Here, give me the baby," I said, taking him from her. He screamed and writhed against me. His fists angry and tight. Brooke burst into tears.

"It's okay, it's okay," Kiersten said as she tried to gather all Brooke's things and shove them back into the diaper bag.

Julian cried harder. He clearly wanted Brooke, but she didn't move. She just stood there with her arms at her side, crying. I pressed Julian against my chest, grateful Asher was still sleeping in his stroller next to me. I rocked back and forth while Brooke stood in front of Kiersten, working herself up into heavier and messier sobs. The soul-sucking kind of sobs.

Kiersten was immediately uncomfortable even though you'd never know it on the outside just by looking at her, but I knew her better than I knew myself. All her insides. And right now, she was freaking out even though she was wrapping her arms around Brooke and telling her not to be embarrassed about it, that it was going to be okay. She absolutely hated public displays of messiness. She didn't like emotional outbursts in public. She had no problem crying and screaming things out, but she liked to do all her breaking down behind closed doors. I got it. I was the same way. That's why we were best friends. But she kept her judgment in check as she continued comforting Brooke.

"It's okay, really, it's not a big deal. Julian's fine. He just got startled. Everything's okay, hon," she said, doing her best to quiet and settle her as quickly as possible. We had a perfect view of the parking lot, and the other moms were pulling their cars into the lot. This wasn't a good start to our meetup. These were supposed to be fun. Light and upbeat. Carefree. A time for us not to care so much. That was the whole point. This would be a huge buzzkill before the meetup even got started, and we might not recover from it. No one wanted that.

"I just—I just—" She took huge gulping sobs as she spoke. "I'm having a really hard time. Abby said she wants a divorce. She actually said those words. Can you believe that?"

God, I hated these moments. Those awkward couple breakup moments when you had no choice but to pick sides. These were the worst. Especially when I wasn't really on her side. I hated even thinking that, and I'd never say it to her face, but Abby had a point. Brooke was a tough person to be around. She was always on the verge of tears. If she wasn't crying, then she was angry, and you never knew what was going to set her off. And honestly, she just wasn't that fun. It wasn't just that she was sober. Abby was sober, too, and she was one of the funnest people I'd ever met. Brooke was just so serious all the time, especially about the kids. Like every moment of their lives hung in this delicate balance between life and death. Being a mom was important, and I was totally down for doing the best possible job, but I had to have a life outside my kid, and Asher's life wasn't this delicate balancing act. As if he were just one wrong parenting choice away from death. No thanks. I couldn't live that way.

I didn't know Brooke before she was a mother, but from what I'd heard, it'd changed her. She wasn't always this way. Part of me wondered if it was hormonal. None of us were as young as we used to be, and things affected us differently than if we'd had kids in our twenties, even if we didn't want to admit it. I'd asked Abby about postpartum depression, but she'd assured me it wasn't that. I wasn't so sure, though. Julian was almost six months old, and she still wasn't any better.

Now this?

Kiersten turned to me, her eyes pleading with mine for help. I jumped in. "Look, I know that's got to be so hard. Like I literally can't even imagine what I'd do if Colin left me for another woman right after I had Asher." I gave her my most empathetic smile, and I meant it. From the bottom of my heart. Losing Colin would wreck me. But eventually, like anything, you've got to get back up. "You must just be obsessed with it. I know I—"

"I am," she interrupted before I had a chance to finish, clearly eager for the opportunity to talk about it. Like she'd just been waiting for the right moment. "I can barely do anything else. I've turned into someone totally pathetic that I don't even recognize. I mean, who is this person?"

"That's a lot." I nodded at her just as Colleen and Taylor approached us. Thank god. I couldn't handle much more. "Hi, ladies!"

"Hi, these cupcakes look so good," Taylor said, pointing to the red velvet ones in the center. The ones with the real cream cheese filling.

Kiersten turned around and smiled. "Eat them all because I'm not taking them home with me."

And she wouldn't either. That's why she stayed so skinny. She kept the sweets out of the house. Not like me. I have no self-control.

Colleen pushed her twin girls in a double BOB stroller. Taylor held her son strapped to her chest in a Moby Wrap. We'd probably never even see him this entire time. He slept most of the day and was awake all night, but Taylor had no interest in putting him on any kind of a regular schedule.

"He's his own person, and I'm not trying to impose society's standards and rules on him. He's going to be raised to be a free spirit," she said whenever anyone asked her why she did the things she did with him. She'd grabbed hold of child-led parenting and taken it to an entirely different level than the rest of us had.

Taylor's eyes took a quick roll over Brooke before she decided to ignore whatever was happening there. Instead, she grabbed one of the cupcakes, then pointed to a spot in the shade of one of the big palm trees. "We're going to go grab a seat over there where it's not quite so hot. Come chat with us later. I want to hear all about the new spin class you're taking."

"I will," I said, keeping the steady rhythm with Julian. He was finally starting to calm down.

Kiersten returned her attention to Brooke. She didn't consider any event a success unless everyone was happy at it, and she made it her personal mission to be sure of it. "Look, sweetie, Rinley and Asher are sleeping." She pointed to where my son lay in his stroller, just in case Brooke hadn't noticed him yet, and Rinley, who was doing the same in hers. "So, why don't you leave Julian with us for a minute and go join them?" She motioned to where Colleen and Taylor were laying out a blanket and setting down their stuff. "Just try to take your mind off things. It might help if you gave yourself a break."

Brooke looked insulted, like Kiersten had suggested she do something awful, but she turned and walked over to Colleen and Taylor anyway. They were in the only shaded spot over here. That's why Kiersten had picked it. She always got here twenty minutes early to stake our claim.

"Wow," I said as soon as Brooke was out of earshot. "That was intense."

"Yeah, she's definitely not doing well. I feel bad for her." Sadness washed over Kiersten's face. "I'm really worried about her. Do you think we should do something?"

I shook my head. "You don't want anywhere near that. It's only going to get worse."

"Yeah, you're right," she said, but she wasn't going to listen. I could tell by the look in Kiersten's eye as she watched her walk away that she was already trying to figure out a way to make things better for Brooke. She made it her mission to heal people even if it meant getting hurt, and there was no doubt in my mind that Kiersten would get hurt in the middle of Brooke's crisis. Because Brooke was unstable, and unstable people were dangerous.

CHAPTER SIX

NOW

JADE

"What happened tonight?" I repeated Detective Perez's question, trying to shift from taking care of Whitney to answering her questions. "I don't really know." I shook my head, but it just made it hurt. I needed water. "It all happened so fast."

And it did.

One minute we'd been in the family room, dancing like we were fifteen again. We were all drunk, except for Brooke. It didn't take much anymore. At least not for most of us. Two glasses of wine usually did it, and we'd gone way beyond that tonight. All the others had left. Only the core remained. Me, Whitney, Brooke, Natasha, Kiersten, Taylor, and Colleen.

We were dancing. Twirling. Spinning. Smiling. Laughing. Having a good time.

The next minute—Natasha's scream that sent all of us running.

"When was the last time you saw Kiersten before the pool?" Detective Perez prompted in a clipped voice. All business.

I flitted through the images from tonight, trying to push the horrible ones from the pool aside, but it wasn't easy. Dead-body eyes seared your soul. "Really, I didn't even know she was gone. I thought she was in the living room with us the entire time. I really did."

I'd talked to her earlier.

"I'm going to run and get another bottle of wine. Do you want anything?" she'd asked.

I'd waved her off, smiling and laughing at Taylor. She was going on and on about her nanny. She'd been worked up about it all night, and she was one of the funniest people when she was mad, especially when she'd been drinking. You never knew what was going to fly out of her mouth, so I was hanging on her every word.

"I could've sworn Kiersten was standing right there next to me, talking with Taylor. She was when the story started," I explained to Detective Perez. Her smooth face was impossible to read.

"When did you notice she was gone?"

"Not until Natasha screamed," I said softly, like I couldn't talk about it too loudly or I'd wake Whitney and set her off all over again. Nobody wanted that.

"And then?" she prompted, motioning with her phone. So far, she hadn't typed any notes. Did she actually have it turned on? Was she secretly recording me? Had she recorded the others?

"I ran outside with everybody else and saw her floating there."

"Had Brooke jumped into the water yet?"

I shook my head. "She made it out there with us. There was a lot of splashing around, though, because Natasha was already in the pool, but she was super hysterical and almost made things worse for Brooke when she started trying to help Kiersten." Natasha had kept grasping at Kiersten's gown and was so focused on it being wrapped around her. Some part of her brain must've thought the gown was choking her, like that's why she drowned.

"Her gown was wrapped around her neck." That's all Natasha kept saying. Then and now. She was fixated on it. I didn't know why people reacted the way they did tonight.

Whitney's hysteria was shocking. It'd taken her longer to get there than everybody else. She'd been in one of the bedrooms, pumping. Somehow, she'd missed all the yelling and commotion in the beginning. When she stumbled out onto the patio, we'd already gotten Kiersten out of the pool. Whitney was shocked to find all of us hovering around Kiersten's body splayed out in the middle. Brooke was frantically trying to do CPR.

"OHMIGOD, KIERSTEN!" Whitney screamed at the top of her lungs. "What's wrong with her? What happened? What are you doing?"

Brooke ignored her despite the fact she was screaming at her within inches of her face. She kept up the steady rhythm of CPR that she'd been at since they pulled Kiersten out. She was focused. Determined.

"You're doing it all wrong. That's not how you're supposed to do it." Whitney tried to push Brooke off Kiersten, but Brooke wasn't having it.

"Whitney, stop, I know what I'm doing," she'd cried, bringing her hands to Kiersten's chest again and pressing down hard.

I shook my head, forcibly stopping the memories. The sound of the crack. Bones made a distinct sound when they broke. I focused on Detective Perez instead.

I pointed to Whitney, still out cold from whatever shot Carl had given her. "Is there any way I can get her home and you can finish questioning us there?" Her partner had already told me no, but she was the one in control, so I thought I'd give it another shot.

"Nope. Sorry," she said, as adamant as he'd been. "We're going to process the scene and try to get people out of here as quickly as we can."

"Has Tommy been notified yet? Does he know?" I didn't want to be here when he found out about Kiersten. I wasn't sure I could go through that.

Tommy was Kiersten's husband. He and Colin were as close as Kiersten and Whitney. They didn't really have much choice in the matter, though. They had to be since Kiersten and Whitney spent so much time together. They joked that they'd picked their husbands on purpose so that they were already friends, too, but I wasn't sure they were joking.

"We don't like to notify family or next of kin of anything, especially things like this, over the phone."

"So, you're just going to wait for him to show up here? The poor man is just going to turn down the street to find emergency vehicles and yellow tape surrounding his house? That's awful. You have to have a better system than that."

I couldn't believe the two of them weren't back yet. There was no way everyone in the neighborhood hadn't posted about what was going on. Nextdoor was probably getting blown up. Somebody had to have texted one of them. Wasn't a chance someone hadn't let them know. Unless they had their phones off. But why would they have their phones off?

"Can you tell me what happened with Brooke?" Detective Perez asked, ignoring my concerns about Tommy.

"That was the scariest part. I'd never seen someone snap like that before."

"What do you mean?"

"She was the one who got to Kiersten's body after Natasha, and she jumped right in the pool with her." I hadn't been far behind Brooke when she took off and made a running leap into the pool. The weird thing about her freak-out was how calm and put together she'd been half a second before it. She'd taken command of the entire situation as soon as she got in the water because Natasha was useless. She had no idea what to do, and she was just standing in the water panicking, twirling in circles in Kiersten's gown.

But Brooke?

She took over like a military officer. She barked orders at Natasha, who fell in line almost instantly. Colleen and Taylor jumped into the water and helped pull Kiersten to the side and hoist her out, but they didn't need to. Brooke probably could've done it herself. It was like she had superhuman strength in the moment. Kiersten's body flopped onto the patio like a limp fish.

Her eyes were empty and glassy. Hair was over her forehead, completely covering her eyes. Lips were a purplish blue. Slightly parted. And she was so pale. Like all the blood had drained from her body as soon as she'd taken her last breath.

Brooke had been so steady and sure. Yelling out orders.

"One. Two. Three. Push. Breathe." As she alternated the breathing and compression sequence.

But Kiersten didn't breathe, and it just went on and on. Nothing happened. Nothing changed. Each second was excruciating. When she let go of Kiersten's head to push on her chest, Kiersten's head rolled to the side.

"Breathe, Kiersten. Dammit, just breathe," Brooke said through gritted teeth. Water dripped from her forehead. Taylor screamed instructions at the 911 operator in the background.

Whitney couldn't take the waiting to see if she'd breathe or move or show any kind of life in between the breathing/pounding. It was too much. She wanted to have a turn.

And Brooke should've given it to her.

But she didn't.

"Whitney, get off her." Brooke yelled at her in the same commanding voice she'd been using when Whitney tried to jump in and take over.

"It's not working. You're not doing it right. Let me try," she cried, trying to push her off Kiersten and away from her body, but Brooke wouldn't let her.

"No," she shouted. Never taking her eyes off Kiersten as she pushed on her chest another time. She elbowed Whitney to keep her back; then she just snapped and started pounding Kiersten's chest with her fists, forgetting all about the breathing part. It was frantic and wild. Smack. Smack. Smack.

"Come on!" she yelled. "Breathe!" She pounded again.

Thankfully, the paramedics finally arrived, but not before Brooke broke Kiersten's rib pounding on her chest like that. We all heard it snap. This awful crack.

Everyone froze, trying to figure out what to do, and then Taylor let out a yelp.

"They're here! Ohmigod, they're here!" she squealed into the phone.

Colleen ran through the gate to the driveway, flagging down the paramedics before they'd even turned down the street. They'd come quietly. No sirens to alert the neighbors or the paparazzi. Jay-Z lived down the street.

It'd stopped Brooke's moment, but I hadn't forgotten what she'd done even if everyone else had. That freak-out was weird. Period. Of course Detective Perez had to ask about it.

"Any idea why she acted like that?"

I shook my head. "I have no clue why Brooke acts the way she does."

CHAPTER SEVEN

NOW

BROOKE

The air was thick, filled with trauma and suppressed sobs. Nobody had said much of anything, especially not to me, for the last hour. At least Whitney finally stopped crying when they brought Jade in the room. I didn't think she was ever going to quit. It's just all so weird because I'd never even seen her cry. Whitney wasn't a crier, but all that disappeared when you'd just lost your best friend. If anyone understood what that was like, it was me. I still didn't get why she was so upset with me for tonight, but how you reacted to trauma wasn't rational. It was totally limbic.

A shiver went through me. Not from the cold, but from the memory. That's how it'd been ever since I came out of the bedroom. I kept seeing myself spotting Kiersten floating in the pool. My mind was stuck on repeat. Those moments.

At first, what I'd been seeing hadn't registered. There she was. Lying facedown. Her long brown hair splayed around her, floating like water snakes. Her arms out to her side.

Why is she swimming like that?

That was my initial thought. And then louder. *Why is she swimming like that?* I made my way toward her like I was sleepwalking. Like I couldn't quite take it all in. As if I was creeping toward the bed to look underneath for the monster. I couldn't stop myself, but I had to know. Each step got faster and faster as the realization dawned on me that she wasn't swimming. Something was wrong. Very wrong.

And then I'd screamed. Just like Natasha. But I didn't remember doing it.

Kiersten!

Her name had cut through the crisp night air.

And then I'd run. I took one look at her awkward body, bobbing, and dove into the water. My dress wrapped around my legs like I was thrashing through sand as I worked my way to her. Panic hammered in my chest. I grabbed her body and tried to pull her toward myself, but she was too heavy. I lifted her head up.

Her face was frozen in terror like she was still trying to breathe. As if she'd died trying to catch her last breath.

"Help!" Natasha screamed, tangled in Kiersten's dress.

I hurled myself at Kiersten, desperately trying to pull her up and out. Our dresses ballooned around us, trapping me. Mine wrapped itself around my legs like rope. Her small frame was so heavy. It was like she weighed three hundred pounds. Someone crashed into the water next to me. Colleen.

"I've got this arm. You grab that one, and we'll pull her on three, okay?" I yelled. She nodded, like there was any other way to answer. We had to move fast. "One. Two. Three."

We lifted and heaved, dragging her through the water. The three feet felt like ten as we crossed to the edge of the pool. Hands swarmed from the side like an angry mob. Everyone grasping and pulling at Kiersten, trying to get her out. Safe. Somehow, we flipped her up and out of the pool. Everyone was gasping and breathing hard.

"What do we do? What do we do?" Colleen cried frantically.

"No! You fucking idiot, I said turn at the end of the canyon. Now you have to turn around," Taylor screamed into her phone.

"Why aren't they here yet?" Jade asked on top of her. "Why aren't they here yet?" she kept repeating to herself.

The world spun and tilted. Wine. Adrenaline. Fear. I felt like I was going to pass out. I reached for the chair next to me to steady myself. Then, quickly knelt down next to Kiersten and put my face close to hers to listen and feel for her breath, but I didn't need to do that. Something was very wrong. She wasn't breathing. She hadn't breathed in a long time. I felt her neck, moving my hand around it. Putting my other hand on her chest for a heartbeat.

Nothing.

I tilted her head back with one hand and plugged Kiersten's nose with my other one. Vomit crusted the corners of her mouth. I held back the urge to gag as I put my lips on top of hers and gave her a deep rescue breath. I moved to her chest, clasping my hands together from rote memory and smashing them down on her chest.

"One. Two. Three." I brought my face back up to Kiersten's. Started again.

"You have to do more. You have to do more. That's not right," Jade said frantically.

"Shut up, you don't know what you're talking about, Jade. That's how you do CPR," Taylor snapped.

Suddenly, Whitney burst through, pushing everyone else aside.

"Kiersten!" She sounded like a little girl. She threw herself on top of her, sobbing.

Colleen grabbed her and tried to pull her off. "What are you doing? Get off her!"

But Whitney ignored her. She grabbed my face and squeezed hard. "You save her," she practically hissed at me. "You save her, do you understand me? She cannot die."

But she had.

And I had failed her.

Just like I'd failed my marriage.

CHAPTER EIGHT

NOW

JADE

The shower beat against my skin. Steam filled the room. The heat scorched me. I stood underneath it, trying to wash away tonight's grime, but it didn't feel like I was ever going to get this night off me.

They'd finally let us leave Kiersten's at 4:00 a.m. The scene with Tommy when they told him about Kiersten was as awful as I knew it'd be. They got home before the police were even halfway through questioning our crew. Wherever they'd gone, they had a good time, because they were stumbling drunk. The two of them always reminded me of frat boys, especially since that's who they'd been to each other all along. Frat boys from Yale. And you saw it. The way they slung their arms over each other's shoulders and had to constantly touch each other. Batting and swatting. Ten thousand shared jokes between them.

We were all there when it happened. But none of us wanted to be.

Halfway through Detective Perez's interview with Taylor, we heard them come home. One of the officers had left their scanner on, and it'd been crackling all night. Nobody missed when the operator announced, "Husband on premises." There were all kinds of codes and numbers thrown in there along with it, but anybody listening didn't miss the most important part—the boys were on their way home.

Two of the officers posted out front brought Tommy and Colin back to the guesthouse. It was a huge flurry of activity and voices. People trying to get in. Others trying to get out. Everyone wishing this night had never happened.

Tommy hurtled his way into the room first.

"What happened? Someone tell me what the fuck is happening." But it was Colin that spoke for him. Tommy was excited. Nervous. Wasted. But he was too scared to ask the question.

Colin's voice rose Whitney from her stupor, and she stumbled into the living room drunk on grief and sleeping pills.

"Baby? Baby?" she slurred, her eyes scanning the room. Her movements slow even though she was frantic. She couldn't see him despite the fact he was standing right there in front of her.

Tommy raced to her. "What happened to my wife? Whit, where's Kiersten? Why won't anyone tell me anything? Please tell me what's going on."

But Whit couldn't talk. She just stood there sobbing.

Carl stepped in. "I'm sorry, sir, but there's been a terrible accident." I was glad it was Carl. It needed to be him. He used that sweet, calming voice. The same one he'd used with Kiersten. "Your wife drowned in the pool tonight."

Just like that. No buildup. No preparation. Just bam. World destroyed.

Tommy's face drained of all color. White. And then he just started to shake. His body trembled like he was freezing or having some strange kind of seizure. He kept opening and closing his mouth, but no words would come out. Whitney collapsed into hysterics again.

Poor Colin. He didn't know if he should go to his wife or his best friend. In the end, he chose Whitney as the rest of us women swarmed Tommy. Natasha held him as tight as she could because after the shaking, there was a kind of heart-wrenching sobbing that I've only ever seen in the movies. I hoped I'd never see it again.

I didn't wake Ryan when I got home. I came in as quietly as I could. Everyone else called their husbands to come pick them up from Kiersten's once we were finally allowed to leave, but I called an Uber. While they were obsessively texting and FaceTiming with their husbands, I left mine alone. I'd been leaving him alone most days. And that said something about where we were at. It was impossible to miss.

I just couldn't be the one to tell him another bad thing. There'd been so much bad news lately, with his mom, Lily, being sick, the new baby. And all those things would be stressful enough on their own, but he'd been out of a job for months again. He still hadn't told anyone he'd been let go from DreamWorks. They laid off half his crew after COVID, and since he wasn't telling anyone, then it meant that it was my secret too.

"Can you please just tell your parents?" I'd begged him the other night. I wasn't sure I could stand all the lying another second. It was getting harder and harder to keep up the facade with my mother-in-law, and she was relentless.

"Absolutely not," he said with the same adamant refusal he'd given the last time I asked. He'd had a chip on his shoulder when it came to his parents and money since the moment we met. It wasn't a chip, more like a mountain. He'd always been in direct competition with his brother too. Who was a genius. A certified one. Mensa and all.

Ryan was hanging on by a thin thread. Telling him another bad thing might sink him. It wasn't like Kiersten was his friend, but she was mine, and we were all close. Close enough that it would affect him. It would give him more ammunition to prove how terrible life had gotten. He wasn't forty yet, but it was looming on the horizon, and if things didn't get better soon, I was afraid of what might happen. It was fine if he ditched me. We'd been walking away from each other one step at a time for years, but I needed him to be there for the girls. More than ever.

The water started to cool. I'd been in here so long. The entire place steamed like a sauna. I fought the urge to escape into the guest bedroom with Iris. Snuggle in beside her with the room-darkening shades drawn tight and pretend like none of this was happening, but no matter how much I wanted to, I couldn't.

I turned the water off and stepped out of the shower to dry. I would power through this day. This vortex that had been swirling around us and our family. I was going to get us out. Somebody had to because I refused to drown. I'd been thinking that exact thing on the way to Kiersten's party tonight. Maybe some part of me felt our world was going to shift. Like dogs that sense earthquakes right before they hit.

I'd never been one to play much of a leadership role. I was more of a worker bee. Growing up in the military had that effect on you. If nothing else, it taught you how to work, and I hadn't missed out on that lesson. Tell me what to do and I'd do it. I'd be the first one done with the job. I wasn't good at being the person to come up with what we were doing, though. Everyone had their gifts. That's not mine.

Except all the changes in our family hadn't left me any choices except to rise up, and today wasn't going to be any different. I would spend the morning with the kids, and if Ryan woke by noon and was ready to join us, we'd be lucky. He stayed up until four in the morning playing video games most nights. He never even played video games in college. He'd reverted all the way back to high school. That's how bad things had gotten.

I wasn't mad, though. I'd moved past being angry a long time ago. Years ago, probably. I was somewhere else now. A place I'd never been, and losing Kiersten tonight only made it feel more real.

CHAPTER NINE

NOW

BROOKE

This was the first time we were all getting together since it happened.

Fifty-two hours.

That's how long it had been.

All I could think about was that poor baby. Rinley. Raised without a mother.

Or a sibling.

Kiersten was pregnant.

At least that's what they said on KTLA last night. I never watched the local news. Most of the time I forgot we even had cable. I hadn't watched it since 2020. Back in the early quarantine days, when the world got flipped upside down and we watched the body count scroll across the bottom of the screen every night. But I'd turned it on again. Ever since the night of the accident.

Because that's where I was getting all my information about Kiersten's case. None of us there that night were talking about it. At least they weren't talking about it with me. Not like this was unusual. I always felt like I was intruding. Like I wasn't supposed to be there. For all I knew, they could've been at each other's houses for days or texting nonstop.

It wasn't all on them. I realized that. I could've reached out, too, but I didn't know what to say. Truthfully, I'd never really been on the inside of the group. Everyone always liked Abby better. Still did, even though nobody would ever admit such a thing.

The West Hollowood Moms' Club was invite only, and I'd only gotten in because of Abby. They invited her. Not me. I'd always been their second choice. She'd brought the invite home to me after one of her events.

"You're never going to believe this, but I have a tennis client who plays golf with Tommy McCann. Crazy, huh? Anyway, he said his wife belongs to a new moms' club in West Hollywood. And when I say new, I mean like nobody's even had their babies yet. Everyone's pregnant, just like us. He swore it wasn't like a regular moms' club. Just very professional women who've shifted into motherhood and want to hang out with other women doing the same thing. Sounds right up your alley, doesn't it? I told them you'd love to go."

So I went. Alone and without her. And even though everyone tried to quickly change their expressions, there was no mistaking the disappointment when I walked up to the fountain that first time that it was me and not Abby. A hotshot sports agent definitely fit their profile. I didn't have any impressive credentials behind my name. At least none they knew of. The fact I'd sold my corporate credit card company for $7 million when I was twenty-three years old didn't faze them. If it wasn't something you could brag about or post on Instagram, they weren't really interested in it.

But I kept going anyway because I wanted mom friends. The original plan was for Abby to take eight weeks of maternity leave, but we all knew how the original plan was working out. I was without a wife, but even worse—I was without friends. I'd left all my people behind when I'd moved across the country to be with her. Everyone in LA had always been connected to my recovery life with her, which hadn't mattered when I thought we were going to be together forever, but it'd left me without anyone, and making friends as an adult was hard. Especially when you didn't have alcohol to break the social barrier. So, I went every week.

We'd started meeting up when we were pregnant. Kiersten and Whitney had been the logical leaders from the beginning. They were the cocaptains of the West Hollywood Moms' Club like they'd been cocheerleading captains at Pacific Palisades High School.

They'd been best friends since elementary school, and their babies were only five days apart. Five days. No way that happened on accident, but they swore to everyone they didn't plan it that way. I didn't believe them. That was too close.

I bet Whitney's pregnant again too.

That's what they released last night on the news—Kiersten had been ten weeks pregnant. I hadn't been prepared for that one. I thought I was unshockable, but last night blew that theory out of the water.

I never saw that one coming.

I guess they gave dead people pregnancy tests, and hers came back positive? What did the others think about it? Did they already know? Whitney had to know. No way she didn't. Nobody's talking to me about it, though.

The only people talking to me were Detective Perez and her people. There were so many different officers working the case, it was hard to keep track of them all, but she was always at the forefront. The one standing behind the podium on TV and giving all the updates too. Constant updates. Naturally, everyone was obsessed with the case. People liked a good sneak peek behind the golden curtain of the elite and privileged. It was more than that, though. They secretly liked seeing us suffer.

Couldn't blame them. I was the same way. Sometimes I still was, even though technically I was one of them now. I lived in their communities and their neighborhoods. We shopped at the same Trader Joe's and ate at the same fancy restaurants, but I'd never felt like a real part of their lives. The feeling of coming out of my own universe and being dropped into theirs never left. I was an alien on Planet White Privilege. I didn't grow up with money, and people that grew up without money had a very different childhood from those that did.

I'd never felt like more of an outsider. Had they all gotten lawyers? Was that what you did in these types of situations? I had no idea what to do when I got Detective Perez's text early this morning.

I'd been trying to get Julian to nurse when my phone buzzed with a text from an unknown number. An 818 area code. I used to stay off my phone in the mornings, trying to give myself space in my head for my own thoughts, but I haven't been without my phone since Abby told me it was over. I didn't want to miss her reaching out to me even though, at the time, we still lived in the same house and I could walk down to her in the guest bedroom and knock on the door if I wanted to talk to her, but I'd turned into someone I didn't recognize. Desperate and pathetic. Hanging on to crumbs. I didn't want to miss the chance if she realized she'd made a mistake and wanted to take it all back. It was pathetic of me, but I couldn't stop it. The text had nothing to do with Abby, though:

> This is Detective Perez. Can you call our office to schedule a time to come in? (818) 922-4185.

It sounded so innocuous. Completely harmless. Until I called the number and a receptionist answered with "Beverly Hills Police Department."

For some reason, I'd assumed we were meeting in an office somewhere. Like maybe she had an office where she met privately with people like a therapist or like in a doctor's office, but no. We were going down to the police station to meet.

And I wasn't the only one.

Within ten minutes of her call, texts started popping off:

Hey. U awake?

Did you get any weird texts this morning?

Do you think we should talk?

It wasn't long before Natasha had officially made it a group text thread labeled THE SIX: Me. Her. Whitney. Jade. Taylor and Colleen. It was an even shorter time before someone said we needed to meet. Nobody disagreed.

CHAPTER TEN

NOW

JADE

Jesus.

I paced the dining room, eyeing the table. What was I supposed to serve? Was serving people too much? Would they think I was trying to have some sort of weird memorial for Kiersten? I didn't want to offend any of her family traditions.

I rearranged the coffeepot in the center and adjusted the tops of the creamer and milk dishes. I laid out a plate of toffee cookies and a few slices of banana bread. That was too much. It looked like I was trying too hard. I grabbed the plates and hurried them back into the kitchen before anyone arrived. I had no idea how these things worked.

What was I thinking, offering my house for us all to meet?

I hated having people over because our house was so depressing. It was dark and dingy, covered in a layer of dust and grime because I couldn't do everything and keep up with all the household duties too. We'd let go of our housekeeper years ago, after Ryan had gotten laid off the second time. And everything was a mess again. Things got out of control so quickly.

Laundry scattered all over the house. No idea which was clean or not.

I'd spent the entire morning shoving stuff into closets and trying to get things straightened up as best I could because my house was the only logical place to meet right now. Taylor's house was being renovated, so they were staying in an Airbnb on the other side of the city. Colleen's kids were still sick with that nasty virus, so no one was going anywhere near her place. And it's not like we could ask anything of Whitney right now. She was a complete mess. Probably would be for a long time.

Would she come today? She didn't say anything in the group text. She only liked comments in the string. The bare minimum to let us know she was still breathing and she'd seen the plans. She was going to come over last night, but she flaked at the last minute. I couldn't tell if I was relieved or upset. My emotions were all over the place.

I'd made Ryan take Lily to the park because I didn't want them around for any of this discussion and figured he'd understand that given how serious this was, but he acted like I'd asked him to take Lily for a ten-mile walk. I would've had him take Iris, too, but she was running a low fever. On top of everything else going on right now, I had a teething baby.

"It's so hot out," he whined, sounding just like the baby. "We'll just go upstairs and stay there the entire time your friends are here. You won't even know we're here. Promise. We'll totally be out of your way."

"No, you're leaving," I said, shaking my head. There was no way I was letting him hang around the house. "Lily needs the exercise. She's been cooped up for two days and hasn't had any activities. The sun is good for her."

I could've said the truth—that they couldn't be here because he'd never leave me alone and stop asking for help with them—but I didn't because that would only lead to a huge argument. He only took care of Lily by himself when he didn't have any other choice. He just wasn't good with little kids. He was an only child, and he'd never been around them, so he was clueless.

He'd been one of those really anxious dads when Lily was an infant, and I'd thought it was so cute. How he worried that he'd drop her when he was holding her or that somehow her neck would snap back if he didn't keep his hand on it just right. He was terrified of changing her diaper. Every time she cried, he thought he was hurting her.

At first it was cute. Until it wasn't.

All my girlfriends and my sisters assured me it would go away over time. That all first-time dads were nervous, and it just took them longer to adjust, especially ones that had never been around kids before. They gave me all the usual platitudes. How we'd been the ones carrying the baby, so we'd gotten used to being a mother and responsible for another human being for nine months already. So I'd been patient, but Lily was three, and it hadn't gotten any better. He still didn't trust himself to be alone with her. Not to mention that we had a new baby. So, I needed him to step up more than ever before.

I hoped he remembered to give Lily her medicine. She was so—I stopped myself.

No.

He was going to have to learn how to be a parent by himself. *He's a grown-ass man. Not a child,* I reminded myself like I'd been reminding myself ever since my most recent session with my therapist. That was the biggest thing she was working with me on—to stop seeing and treating my husband like one of my children and start treating him like a responsible adult. It was definitely taking some getting used to, especially when he didn't act like one.

I shoved the familiar resentments down. I had to focus. This was way more important.

The door buzzed, and I hurried to answer it, casting one final look at the table behind me and deciding at the last minute to grab a bottle of wine and put it next to the other beverages. It was only eleven in the morning, but some days called for day drinking, and this might be one of them.

CHAPTER ELEVEN

NOW

BROOKE

Jade opened the door with a weird smile on her face, and I gave her an equally awkward one back. I held out the flowering plant I'd picked up from Gelson's on the way over and gave it to her. It felt strange to come empty handed, and I had no idea if a flower was appropriate, but I didn't know what else to bring.

"Thanks." She took it from me, a natural evasion of the weird hug we would've felt obligated to have if she didn't. She hurried through the foyer and into the dining room, and I followed. She set the plant on the table next to the cream and sugar, then turned around and asked, "Do you want coffee? Water?" She pointed to the bottle of wine that was next to the coffee. "Wine?" She giggled, and I giggled back. Some of the nervous tension eased, and then somebody else rang the doorbell, thankfully shifting the attention from me.

Jade headed to answer it, and I was grateful for the second to catch my breath. I grabbed a bottle of water instead of the coffee. I really needed the caffeine, but my stomach was already a twisted, knotted-up mess. Colleen and Taylor walked into the dining room together. Both of them were crying, their arms wrapped tightly around each other.

"I just feel so bad for the baby." Taylor sniffled. Her eyes were so swollen and red they looked painful. She'd clearly been crying all morning. Maybe for days.

I still hadn't cried. I hadn't told anyone that, and I wasn't going to. Not because I was stoically keeping it together. Being brave and strong, and all that crap. I just couldn't cry. It was as if all my emotions had locked themselves up inside me without my consent.

Colleen handed her a tissue and rubbed her back while Taylor blew her nose. "I still can't believe she was pregnant." She noticed me and gave me a weak smile. "Hi."

"What?" Whitney's voice screeched from the entryway, stopping all of us in our tracks.

The three of us whipped around to face her. I hadn't even heard her come in. Colleen and Taylor kept looking back and forth between her and each other, waiting for the other to speak, but neither of them wanted to. I gripped my water bottle so hard it crackled. How could she not know? It'd been the biggest headline in the local media for the last twenty-four hours. Her pregnancy had even made national news.

But she wasn't doing well. Not at all.

Her hair was dirty and matted, twisted in a knot at the back of her head with half of it hanging out. Wrinkled sweatpants hung on her waist and dragged on the floor while she walked. Her white T-shirt was stained with all kinds of different fluids and marks.

Jade swooped in from the kitchen to rescue the moment. She put her arm around Whitney's waist and steadied her on her feet. "Sweetie, let's go into the living room, where we can sit," she said, moving Whitney away from the table in one movement before she had any chance to protest. Whitney shuffled her feet like she was in a trance and allowed herself to be guided by Jade into the living room. Jade sat her down on one of the couches in front of the fireplace and patted her on the knee. "I'm going to get you some water. Just sit tight." She motioned for the rest of us to join her, and we hurried to surround her like a swarm of bees.

"So, you didn't know she was pregnant?" I said quietly after a few beats had passed and no one had spoken.

"Ohmigod, I really can't believe she was pregnant." Whitney cried like she'd already forgotten about it and I'd just reminded her. She brought both hands up to her eyes. Crumpled-up tissue balled in her fists. "I had no idea. Why didn't she tell me?"

The others gave me dirty looks, and my cheeks burned with embarrassment. I never said the right thing. Not in this group. But I thought talking about it might help her. Wasn't that what we were doing here? Processing what had happened? Trying to help each other through it? Seemed like talking about Kiersten's pregnancy would be a logical part of that.

Before Jade had a chance to come back, the door buzzed again, and she let in Natasha. Natasha was silent as she walked in, taking in the scene in front of her: Whitney shell shocked on the couch. Sandwiched between Colleen and Taylor. Their arms slung over her shoulders. She looked so small. Frail.

"Hi, everyone," Natasha said in a soft voice, skipping the coffee and making a beeline for the chair in the corner. A safe space to hide. Be part of the conversation, but not quite. I wish I'd gone there, but instead I was stuck standing awkwardly next to the media console.

Whitney was upset, but she wasn't crying. She was quiet. I wasn't sure which was worse. The vacant, detached stare from today or the hysterical shrieks from the other night. It was hard to be around someone who'd let themselves fall apart when I was working so hard to keep it together.

Jade moved to the center of the room and stood in front of the fireplace. She tried to look comfortable, but I could tell she wasn't. We rarely had meetings here, and it all seemed out of place. Only drawing more attention to the fact that Kiersten was gone since her house had been where we'd spent the most time. Jade's eyes swept the room, taking a moment to latch on to each of us before moving on. "Okay, so it sounds like the police have called everyone in the party back in to be interviewed. They—"

Colleen jumped in. "Everyone? Like all the people at the party?" Jade nodded. "Even the ones that weren't there when it happened?" Jade nodded again. "But why would they be interviewing everyone that was there?"

Jade shrugged and looked around the room. Waiting for someone else to offer an explanation, but I didn't have one. It didn't make sense to me either. Maybe they didn't know we were the only ones there at the time? But we'd told them that already. And besides, they had all the camera footage. Did they think someone pretended to leave and stayed behind? But Kiersten had been the one to see them all out. I remembered because afterward, she'd come out to the pool and announced, "Everyone's gone, bitches. Now we can really party."

I'd just been so happy to be included at the after-party. It wasn't like anyone asked me to stay, but nobody asked me to leave either, which was a good sign. Maybe they were going to forgive me for how I'd acted the last time we'd gotten together. I'd stayed sober all night, and I'd made a point to be sure everyone saw that I was only drinking water. Just because you fell off the wagon once didn't mean you had to fall off again.

"Are you sure?" Natasha piped up from the corner, interrupting my thoughts and bringing me crashing back to the present moment.

"Positive. Tessa texted me this morning after we were all chatting. So did Ebony. Everyone is going in today. Sounds like Perez has back-to-back appointments."

"At least they're thorough," I said. Colleen and Taylor exchanged glances like I'd said something wrong again. That was it. I was going to sit here and not say another word for the rest of the time. I didn't even know why I bothered with them.

Taylor dropped her voice low like someone was close and might overhear. "Do you want to know what else I heard?" She paused for dramatic effect because of course we all wanted to know. "They know we had edibles too."

Colleen burst out laughing, and Taylor immediately looked hurt.

"What?" she asked, her lower lip wavering like it did every time she cried.

"It's just that edibles? Everyone does them now. We were a bit tipsy. They made us tipsier. That's all. You just said it so scandalous." Colleen giggled. Taylor still looked hurt.

Natasha was looking back and forth between them like she didn't know what she thought. "They—"

"She never told me she was pregnant," Whitney interrupted, sending the conversation into silence immediately. The empty space grew more and more uncomfortable.

Natasha took a huge breath and finally broke the silence. "So, it's true? I was hoping it wasn't. I was hoping it was something they'd just made up. You know how everyone likes to talk and blow everything out of proportion."

"She never told me she was pregnant," Whitney said again, like maybe we hadn't heard her the first time.

Taylor rubbed her leg gently. "I know. It makes it harder. The thought that it wasn't just her. Like she was going to have a baby. That's why I know it wasn't suicide."

Whitney's head spun to face her. "Suicide? Someone is saying she died by suicide? Are you out of your mind?" She looked like she wanted to come at her.

Taylor's cheeks flushed. "I . . . I mean . . . I didn't say that. Somebody else did. I just . . ." She scanned the room. Desperately pleading with all of us to jump in and help her, but I couldn't save her. I had no clue what to say. I was just glad Whitney wasn't coming at me this time. Taylor finally just had no choice but to continue. "Someone said it in one of the group chats that's going around—"

"Which group chat? There's another one besides the joggers?" Jade interrupted. Being the one to know all the mom groups was her role. She hung with all of them. If you wanted to know which story time was happening at which library, she could tell you without even having to look it up.

"No, not that one."

"Which one?" Jade pressed.

Taylor looked slightly annoyed that she wouldn't let it go. It wasn't a competition. She could have other mom friends. Be in different groups. "Just Raquel, Zoe, and Emily. For some reason, we all ended up in a chat together."

Jade still looked bothered.

"So, one of them said it?" Whitney looked annoyed. Or hurt. I couldn't tell which. Taylor nodded. "That's the stupidest thing I've ever heard. Kiersten would never commit suicide. Never. She was like the happiest person on the planet."

"Sometimes the happiest people on the outside are the saddest ones on the inside," Colleen said, sounding like an Instagram post.

Whitney shook her head. "Nope. If you think that, then you didn't know her at all."

Colleen was right. Look at Robin Williams or all the other comedians that had experienced death by suicide. I wanted to jump in, except I wasn't saying another word today.

"Whoever said that is just dumb," Whitney continued. "Who throws themselves a party and then decides to off themselves at the end of it?" She looked disgusted, but there was life in her body and behind her words for the first time since the accident. Power was slowly returning to her body.

That was good. We needed her.

"So, what do we tell the police?" Natasha asked, coming forward to stand next to her. She'd noticed the change too. Whitney was magnetic when she was present, and she was back. At least for the moment.

"The truth," Whitney said. "We tell them the truth."

CHAPTER TWELVE

THEN

BROOKE

I tiptoed my way inside the house, not wanting to wake Abby or Julian after my night out with Whitney and the girls, but I was quiet for nothing. It didn't take long to realize they were gone. At first, I thought she'd taken him with her, but she left a note on the counter saying she'd dropped him at her mom's. An old-school note written on a Post-it because if she'd texted me, there would've been a conversation about it, and she didn't want to talk to me. Not in any real way.

I'd spent the first ten minutes at dinner telling Kiersten all about what was happening and how I couldn't get Abby to talk to me about anything in our marriage. I just needed her to talk to me. She'd loved me once, and love like that didn't just die. Her love for me was in there somewhere. That's what I'd told Kiersten, and she'd agreed with me. We stopped talking about it as soon as Whitney sat down beside her, though. Whitney hated talking about Abby, and it was so obvious that she was disappointed when I told her that Abby wasn't coming.

I crinkled the note into a ball and chucked it into the trash. Abby hadn't bothered telling me where she was. I'd never been one of those women that kept close tabs on my partner, but I was obsessed with her

Keep Your Friends Close

every move. Full-on stalker mode. I'd broken into her phone, watched all her social media activity from spammer accounts. I'd even reached out to her as another girl just to see what she'd do. It'd taken me an entire weekend to create a fake IG account. I didn't want to make it obvious. I couldn't have her be the first person I reached out to, so I spent all weekend interacting with all these other people and accounts instead. She'd never responded to any of my DMs or even liked a single post. I'd physically followed her in the car more than once. Actually gotten into my car with Julian strapped into the car seat and shadowed her like a private investigator. I was out of control and didn't know how to stop myself.

Not that I could confront her with anything I'd found. That was the problem. She valued her privacy, and I'd crossed every single boundary we'd ever created. Installing a hidden keylogger app on her phone was an entirely different level I didn't even know I was capable of. I kept telling myself to quit, but I couldn't. That's what happened when your world fell out from underneath you without any warning. Her announcement that she was leaving me. That she didn't want to be married anymore was about as unexpected and dramatic as if an actual bomb had landed in our kitchen.

"Come on, there had to be some kind of sign. Something . . . ," my best friend said after she'd forced me out of the bed I'd been in for three days. That's where I went in the days following my earth shattering. Straight to bed. I'd still be there if it weren't for Julian. Taking care of him was the only thing keeping me breathing. I loved him more than I loved myself.

"There was nothing. Not a single one. We were happy. I thought we were happy," I said to her that day just like I said to everyone else that asked afterward whenever I told them we're separated. They all asked the same question, and no one ever believed that I had no idea and that there weren't any signs, but I didn't and there weren't.

"I don't understand," I'd said in the seconds after Abby told me. Her words wouldn't register. They didn't resonate with any part of the reality I'd dreamed for my life. The one we'd worked so hard to create together. They just didn't fit. They were wrong.

She peered at me with the same hazel eyes—one slightly smaller than the other—that I'd been gazing into for over eight years. She looked the same. Her face was the same. Her lips, too, as they moved, speaking the words a second time: "I can't do this anymore. I don't want to be married to you."

It was incredibly disorienting. As if I'd left my own body. Like my head just detached from my body on a string, floating like a balloon. I couldn't cry. I couldn't move. I could barely breathe. All I could get out still, again, a second time, was "I don't understand."

And then, anger and irritation filled her face in a way I'd never seen before. I reached for her like I was reaching out for a ghost, as if I knew whoever she'd been to me was already gone. "Abby?"

It came out almost a whisper.

Next came the tears. A flood of them. Hot down both cheeks. Normally, this was the spot where she'd crumble. No matter what kind of a fight we were having.

"I hate when you cry, baby." That's what she'd always say.

But she didn't say that. She didn't say anything. She just looked at me with a cold, detached stare as if all she wanted was for me to stop.

I brought my hand up to my mouth. "Ohmigod." This was happening.

Those first few days afterward were still a blur. I didn't know how I stayed sober through them. I'd never lost anyone close to me before, but I imagined this was what it felt like. As if all the color and the air had been drained from the universe. A huge gaping hole inside you where the person used to be. The most treasured spot they used to hold.

That was the part about death that nobody discussed—how incredibly disorienting it was. And it didn't matter what anyone said; I lost

Abby that day. Whoever she was to me died in that instant. As real as if a police officer had knocked on my door and told me that she'd been hit by a car.

There were moments I wished that were the case, like it'd be better if she were just dead. It was worse having to live with her ghost. Her pretending like I didn't exist. That what we'd experienced wasn't real. She looked at me like I was crazy whenever I approached her about anything, really cornered her.

"What about our vows?" I'd screamed at her once, waving them in her face. I'd printed them out earlier that day. But I didn't need to print them. I knew every single one by heart since we'd written them together. Practiced them until they were perfect. *I promise to stay even when it gets hard. Even when things change and I don't understand.* I threw it at her. "Remember that, Abby? Remember?"

"You should call your therapist," she said.

It wasn't what she'd said—it was how she'd said it. Her words weren't mean. She hadn't meant them that way. She'd said them like you'd say to a casual friend or an acquaintance. Someone you were concerned about but whose problems you didn't want to be bothered with, and you didn't want to seem like a total asshole by just blowing them off.

"I hate you!" I'd yelled at her.

All the memories violently assaulted me like real intruders as I walked through the house making my way to the bedroom. We'd bought the *Hamilton* tickets six months ago at one of the first moms' club charity events that we went to. Back when we went to everything together. In our old life, she would've been there tonight too. Right in the center.

I'd asked all the other girls if they'd talked to her even though I promised myself the entire drive over that I wouldn't. They all said the same thing. It was the identical reply no matter what or who I asked, as if someone had given them a script for how they're supposed to handle me.

"I'm sorry, Brooke, but I just really don't want to get in the middle of your divorce."

I didn't know which bugged me more. The fact that no one wanted to be there for me and hear my side. Or the fact that they called it getting in the middle of our divorce instead of our marriage. They all knew it was over too. Just like that. How was it possible?

I still didn't know.

Nothing was right with the universe.

CHAPTER THIRTEEN

NOW

WHITNEY

Carl wasn't in the room this time to give me drugs to calm down. Just Colin for a brief second. He'd walked me inside the station but wasn't allowed to go back to the interview room with me. I'd never been inside a police station before. The headquarters of the Beverly Hills Police Department looked as gorgeous as the houses surrounding it. It was hard to imagine criminals inside something so pretty.

It was just Detective Perez in the room. The guy helping her out the night at Kiersten's wasn't here. Good. I didn't like him anyway.

"Have a seat," she said, pointing to the chair in front of her Restoration Hardware executive desk. It was as nice as the one at my house. Beverly Hills treated their officers well, especially the ones as decorated as she was. Lines of distinguished service medals and awards, including Detective of the Year, hung on the wall behind her. They sat next to her NYU degrees. She'd graduated summa cum laude, followed by a criminal-justice fellowship at Cornell. She watched me take it all in, her lips in a half-turned-up grin. She was impressive, and she knew it. She gave me a few more seconds before asking, "How are you doing?"

"I'm okay," I said because what else could I say? That I was a complete and total wreck who hadn't been able to feed my own baby since my best friend died? That I hadn't had enough energy to take a shower before I got here? How every time I thought about Kiersten being gone, I wanted to disappear from the planet?

"Great." She leaned forward into her desk. "I know this is hard, so thank you for coming in. We weren't able to talk much the night of the party, so I appreciate you taking the time to come back."

"Anything for Kiersten," I said. "Do you know what happened to her yet?"

I was still reeling from finding out she'd been pregnant. We did every single step of our first pregnancy together, from the maddening infertility treatments in the beginning, through the awful morning sickness when we finally got pregnant, and all the way to delivery. Our deliveries were so close together that we overlapped in the hospital for two days. We'd been more like each other's birth partners than our husbands were, and she hadn't said one thing to me about being pregnant. Hadn't hinted they were even trying.

Why?

Kiersten didn't do anything without a reason. She planned her life and her days down to the smallest detail, but I wasn't the only one totally surprised about it. Tommy was just as shocked when he heard the news.

"We weren't trying to get pregnant, Whit. We were barely even having sex," he'd said last night. We spent three hours on FaceTime. Most of it without talking. We just didn't know what else to do with ourselves in the middle of the night while the rest of the world was sleeping and our world was ending.

Most guys complained about not getting enough sex, but he wasn't lying. Rinley was only four months old, and Kiersten had barely been given the all clear to have sex again. Your first time after giving birth was a lot like your first time having sex—painful and disappointing. We'd

66

both said the same thing—we weren't going there again for a while. Not until we felt better and our vaginas healed. It must've happened the first time they had sex because as far as I knew, they hadn't had sex since.

And there was absolutely no way the baby was anyone else's but Tommy's. Even though that's what everyone was probably saying, but Kiersten wasn't the cheating kind. She didn't have an unfaithful bone in her body.

It was driving me crazy not knowing why she hadn't told me, but the only logical thing I could come up with was the same thing I'd told Tommy last night: she didn't know she was pregnant. Especially because she'd been drinking at the party.

I kept going over that night. Retracing. Rewinding. Slowing things down. Every little step. Trying to figure out how she could've possibly drowned in that pool. I came to the same conclusion every time—there was no way she just drowned on her own. I couldn't wait to hear what Detective Perez knew and where they were in the investigation. Hopefully, she had answers, but she shook her head in response to my question.

"We're waiting on some test results from the medical examiner. Those should tell us more about what happened," she said.

"What results?" I asked. Tell them more about what? What were they looking for?

She gave me a vague response: "Oh, you know, just the standard ones." As if I knew the kinds of tests they ran when somebody died or there was anything standard about this, but I didn't push her. She didn't look like someone that liked to be pushed.

"Since you were struggling so much the other night, we didn't get a chance to talk, which again"—she paused and made eye contact—"I'm sorry that you're having to go through such a painful and difficult time."

"Thanks." I nodded.

"It gave me an opportunity to talk to the other women that were at the party, and everyone's pretty much said the same thing about you and Kiersten."

"What's that?"

"That you were really close. How the two of you have the kind of friendship most of us only dream of having." My eyes filled with tears as she spoke. That's why this was so hard. Right there. She continued, "So, I figure you probably know her better than anyone else. Maybe even her husband." She gave me a knowing look. She wasn't wrong. "So, I'm just going to ask you, What do you think happened to Kiersten Friday night?"

"See, that's the thing, Perez. Can I call you that? Is that okay?" *Detective Perez* was just so formal. Made her sound like a teacher, and I didn't like that. She gave me a clipped nod, and I continued. "I've gone over that night like a thousand times. That's all I do. And there's no way Kiersten jumped in the pool in the middle of her own party and just drowned." I shook my head at the ridiculousness of it. "First, she's an amazing swimmer. I already told you that, but just in case you forgot, she was. Second, why would Kiersten leave her own party and go all the way out to the pool by herself? For what? She'd never do something like that. Not without a reason. And look." I held my hands up. "I'm not saying she'd never jump in the pool. She could be wild, and she might jump in the pool if she was drunk, and you already know we were pretty wasted that night. So, Kiersten jumping in the pool? That's actually a possibility. But here's why that didn't happen." I shook my head to emphasize the point. "No matter how wasted Kiersten was, there's no way she's ruining that dress. Even in her most drunken moment, she's taking that thing off and then jumping in the pool. No way in hell when she's wearing a Valentino."

"I can certainly appreciate that." Perez smiled, and she wasn't lying. I'd spotted the Harry Winston watch peeking out from underneath her cuff.

"It's super weird that she'd be by the pool in the first place. Like why would she abandon her party and head out there by herself? I know you don't know her, but that's not like her at all. She'd never leave a party, especially one she was throwing. And besides, it was just us left. The real party was just getting started." I paused, pushing down the emotions threatening to break their way to the surface. Talking about this with her made it so real. "What if someone else was involved?"

There, I'd said it. Had I been thinking that all along?

She leaned across the table, meeting me halfway. "I'm going to level with you, Whitney, because you were her best friend, and I can tell she felt as strongly about you as you do about her. We've been approaching this from the very first night as if someone else was involved."

"You have?" She nodded. Smiled at me. Pleased she was letting me in on a secret. I slowly sank back in my chair. I'd said it, but I wasn't really sure I meant it. Hearing her say it back freaked me out a little. "How come? I mean, Why? Does everyone know that? I—"

She raised her hand to stop me. "Again, we're in the beginning phases of the investigation and we don't have an official medical exam-iner's report yet, so most of your questions, I'm not going to be able to answer. However, I just happen to be friends with him, and he owes me a favor, so he told me his initial findings. Oh, and also, can't believe I forgot that part—the fact that she was pregnant." She paused and gave me her most penetrating stare yet. It made it hard to swallow. "You knew she was pregnant, right?"

"Of course I did," I lied. I wasn't about to get hung up on trying to explain why Kiersten hadn't told me she was pregnant. There was a completely logical reason for it, and I wasn't wasting any of our limited time on that. We needed to figure out what happened to her.

"Any idea who the baby's father was?"

I balked on the inside but smiled on the outside. "Tommy, of course," I said, giving her a penetrating stare, so there was no mistak-ing there weren't any other options. There's no way she had a secret life. None. I was with Tommy on this one.

Detective Perez nodded and quickly continued, "Besides the preg-nancy, their findings were consistent with our line of thinking that she wasn't outside by herself." She cleared her throat. The telltale sign that someone was going to deliver big news. "They found a large laceration on the back of her head and concluded cause of death was due to blunt force trauma secondary to drowning."

"What do you mean? Like she fell? She fell and hit her head and then what? She was so disoriented from the fall that she stumbled into the pool and drowned?"

"No," she said. "The injury is consistent with being hit with an object."

"So, someone hit her and then dragged her into the pool?" I couldn't wrap my brain around any of this. It didn't make sense.

"That's a possibility. It's also possible that they knocked her out and left her there. She could've stumbled into the pool after she regained consciousness. We can't forget that she'd been drinking too. Had she taken any of the edibles?"

"I'm not sure." We'd all eaten edibles that night. Colleen brought the ones she always got when she and her friends did their girl trips to Palm Springs—Elev8. "Kiersten's never been one to actually eat them." Perez gave me a funny look, and I explained, "I didn't know that, though, until a couple years ago because she always took them and acted high. But then one night when we were really drunk, she told me she rarely ate them. She'd take like the tiniest nibble and then get rid of the rest without anyone seeing. Sometimes she didn't even do that. She put the whole thing in her mouth and then spit it out as quickly as she could before any of the THC seeped into her tongue. I bet she didn't even eat any of it that night." Perez scribbled something on the notepad in front of her. I was dying to know what she'd written. Was it about what I said or something else? I waited for her to finish before going on.

"Here's the other thing about Kiersten being in the pool. Wouldn't she have screamed or yelled for help? Someone would've heard that. Maybe not with all the music, but the bathroom off the baby's room faced the pool, and Brooke was in there. Plus, we were going in and out of there all night. Someone would've noticed or heard her screaming."

"No." She shook her head again. "The images of people flailing their arms and screaming wildly for help while they drown are only for the movies. Drowning is actually a very silent death. You can't scream for help when you're desperately trying to breathe. And the first time you do, you take more water into your lungs. People usually slip away quietly without a sound."

It seemed so lonely. She was just out there, steps away, without any way to call for us. The familiar crushing sadness returned to my chest. Tears wet my cheeks.

Perez continued. "We're considering lots of possibilities, but the most likely is that she wasn't out there alone. We've narrowed down the window of time that it happened. It's amazing what science can do now, right?" she said with a strange glint in her eye. One I'd never seen before. "What were you doing between ten forty-five and eleven the night at the party?"

"What was I doing?" I balked and pointed to myself.

"Yes." She cracked her knuckles. She'd shifted into total police mode. "We've reviewed all the security footage both inside and outside of the house that night. After the last worker left at ten thirty, nobody else enters the house until the paramedics arrive. That much we know for sure because every entry is on video. There were only six of you in that house when it happened, well, seven if you count Kiersten."

"You think I killed my best friend?" I snorted. All respect I'd held toward her for being such a badass was gone. Poof. If she thought that was what was going on here, then she was way off base. Had she been trying to pin this on me the entire time? "Kiersten was closer to me than anyone. We've been friends since kindergarten. Did you know that?" Of course she didn't. She didn't actually know anything about us. Only the judgments she'd made based on her own opinions and what everybody else was saying about us, and they were saying a lot. The media hadn't shut up about it. "Nobody ever believes me, but I was super shy when I was young, and my first day of kindergarten was terrifying. My mom had to drag me through the door and tear me off her. I was standing there terrified, but I wasn't crying because I held it in. Even back then. Anyway, Kiersten saw me, and she could tell how scared I was even though I wasn't crying. She walked over to me and took my hand without saying a word. She led me over to the carpet for circle time, and she's walked me through every hard thing in my life ever since, so what makes you think for one second I would ever do anything to hurt her?"

Her face softened as my words landed. They melted her reserve. You could feel my love for Kiersten in every word, and if she couldn't, then she was oblivious and they needed to put somebody else in charge of this case.

She put her hands up and pushed her chair back. "Okay, okay," she said, her body posture conceding defeat. "I get it. You loved Kiersten and would never hurt her. So, if you didn't, then who did?"

I didn't need any time to think about what I said next: "Look at Brooke."

Perez raised her eyebrows at me. Surprised that I'd given her a name so quickly or by the fact that I'd said it was Brooke. Either way, it didn't matter. If anyone in that house was a murderer, it was her.

"Here's what I'll tell you: if you're looking for anyone that's unstable in our group, I'm going to save you the time—Brooke's a train wreck." That wasn't anything like we'd planned on yesterday. Wait and see what they had to say. Well, I'd waited, and I didn't need to see anyone else.

"Why do you say her?" Perez asked.

"She's been unhinged for months. Ever since her and Abby broke up. She even started drinking again over it. Nobody even wanted her there that night after the drunken scene she'd made at the last party she showed up at, but Kiersten was way too nice to ask her to leave."

"Are you sure about that?"

I raised my eyebrows at her. "What do you mean?"

"Maybe she *did* ask Brooke to leave. It didn't go well last time someone asked Brooke to leave a party, did it?" she asked pointedly. "Maybe something worse happened this time."

CHAPTER FOURTEEN

NOW

BROOKE

Abby sat shaking her leg next to me. So strange that they'd invited her in to talk too. I'd had no idea. I was surprised when I walked into the waiting room to find her sitting here. She wasn't even at the party, so what could they possibly want from her?

She'd given me a nod when I walked through the door, like we were some strange acquaintances, not two people who'd sworn to spend the rest of their lives together and had a small baby at home. It was her egg. I'd carried her egg inside me. Because it was important to her that she felt like she had a part of it. Now I just wanted to slap her, but instead I sat next to her because as much as I hated her, all I wanted was to be near her.

"I didn't know you were coming," I said, like this was some kind of awkward first-date encounter.

"I didn't have much choice," she responded, not looking pleased. She motioned for me to come closer as she leaned over to whisper. "Don't you think it's weird that they called me to come in? I mean, I wasn't even there."

But I couldn't focus on anything she was saying. All I could focus on was the smell of her. The tinge of sweat mixed with coconut oil because she refused to wear antiperspirant, coupled with a hint of lavender from the baby lotion she wore because it was the only lotion that didn't make her sensitive skin break out. Memories flooded me— Sunday mornings in bed, fresh-out-of-the-shower hugs before work. Late-night cuddles. Binge-watching Netflix on the couch. All of it. And it was just gone. Gone like she was.

"Don't you?" Abby nudged me.

I dragged myself from the memories, tried to be present. Not look like a basket case in front of her. She hated my emotions. Those had always been tough with her, and she'd told me stories about how the women she used to date always complained about her getting turned off whenever they got emotional, and I'd never believed her. That's not who she was—had been—with me. But I was seeing it now.

"What could they possibly want with you?" I agreed with her. "They—" An officer stuck his head out from the hallway, interrupting me, and motioned toward her. "Good luck," I called out as he led her away. Embarrassment flooded me.

Good luck?

Why would I say something like that? Oh well. At least I hadn't cried. That mattered. I eyed the clock above the receptionist's head: 3:45.

How many people had they interviewed today? Where were we on the order of things? Were they interviewing everyone's spouses or just mine? I still couldn't shake the feeling that it was too strange for her to be here. I pulled up THE SIX group text chain. I typed and erased until I finally settled on this:

Hey! Just got to police station 🚓. Abby went in first. So strange that she's here. Anyone else's husbands come? Just seeing if we're being discriminated against 😜

Hopefully, trying to make light of it wouldn't make it seem so serious? I hit send before I could change my mind. The minutes dragged, and nobody had responded by the time they brought Abby back out. Her eyes met mine in the waiting room, and she gave me a quick nod as if to say it wasn't so bad. She looked okay too. I held back from giving her a hug even though that's all I wanted to do.

Be cool, Brooke. Be cool.

I waved and gave her a small smile. She smiled back, and I tried not to burst inside. To keep my face straight until she'd left the building. Emotion. The teeniest piece, but it was something, and I couldn't remember the last time I'd gotten anything from her. She headed past me as the officer motioned for me to follow him next.

He led me down a wide hallway that opened up to offices on each side. Detective Perez's office was much nicer than anything I'd expected.

"Sit," she said, motioning to the leather chairs in front of her desk.

"Thanks," I said to both her and the man who'd escorted me here. All my nerves were gone. I was giddy from Abby's attention, but I tried not to show it. The last thing I needed to do was seem happy to be here.

The leather was still warm from Abby's body. How many of us had cycled through this chair today? By the looks of it, a lot because Detective Perez was exhausted. There were dark circles underneath her eyes popping out from drinking too much caffeine.

"Thanks for coming in, Brooke," she said.

"You're welcome," I said, doing my best to stay focused on looking serious and not smiling.

"How have you been doing?"

I averted my eyes. I wasn't getting caught in that stare. Not this time. "It's been tough."

"Sounds like lots of things have been tough for you lately."

"Did Abby say something? What'd she say?"

"I'm just going to get right down to things. Pretty much everyone I've talked to today has expressed concerns for you, Brooke."

I didn't care what everyone else had to say about me. They could say whatever they wanted to. I wanted to know what Abby said. Did she tell her I was struggling? Did she say it because she was worried about me? Did that mean she cared? If she said something, then that had to mean she cared, didn't it?

"My wife and I have been having some problems."

"Problems?" She wrinkled her forehead. "From what I understand, the two of you are going through a pretty painful divorce."

She said the two of us. What if Abby said it was hard? Was it really hard for her? Maybe she was second-guessing herself. It took me a beat to realize Detective Perez was still waiting for me to speak.

I nodded quickly. "It hasn't been easy."

"People are concerned about you."

"Which people? Who said something?" I sounded paranoid, but not for the reasons she thought.

She laid her hands on the table and slowly twiddled her thumbs in the most maddening way. "I'm not really at liberty to let people know what others in an active investigation have said about them, but what I can tell you is that everyone I've talked to so far has expressed some concerns for your mental health."

I tried not to beam. I folded my hands tightly on my lap. That included Abby. She was concerned. My spirit wanted to leap out of my body and dance around the room. There was still hope. As long as she still cared, there was still hope and I was going to hold on to that thread no matter how thin it was for as long as I could.

"How do you feel about your mental health?" Detective Perez interrupted my thoughts again.

I shrugged. "It's no secret that I've struggled, but everyone struggles when they're having marriage problems and especially when they're new parents." Did she forget I have a six-month-old baby at home? One that I was primarily responsible for?

"I understand those things are tough. I do." Her face was hard to read. Her eyes nearly impossible. "Do you think they've been more difficult for you than most new parents?"

I shook my head. If anything, I was coping better. Something like this would destroy most people. But it hadn't destroyed me. I was still moving and breathing. That said something.

"Can you tell me about the incident that happened on the fourth of September at the Griffins' party?" She glanced down at the file on her desk, splayed open in front of her. I hadn't noticed it until now. Did she write down the things everyone said?

"Who said something about the Griffins?" I asked, shifting in my seat to try to catch a glimpse of the notes on her desk. I'd only acted that way once in my entire life. Even at my worst drunken moments, I'd never been violent. My therapist agreed that it was only because I'd drunk so much so fast after so many years of sobriety. She said I was lucky I didn't have a seizure. I'd surprised myself as much as anyone else that afternoon.

"Multiple people." Detective Perez folded her hands atop her desk.

The utter humiliation of that day and that moment rose in my chest. It burned my cheeks. "That day was completely out of character for me. You need to know that. I don't want you to think I go around acting like that all the time."

"From what I hear, you'd been sober for many years up until recently, right?"

"Eight years," I said.

"That's how you and Abby met? In treatment?"

I nodded. That was the part that was so hard. She'd been in treatment for two weeks when I got there, so she had a few days before me, but she'd been a part of every step of my sobriety journey. I didn't know this life without her.

"And now you're sober again?" she asked like she wasn't sure.

"Twenty-seven days." I couldn't believe I was back to counting my sobriety in days. "I haven't touched a drop since the party." Kiersten's party had been the chance for me to redeem myself. I hadn't seen most of them since the incident, and I desperately wanted to make things right.

Detective Perez shrugged like she didn't believe me or it wasn't a big deal. I couldn't tell which. "My pop's been in the program for years. Relapse is part of the journey."

I shook my head. "Not mine." Which sounded completely hypocritical, but whatever happened at the Griffins' wasn't me. It was some sort of weird trauma response to everything happening.

"Okay," she said in the most noncommittal way, wearing her impossible-to-read expression. "I'd still like to hear what happened at the Griffins'." She said it like I had options, but we both knew that wasn't true.

"It was such a terrible day," I said, grimacing. "It just sucks that whenever two people split up, people have to choose sides. I mean, everyone always says they won't, but that never happens. Everyone always picks."

"And they picked Abby that day?"

They picked Abby every day. That's what I wanted to say, but I held back. "The Griffins were having a big gender-reveal party, and they'd gone all out for it, you know? One of those ridiculous over-the-top ones? All the women from our moms' club were invited, and everyone went."

"Yourself included?"

That was the thing—I never received a formal invitation. So, Abby thought I shouldn't be there. Whitney agreed with her. She always agreed with her. There'd never been a doubt she was Team Abby.

"Technically, I wasn't invited. They invited Abby, but everyone knows if you invite one spouse, it's super rude not to invite the other."

"Yes, but she's not your spouse anymore."

Did she really need to drive that point home?

"Yes, but it was for the kids and about the kids, so whenever that's the case, it goes without saying that either parent can bring the child to the party, you know what I mean?" Except she probably didn't because she didn't have kids, and people without children have no idea what it's like.

"You didn't have Julian that weekend, though, did you?"

I shook my head. She was as bad as Abby. Was she really going to make me say it?

"So, then why did you go?" she asked.

She was.

"Because I wanted to see Abby." I hung my head. I'd clung to my reasoning with both Abby and Whitney even though they were right. For some reason, Whitney had been just as mad about me showing up uninvited as Abby had. Abby had stormed off and left after I'd created a huge scene, but Whitney was the one who confronted me. She didn't exactly confront me. More like went ballistic on me afterward while I was trying to clean up.

"Seriously, Brooke! You need to leave. That was totally uncalled for." She'd barged into the bathroom after the scene I'd just created in the backyard.

"I didn't mean to. It just happened," I cried as I frantically splashed cold water all over my face, trying to get myself to calm down. Angry red blotches dotted my skin. Mascara trailed thick under my eyes and down my cheeks.

"You can't show up uninvited and attack people. What the hell is wrong with you? You literally ruined the entire party." I'd never seen Whitney so mad.

"I didn't mean to. I'm sorry," I cried, but that didn't make what I'd done any better.

It'd never dawned on me that Abby would bring Liza to the party. Never once. I'd expected her to be alone. Nothing could've prepared me for the wave of emotions that overtook all rational thought when I saw the two of them together. It was one thing to see it on social media. But in real life?

It was a straight sucker punch to the gut.

And I needed immediate anesthetic.

It'd been eight years since I took my last drink. Eight years. One month. Fourteen days.

I hurried over to the outside bar and asked for a shot of whiskey. The bartender gave me the strangest look and glanced around like he wasn't sure whether there was someone filming the entire thing as a joke. He stood underneath the huge bouquet of pink and blue baby balloons and pointed to the pitchers on the table. "We have some mimosas," he said with a forced smile.

"I need something stronger."

Judgment clouded his expression as he pointed to one of the other pitchers. "There's vodka in that strawberry lemonade," he said.

"I'll take the vodka." If he didn't give it to me soon, I was going to jump over the table and grab it myself.

"You can't . . . I mean . . ." He looked around, hoping one of the caterers would come to his rescue.

I didn't let him finish. I put my hand on the table, and he sensed I wasn't playing around. He looked at me like I was crazy while he quickly filled a glass with ice and started to pour.

"Fill it up," I barked, not recognizing the sound of my voice.

He didn't try to hide his disgust or his disdain as he handed it to me. I swiped it from him and hurried away from the table as fast as I could. I didn't care about his judgment. Only relief.

The vodka burned my throat on the way down.

I stood off to the side, where I had a perfect view of the two of them. I watched the way Abby placed her hand on Liza's lower back and carefully guided her through the crowd. Liza looked stunning. There was no denying that. But her low-cut top with her cleavage spilling out was more appropriate for a night at the club than it was with a bunch of babies and toddlers running around. I couldn't help but giggle as her long heels kept getting stuck in the grass. She kept tugging her dress down and pulling her shoes out of the mud. It made me feel better that she was so uncomfortable.

But then Abby brought her over to the gender-reveal cake, and she started whispering in her ear. She had no right flaunting her in front of me like that. I took another big swallow. My tongue had already gone numb. I took one more, then another. All my thoughts finally coming together as one voice.

They were practically making out. How inappropriate. Maybe it was time they knew that I was there. I drained the rest of my glass and tossed it into the bushes before marching over to where they stood next to the gender-reveal cake. Abby's eyes widened in horror and surprise as soon as she saw me.

"Hi, Brooke," she said nervously, her eyes darting over to Liza and back to me. "What are you doing here?"

"What am I doing here?" I pointed at myself. "What are *you* doing here with *her*?" I spat out *her* like it was a dirty word.

Abby stepped back and frowned. "What am I doing here? Um . . . I'm at the party I got invited to."

"What is she doing here?" I waved my finger at her. Liza stood next to Abby, draped on her arm like a fancy purse.

Abby grabbed my elbow and hissed in my ear. "Can you not make a scene? Seriously. I have clients here. This is embarrassing. You—" She suddenly snapped back. "Ohmigod. Have you been drinking?"

She leaned in like she was going to smell me, and I jerked away, shoving her off me. "Oh, this is embarrassing for you, Abby?" I raised my voice even louder. I hoped every single one of her clients heard. People needed to know what she'd done. That she was abandoning her family. Leaving everything we'd promised to build and do together.

"I'm sorry if this is too uncomfortable for you to have your girlfriend meet your wife."

Liza stepped forward. Her expensive perfume assaulting me. She wrapped her arm around Abby's waist. "I'm sorry, but you're not her wife. Not anymore." She'd batted her long fake lashes at me and smiled at me like she'd won a prize.

My blood boiled at the memory. "I couldn't tell you what happened next," I explained to Detective Perez. "One minute I was standing there confronting Abby, and then as soon as Liza stepped forward and said that, I just lost it. I went at her."

I'd never attacked anyone in my life. I'd never been in a fight. All the kids in the neighborhoods I grew up in used to fight, but never me. Violence scared me. There was no one more terrified of my behavior that day than me. That's why I hadn't taken a drink since. I'd gotten back on the wagon as fast as I'd fallen off it.

She didn't pick her head up while she read from her notes. "A couple people have said that you suddenly grabbed Liza by the throat. That Abby had to wrestle you off her and then you tried to punch her. Do you remember any of that?"

I didn't remember any of it, but I'd seen the video. The one Abby sent me that night that someone had taken during the party. They'd had multiple photographers there that night, and someone caught the entire incident. She'd sent me the video along with a text. Two words.

Get help

I wasn't going to lie to Detective Perez. She'd probably seen all of it too. I didn't have an explanation for my behavior, but I had to try. "It all happened really fast. You know how people say they saw red right before they lost it? Well, I didn't see red. It was like just blinding white and then nothing until I was wrestling with Abby on the ground." The gender-reveal cake was all over me. Blue.

It was blue. Another baby boy.

"And that was when?" She glanced at her notes again, but she probably had them memorized. "Three weeks before the party at Kiersten's?" I nodded even though I didn't want to. I knew where this was going, and I didn't like it. It was what I'd been afraid of. "The other girls said that no one had talked to you since the party, and they were surprised you were at Kiersten's. They didn't think you'd show up at any of their functions after that."

"I went to the party because I already had the invitation, and once you've been invited, they don't send you uninvite cards." There was no way I was going to let that horrible moment at the Griffins' be the last image they had of me. I needed a chance to redeem myself.

"Had you seen any of those women since the gender reveal?"

"I ran into Colleen at Ralphs, and once I saw Natasha running down Laurel Canyon, but other than that, no."

"So, the party was the first time?" I nodded. "How'd that go?"

"Well, not so good." I gave her a funny look. The truth was I'd done a great job that night. I swore for three days that I wasn't going to talk about Abby or what had happened at the Griffins' the entire night. I was going to pretend like it never happened and show them I was sober again. That I was right back on track. I made a point of making sure everyone saw me drinking water. And if there hadn't been the accident, I would've considered the night a success.

"It must've been really awkward and painful."

"It was," I said curtly, but I was done talking about it. It wasn't like she was a friend. She didn't really care about me or what happened to me. Only finding out what happened to Kiersten. Asking questions and pretending to care about people was her job. "But are we really going to spend all of our time talking about that?"

For a second, she looked surprised. I might look mousy, but I could stand up for myself when I needed to. I hadn't gotten to where I was by letting other people walk all over me.

"Definitely, yes." She cleared her throat. "We're calling everyone back in because things have shifted for us in the investigation." Her tone shifted too. "We're no longer looking at this as an accidental drowning. Kiersten was unconscious when she went into the pool. She'd been knocked out before she was thrown in. Cause of death was likely blunt force trauma to the head. Followed by secondary drowning. Which she likely was not even aware of." She rattled off the facts quickly, then gave me a chance to absorb what she'd just said.

"She was unconscious before she went into the pool? How do they know that?"

"There was barely any water in her lungs. It's called dry drowning." I raised my eyebrows at her, and she explained. "Basically, since she was unconscious when she hit the water, she would automatically still breathe instead of holding her breath like you would do if you were conscious. The brain automatically takes in a short breath. Water rushes in, but then, the throat closes up instinctually. They'll know for sure once they get in there more, but the lungs were only half-filled with water."

"So, you're saying that someone hurt Kiersten? Before she drowned?" I couldn't say what I thought she was saying. The implications of something like that were impossible. Who would do such a thing?

"Yes, that's what I'm telling you. This has officially become a homicide investigation." She laid her hands out in front of herself on the table. "Want to hear something interesting that I've noticed?" She gave me an intense look, followed by an equally intense smile. I nodded slowly even though I wasn't sure I did. "Jade and the others all refer to Whitney as Whit. You're the only one that uses her full name. Any particular reason for that?"

Obviously, there was, or she wouldn't have brought it up. Everyone understood the implications.

"I've just never been super close with anyone in the group, you know?" I might as well tell the truth. There was no point in lying. They were going to find out everything anyway. Probably already had. "We come from very different worlds."

That was an understatement.

Detective Perez nodded. "I see that." She thumbed through the folder in front of her on the desk. It was strange to see her outside her uniform. She looked like such a regular person in her blue jeans and red Converse. You could tell they were her favorite pair. Holes in the corners so worn you could see her socks peeking out. But her hair was still up in the tight ponytail she always wore. I wonder how it felt when she finally let it down at the end of the night. Was it like walking into the house and taking off your bra?

I needed to focus.

"You're originally from Arizona," she said. "You were raised by a single mom and traveled most of your childhood. From coast to coast and even a brief stint in Alaska. Must've been great to see so much of the world, but also hard to ever feel settled. Except you're pretty resilient because you went to college at seventeen and graduated summa cum laude. A fellow Phi Beta Kappa." She gave a quick nod to her plaque on the wall behind her—the same gold emblem as the one in my office.

It was slightly off-putting how much she knew. Like someone had given her the CliffsNotes of my life. How had they done that so quickly? Were they doing the same rigorous checks with all the others? What had they found once they started digging? Nobody was without secrets. Especially not these women.

"I'm not one of them," I'd said to Abby after one of our first big moms'-night-out adventures while we were all pregnant. We'd gone to see Hippo Campus at the Greek. She'd had a ball, but she was like that. She could have fun with anyone. Turn into whoever she needed to be at the moment, but it was so hard for me to pretend like I cared about the shows they were watching or who'd designed their new kitchen.

But I'd stayed because it was convenient and easy. And because Abby liked the group and she wanted me to. How many things had I done because she wanted me to? I was still doing them. A teeny-tiny voice piped up that maybe my relationship with Abby wasn't as healthy or as perfect as I'd made it out to be before all this. But I quickly silenced that voice like I did every time she tried to rear her ugly head.

I'd made sacrifices for love, that was all. We all had.

"Brooke, I'm a straightforward person. There are lots of officers that play all sorts of games with suspects. They use all kinds of tricks and techniques, but here's what I've found." She took a deep breath and gave me a calculated look. "Most people just like to be talked to directly, and they're waiting for you to ask the right question, so they can tell you the truth. Keeping secrets is poisonous. Not to mention hard work, and most people are dying to relieve themselves."

But that wasn't my experience. That wasn't what was happening here. Nobody had any demons they needed to exorcise. I gave her a blank stare back. What did she expect me to say? Did that work with other people? She kept going after I didn't fill in the silence.

"I sat all your friends down and had similar conversations with them, where I explained what really happened to Kiersten. Do you know what each one said when I asked them who they thought of the six of you might be capable of hurting another person?" Her eyes drilled holes into mine. I forced myself not to look away. "They all said you, Brooke. That you were the one who was capable of hurting Kiersten." She let her words fall into the room and watched their effect on me. But I wasn't surprised.

"Did you expect me to be shocked?"

"No," she said quickly, but I could tell she did. "I just wanted you to know that your friends think you might've had something to do with Kiersten's murder."

I still couldn't believe we were calling it a murder.

"Who told you that? Whitney? Jade?" I narrowed my eyes. "Colleen? All of them? I bet it was Whitney." I leaned across the table. Closer to her. "You think every one of them is so tight and close, huh?

That I'm this huge outsider? But they all just love and support each other so much? Like one big happy family?" I gave a sarcastic laugh. She straightened up quick, immediately interested.

"What are you trying to say?"

"Everyone pretends like Whitney and Kiersten were super tight, and they were, or they are, but what I'll tell you is that they weren't getting along."

"Whitney and Kiersten?" she asked like she didn't believe it.

I nodded. I had her attention now. Full on. "They'd been fighting for weeks."

"But I thought you hadn't seen anyone in three weeks?"

"I hadn't, but it'd been going on for the past month or so, and there was still lots of tension that night. They might not have let me close to them, but I was always watching." As soon as I said it, I realized how creepy it sounded and quickly changed it up. "I pay attention to what's happening with people, and it's way easier to see and notice things when you're on the outside of them. You can't see things when you're in the center." I had a point, and she knew it. It was the entire reason she could do her job. She knew all about being on the outside looking in.

"What was going on with Whitney and Kiersten?" she asked, leaning forward. This was new information. Clearly nobody had told her. Why hadn't they told her? Everyone knew it was happening. It was impossible not to notice, and they all talked about it. I overheard them.

"Being around Whitney and Kiersten had started to feel like being around your parents after they'd had a huge fight. You know how that is when you're young? Anyway, something big had happened between them because you could feel the tension and the intensity. Everyone did. Everyone talked about it, but nobody knew what it was."

"What kinds of things did you notice?" She picked up her pen and scribbled. She'd never done that. They weren't just going to pin this one on me since I was the easiest target. No way.

"First, the two of them were always together. Kiersten and Whitney were practically attached at the hip. They went and did everything together. They spent more time with each other than they did anyone else, but then they stopped hanging out like that and started showing up to stuff separately. Driving in different cars. Barely talking to each other. They were almost always the last to leave any event or whenever we hung out, but suddenly, it wasn't like that anymore. They didn't even sit by each other and rushed to leave."

"Do you have any idea what it was about? Did they ever say?"

I shook my head. "They never told me." I'd been clear with her about being on the outside, so obviously I wouldn't be privileged to such insider information, but even though Perez was a detective, my therapist was definitely a better listener. "But I wasn't the only one who noticed, and even though they didn't tell me and we weren't talking about it, the others were. I overheard Colleen and Taylor in the parking lot after we left Starbucks." They hadn't known I was there. That's the thing about being invisible. "Whatever it was, there were lots of awkward moments between them and Jade."

"What was going on there?"

"First thing I'll tell you about that group of women is that they're very possessive and they don't like to share. Whitney started spending more time with Jade, and that made Kiersten super jealous. When they showed up together at Colleen's for book club, Kiersten looked like someone slapped her. She got so upset she had to leave the room." She made a mad dash to the bathroom, excusing herself quickly, saying she needed something to drink. Her eyes were puffy and red when she got back, so I know she went to the bathroom and was crying in there. She left early that night.

"So, what are you saying?" she asked.

"All I'm saying is that something was definitely going on there and things weren't right between Whitney and Kiersten. They hadn't been for a long time." I shrugged nonchalantly. "Maybe you should ask Whitney about it."

CHAPTER FIFTEEN

THEN

WHITNEY

I hurried to meet Kiersten. I was over twenty minutes late. She hated when I was late. Little Miss Punctuality. We'd barely talked in three days. Both of us so busy.

I whipped open the café door and made a beeline for our table. The one underneath the fern hanging in the corner. Her eyes lit up when she saw me, and relief immediately flooded my body. I reached over and gave her a quick hug before grabbing my chair on the other side of the table. I didn't need to get my order. She'd already done it—perfectly prepared it just the way I liked it. She even had my croissant wrapped in a paper towel so that it'd stay warm for me.

"Gimme one sec," she said, glancing up, then quickly back down. Her fingers flew on her phone. "I'm just finishing up this email with a client."

I gazed out the window and took a sip of my coffee, debating whether I should tell her about Colin, while she typed. I wanted to. Just to unload. Get the awful secret off my chest, but you know what? She had to be as sick of hearing about our pathetic cycle as I was talking about it.

I didn't get his "addiction." Heroin. Crack. Pills. Shit, even alcohol. I understood all those. Every single one. The need to get obliviated. Feel good. Who didn't like that? Everyone wanted to feel good. Everyone wanted to escape reality every now and then. That was human. Of course, there were people who missed the mark. Right? The high felt so good so they just wanted more and more of it, until eventually they couldn't get enough? Until eventually it didn't feel good.

And that was the thing. All those drugs felt good. I didn't understand how gambling felt good, no matter how many times the doctors and specialists tried to explain the high. Nothing changed the fact that you weren't taking a chemical into your body. You were sober. Period. It didn't matter how many family-education classes they made me sit through or how many times all those fancy doctors from all over the world explained that gambling altered the brain just like drugs. Gave them the same adrenaline rush.

Excuse me. No.

I'd done drugs. Gambling didn't feel like a drug.

Gambling felt like an irresponsible choice, especially when you had a family. And you couldn't physically get addicted to it like you could other things, no matter what they said. I didn't actually buy any of their theories, but I had to pretend like I did or else I just looked like the bitter, angry wife that couldn't forgive her poor drug-addicted husband. But see, that was the point.

I'd have an easier time forgiving him if he was addicted to actual drugs. Then all his behavior made sense. Then he wasn't in his right mind. Fury rose in my chest.

Kiersten had been through it with me so many times before. From the first structured intervention we'd done seven years ago. God, how had it been seven years already? I was so lost and confused back then. Just figuring out he had a problem gambling. One he'd had since his freshman year of college. I had no idea how massive it'd grown until I discovered he'd secretly gambled away our Lake Arrowhead property. Gone. Just like that.

And I'd known nothing about it. He'd kept all of it a secret. That changed everything.

Everyone saw him through that round of treatment. His first intervention. We treated him like a real drug addict then. Because that's what the doctors and therapists told us to do. The ones with the fancy degrees and long lists of initials behind their names. That's how they explained things to us. Thankfully, I didn't have to do any of it alone. Kiersten and Tommy went to all his family therapy groups in the beginning too. For years, we'd all gone together because they were as close to us as our biological families, but we'd stopped going after he cycled through his sober/relapse routine a couple more times.

But in those early days?

We were all on board. His biggest cheerleaders. All of us were convinced his recovery was solid and he was going to be the one to beat the odds. Until he had a work birthday party at the Santa Anita horse track. I told him not to go. I begged him to stay home.

"I don't think it's a good idea," I said when he mentioned it to me as he was getting ready to leave. My gut twisted. So many red flags. First, that he'd casually dropped the news right as he was walking out the door to leave, so there wasn't a chance to have an actual discussion about it. He'd told me all about the party, but he hadn't told me it was happening at the racetrack, and that's not how we did things. Complete transparency and honesty. That's how recovery in our marriage worked.

He balked, wrinkling his face at me. "It's fine. All we're going to do is be in these super-uncomfortable suits while we drink lots of beer and smoke cigars in some sweaty box," he said without looking up at me. He just kept on tying his shoes like it wasn't a big deal.

"You're going to the racetrack. The whole point is to bet on horses." I tried to keep the fear and nagging out of my voice, but I couldn't. Everything about it felt wrong.

"I'm not into betting on horses." He rolled his eyes and looked insulted. "That was never my thing. Don't worry about it."

But I did. The entire time he was gone.

He stumbled home at 4:00 a.m., down $10,000, like he was stumbling home from the bar. I'd been so devastated. I'd cried for a week straight and lost five pounds because I was too anxious to eat.

I didn't get devastated like that anymore.

Now I was just tired, and I didn't want this to be my life. I didn't want this to be happening again. Not another round.

"Okay, I'm done." Kiersten broke into my thoughts. She plopped her phone in her purse and turned her full attention on me. "We've barely talked since last weekend, so tell me everything that's happening." For a second, I wanted to cry. My emotions were so near the edge. She noticed immediately. "What happened with Colin? You said it was something big?" Her eyes filled with concern. I'd texted her last night after I found the receipts, but I hadn't said anything about them. Only that there was drama with Colin, but I couldn't talk about it then.

I opened my mouth to tell her everything—the hidden receipts stuffed in his gym bag, the fact that he hadn't been actually going to the gym, that he'd been lying again, all of it—but I stopped. I couldn't go through it again. Not one more time around the same mountain.

"Oh, nothing." I laughed it off, reaching across the table and squeezing her hand. "I was super hysterical and crazy because I had PMS. I got my period right when I was going to bed, so of course I'm back to my right mind this morning. You know how it is"—I cocked my head to the side and gave her a wicked grin—"he said something totally stupid and insensitive last night, and I was ready to divorce him. That or murder him."

She burst out laughing. "You really are a complete maniac when you have PMS. Remember when you got so mad at me in college over the bagels?" She quickly launched into one of her favorite stories about me. How I'd lost it and thrown a plate at her head. She always got all dramatic when she described the plate smashing against the wall behind her. All in a fit of hormonal rage over the fact that she'd eaten my last bagel without buying a new one.

I listened to our familiar story and laughed along at all our favorite parts. I kept my mouth shut about Colin. I'd never kept anything from her. Not once. That's all I could think about on the drive home. We didn't have secrets. But maybe we could have this one because I didn't want to talk about my gambling-addicted husband. I was so sick of his problems, and I didn't want them as mine anymore. I was done. And if I never told her, then she never had to know, and if we never talked about it again, then it could just be his problem. Maybe that was the trick. Pretend the problem didn't exist.

Was that possible? Could you really do that? Ignore a problem until it disappeared?

CHAPTER SIXTEEN

NOW

JADE

I hurried to the coffee shop to meet Whitney. Was this smart? I had no idea what I was doing. All this was new territory.

Nobody talked at all today. Radio silence from the six. I thought about texting the group chat about every ten minutes, but what was I supposed to say? How did you even start that conversation?

> Hey everyone! They think one of us killed Kiersten. So what do you think?

Nobody would respond to that text, for sure. And what else could I say?

> What's up? How's everyone doing?

That's entirely too casual and open ended. I considered a heavier *hey* with three dots, but that felt wrong, too, and there wasn't an emoji to fit this situation, so I never sent anything. I was so relieved when Whitney texted to meet up that I immediately said yes. But I agreed without thinking about it. Was it smart to meet in public tonight? How would that look to the investigators? Was it okay that we were together?

Detective Perez wasn't joking around today. She was 100 percent serious about looking at every single one of us as suspects. It had turned into a real-life game of Clue that nobody said they wanted to play. I certainly didn't.

Ryan took over with the kids tonight without me even having to ask him. It was the strangest thing. I was so worried finding out about Kiersten would push him even further into the depression pit, but it's done just the opposite. It's lit a fire underneath him because her death scared him. Made him realize how fragile life was.

Whitney spotted me through the window and gave me an enthusiastic wave. It was too late to back out, so I waved back and hurried inside. I was surprised she'd beat me here since she was usually at least fifteen minutes late to everything.

She'd transformed in the last forty-eight hours. She still wore her familiar comfy clothes like an old blanket, but she'd showered and brushed her hair. Put on clean clothes. That was good. Baseball cap slung low. Ponytail pulled out the back. Just like she looked when we did our beach cleanup walks for Heal the Bay.

I slid into my seat and set my purse down in the chair next to me.

"What the fuck is going on?" She didn't waste a moment on small talk. There was no time for that. Our friend was dead, and they thought one of us killed her.

I shook my head. My eyes nervously darted around the coffee shop like I had something to hide. All Detective Perez's questions had made me so nervous. Funny how being treated like a suspect made you feel like you'd done something wrong. "It's so weird. I'm like a total paranoid speed freak suddenly."

"Ohmigod, me too," she said. Her eyes were as wild and panicked as mine probably were. She whipped a smile on her face as the barista brought us over our coffee, though. We were regulars here, and so was our server, Molly. She was twenty-two years old and always super chatty, but she took one look at us, set our drinks on the table, and quickly walked away without saying a word. I waited until she was out of earshot before speaking.

"That's how I've been feeling ever since I met with Detective Perez today. Like I can't even believe this is happening. None of it feels real."

"Do you know what I am?" Whitney cocked her head to the side. Her eyes were lit. "I'm pissed. I was devastated when I thought some terrible accident killed Kiersten, but the fact that somebody did this to her? That somebody took her life on purpose?"

Her voice rose with every word. By the time she was finished, the couple at the table at the back of the restaurant was already giving us the eye.

"You really think that? Like someone took her life on purpose?" I asked.

She shrugged and looked bewildered. Then motioned for me to come closer and whispered, "How messed up were you the night of the party?" That wasn't the question I'd expected her to ask. It caught me off guard, and it took a second for me to recover.

I shrugged. "Not any more drunk than anyone else?" What was she getting at? Had she heard something? "It's not like I counted my drinks or anything, but it was probably no more than three?"

"Did you have any gummies?"

I felt like a teenager getting the third degree from my mom after coming home from a party. "Again, no more than anyone else, detective." I couldn't help myself. She couldn't really just barge in here and start drilling me with questions about how sober I was that night without telling me why.

She gave a furtive swoop of the café before going on. "Okay, so you might not have been wasted that night, but I was, so lots of my memory is blurry. I only remember bits and pieces from after dinner, and I probably made a huge mistake by telling Perez that."

"You told her you didn't remember?" I wasn't surprised. Whitney liked to party. We were always filling in the missing pieces of her memory from our nights. It was part of the whole experience. Like a game we all played together the next day.

"It's not like I have anything to hide." She nodded. "Besides, I'm totally out of the suspect equation, anyway. Nobody can even look at me as having anything to do with it."

"What do you mean?" I asked. I wasn't so sure about that. They were looking at all of us, and they'd probably be looking at her even more since she was the closest person to Kiersten. Sort of like how the husband was always a suspect in murder investigations? She was the next closest thing.

"My boobs were killing me. Like rock-hard, leaking-everywhere killing me. That's what I remember. I'd pumped before I left and thought I'd be fine without pumping until I got home, but all of a sudden, it was just too much. I was so uncomfortable. So, I went looking for Kiersten's pump to use hers, and after I found it, I sat in the guest bedroom and pumped. Honestly, I have no idea how long I was in there. I just remember being so tired once I sat down. You know when it all hits you? And that's when I felt really wasted. I might've even closed my eyes to rest them for a second."

Passed out. That's what she meant. The polite way of saying she passed out.

"Well, I wasn't passed out when it happened," I half joked, getting back to her original question.

"Where were you? What do you remember?" she asked, leaning forward again.

"Taylor. I just remember Taylor telling her crazy story, and I thought Kiersten was with me too. I really did. Isn't that weird how you can put people in a memory? Like I could've sworn she was there with me for the entire conversation. When Natasha screamed and we ran outside, I turned around expecting to find her. It took me a second to realize it was her floating in the pool, you know? Honestly, I never noticed she was gone."

"Do you remember anyone else being gone around that time?"

This was like being interviewed by Detective Perez again. She'd asked me all the same questions.

"I don't, but only because I wasn't paying attention."

"Well, if you were talking to Taylor the whole time, and you're sure you were talking to her the whole time?" She raised an eyebrow.

I nodded. "Positive."

"And I was pumping in the bedroom . . . then that only leaves Colleen, Natasha, and Brooke." She let the implications of her statement hang in the air.

I'd done the same scenario math as her. Multiple times this afternoon.

"It's really weird to think of any of them as being . . . as being . . . a murderer?" It didn't even sound right.

She nodded her head in agreement. "It is, right? Like Natasha? Hurting anyone? Come on, I'm sorry. Or Colleen? Her entire backyard might as well be an animal rescue. They have like seven different animals."

There was one other name on the list. We stared at each other from across the table. We might not be as close as her and Kiersten because nobody can compete with that, but we knew each other pretty damn well and we had our own shared history. Well enough to know that we were both thinking the same thing.

"What about . . ." I let my question trail off. I didn't have to say it out loud.

"I told Perez that if she thought it was one of us, then Brooke was the only one who could've done it," she announced like she wasn't the least bit sorry she'd told her.

I reached my hand across the table and grabbed hers in mine, squeezing tightly. "Okay, good. I'm so glad to hear you say that because

I was feeling like the absolute worst person in the world for saying that to Detective Perez, but you know what?" I didn't wait for her to answer. "As soon as she brought me in and told me what had really happened to Kiersten, Brooke popped into my head. Immediately."

"Me too!" she exclaimed.

"And I told Detective Perez that. Not that I think she's this mean, malicious, evil killer. Not at all. I really don't. But she's unstable, and unstable people do unstable things."

"Right? And she's already freaked out and totally lost it once. You saw how she put her hands around Liza's neck." She widened her eyes dramatically.

"Exactly."

"You know what I was thinking?" Whitney asked, dropping her voice to a whisper. "What if we were the ones to talk to her? Like really tried to get her to talk about it?"

"Like try to get her to confess?"

She nodded and gave me a wicked grin.

"Do you think she'll tell us?" Would I? If the shoe were on the other foot, would I trust Whitney? Would I trust me?

"She's probably so racked with guilt she's just waiting for us to ask her about it. You know? They say that the only reason some people are not caught for their crimes is because nobody ever asks if they committed them."

I tried not to smile. She was quoting Detective Perez. She'd said the same thing to me. "You really think she'll tell us if we ask her?" I asked.

"Obviously, we're not going to just drill her about it like we're trying to get her to confess, but we can try to get her relaxed enough to start talking, and see where things go from there." She shrugged. "I don't know what'll happen, but it's worth a try, isn't it? What do we have to lose?"

CHAPTER SEVENTEEN

NOW

BROOKE

My stomach churned as I pulled into Whitney's driveway. How was someone going to call you a murderer out of one side of their mouth and in the next, invite you over to their house for coffee? Come on. How stupid did she think I was?

She thought I did this. That's exactly what this meant, and if that's the direction she'd taken, then you could pretty much bet all the others agreed.

Except there was this teeny part of me that worried Detective Perez might've made it all up. If she'd said those things about Whitney and made it sound worse than it was to stir things up between us. What if she was trying to get people upset? Make the members of the tribe turn against each other? It was the oldest trick in the book.

And I didn't want to get played.

I'd said no to Whitney's invitation at first. Immediately, without thinking, the moment I'd gotten her text. And I'd spent the next five minutes spinning out in rage. Of course I was the one they pointed the finger at. Single mom. Because that's what I was now. The divorce petition had come in the mail yesterday. It was official.

A divorced single mom with a shady background.

I wanted to punch every single one of them in the face. It wasn't a shady background. It was a poor one. There was a difference, but they didn't know that. I was just the outsider. The weirdo. The one that didn't know or follow any of their stupid social rules. That's who I'd always been with them.

Yuck.

I hated it. Hated them.

Despite my feelings, I punched in Whitney's gate code and drove up the long winding driveway. Jade's silver Mercedes was already here. Why was I not surprised? What was I doing? These weren't my friends or my people. Whitney was probably going to have her phone in her pocket the entire time recording. Or have Colin figure out a way to record audio in the house. But I couldn't leave. I had to know what they knew. What if they knew something I didn't?

Whitney opened the door into her grand entryway. I'd been blown away the first time I came to visit. Her home was so beautiful it'd been featured in magazines, and it was regularly rented out for commercials. Every single piece was perfect. Meticulously designed. Stunning.

"What does her husband do?" Abby had whispered to me as we walked through the foyer into the formal living room—all nine hundred square feet of it. With floor-to-ceiling windows that revealed a sparkling pool and tennis court in the back. The most glorious garden of rare flowers and cacti that you'd ever seen to the right of them.

Colin was a successful Medtronic salesman, but as it turned out, Whitney was responsible for just as many square feet and custom-made tiles in the house as him. She was the president of an elite talent agency that she'd built from the ground up twenty years ago. There was no doubt she worked hard, and she hadn't skipped a beat even after she had Asher.

She swung the door open wide. It was like a transformation from our meeting two days ago. She looked like the old Whitney. Her hair was tousled and feathered back. The classic curtain bangs she'd rocked since I met her. No matter what she wore, she always looked good, and today was no different. She was in Alo cashmere from head to toe. But even though she looked like herself, her voice was like this weird octave off, and her eyes were too wide. Trying too hard to look normal.

"It's so good to see you. Come in," she said, hurrying me inside.

The door latched behind me, and suddenly, I couldn't breathe. I'd come out of anger and curiosity, so I hadn't thought any of this through. All I'd done yesterday was go over every interaction with Abby at the police station. I'd analyzed every detail: from the way she'd crossed her legs while we were in the waiting room to her expression when she said goodbye. I hadn't given a second thought to Detective Perez's veiled accusations against me because there wasn't any merit to them. I hadn't done anything wrong, so I didn't have anything to worry about.

But I realized if I didn't hurt her, then it meant someone else had. Someone at that party. Just like Detective Perez said. One of the other five. Two of them were here. What were the odds one of them was the guilty one? And if they were, why'd they invite me over?

Suddenly, this didn't feel like a good idea anymore, but I followed Whitney through the dining room anyway. She chattered on about something, but I couldn't keep up. Not with her conversation or my steps.

What if one of them had done it? What if they were leading me here to do the same thing they'd done to Kiersten? Why? Could they be that vicious? I really didn't know them at all. Not really.

Sweat clung to me. Jade sat in the living room looking just as Stepford Wifey as Whitney. She didn't have that trying-really-hard-to-keep-it-together look like Whitney, but everything else was the same. They were performing, and they were definitely orchestrating their own show. I'd thought it was to question me about my involvement. Like they really thought I did it, but what if they were the guilty ones?

What if I was next?

I tried to still my pounding heart. I was being silly. Too overdramatic. My throat closed at the same time that I felt like I was going to throw up. The familiar swellings of a panic attack. I hadn't had one in years.

I tried to calm my breathing while Whitney asked what I wanted to drink, and somehow, I responded "Water" without even trying. And I looked normal. I must've looked normal because no one was asking me what was wrong. Why weren't they asking me if anything was wrong?

Settle down. I needed to relax. I was just being paranoid. This was what Detective Perez wanted. But one of us was guilty, and it wasn't me. Which meant it could be them. And now I just wished I hadn't come. I didn't want to play with the mean girls. I wasn't cut out for it. Not in high school and not now.

CHAPTER EIGHTEEN

NOW

JADE

Brooke walked into the living room with Whitney, looking like she wanted to bolt. Her eyes were wild. Her face stricken. This was a bad idea. Why had I agreed to it?

I hopped up and gave her a quick hug. She was stiff and smelled sweaty. She took a seat on the club chair next to the fireplace. She perched herself on the edge. Whitney ran off to grab her water.

"You doing okay?" I asked, doing my best to sound friendly and nonthreatening. She already looked spooked.

"I'm all right," she said without really looking at me. She did that thing where she looked at your face but you could tell she was looking above your eyes at your forehead.

This was only going to get weirder. She obviously knew something was up, otherwise Colleen, Natasha, and Taylor would be here too. "We tried to get the others, but Colleen came down with whatever yuck her kids had, and she hasn't been able to get off the toilet all day. Taylor's not answering her phone."

The Colleen thing was feasible. Taylor not so much, but I had to address the elephant in the room and give her something. I didn't say anything about Natasha not being here, hoping she wouldn't notice I'd left her out.

"I hear that flu is really nasty," she said like we were two strangers meeting for the first time in the checkout line at the grocery store or a doctor's waiting room. "People are getting sick, and it's super contagious."

"Yeah, I'm sure we're all probably going to get it."

"Here you go." Whitney breezed back into the room and put an end to the awkward moment. Brooke grabbed the glass and drained half of it immediately.

Whitney plopped down in the chair next to her. She was acting just as weird as Brooke. It was like she was a windup doll and someone had wound her up all the way. This would impact her more than any of us since Kiersten was the closest thing she had to family. She didn't have parents. They'd died in a car accident when she was three, and she was raised by her grandparents. They'd both been dead for years now. My heart ached for her. Tears filled my eyes.

"Are you okay?" Whitney asked Brooke just like I had.

"I'm good now. I was just thirsty," she said, but her eyes didn't look any less wild, and her posture wasn't any more comfortable.

Whitney was perched on the edge of her chair in an almost similar position. Except she had her legs crossed at the ankles and her hands folded on her lap like a talk show host about to start her interview. "Okay, so Colleen and Taylor—"

"I explained to her why they couldn't come," I interrupted. We hadn't talked about the others beforehand. It'd never dawned on me while we were plotting how all this would go down, but I didn't want her to undo what I'd just done or make Brooke think we weren't on the same side.

Whitney gave me a twinge of a frown, but quickly moved forward. "Anyway, yes, so you know why they can't be here. I wish we all could. How did your meeting with Detective Perez go?"

"Um . . . I don't really have anything to compare it to, but I guess it went okay?" The last part came out sounding like a question instead of a statement.

"What'd she ask you about?" Not only did Whitney look like a talk show host, she was talking like one too. And going against everything we'd said we weren't going to do. Beginning with not drilling Brooke with questions so she felt like we were interrogating her. We wanted her to think we were her friends.

She gave a weird face. "She asked about what I was doing and who I was with during the time that Kiersten disappeared. She—"

"Where were you?"

Brooke's face immediately flushed. "I . . . I mean . . . it's kind of embarrassing."

"Don't worry about it. It's just us," I said, giving her a friendly squeeze on the knee. That's what we were supposed to be doing. Befriending her, not putting her on edge. I gave Whitney a look over Brooke's shoulder, hoping she could read the meaning behind it. She needed to chill, or we weren't going to get anything from her.

"I don't normally eat all of that spicy food, and let's just say, the food and the drinks weren't agreeing with me. I was in the bathroom. I'd just come out when Natasha screamed."

Was she really? Did I even speak to her at the party? I racked my brain trying to remember, but I kept coming up empty handed. We might not have talked that night. I'd clapped when she'd received her Most Likely to Give Their Child an Anxiety Disorder award. It was one of the funny ones. Really, all of them were supposed to be funny—Most Likely to Forget Their Child at Preschool or my favorite: Most Likely to Lose Their Shit While Driving. Brooke had gone up front and taken hers from Kiersten, but she didn't look happy. That's what I remembered. Everyone else had laughed about their awards. She was the only one that hadn't been amused.

"Really? How long were you in there?" Whitney asked like it was something she was actually curious about, but it was obvious why she cared.

"I don't know." She looked even more flustered. "I didn't really pay attention at the time."

"It's okay. Don't worry about it." I shot Whitney another look. I scooted closer to Brooke. "I still can't believe this is happening. I keep thinking we're going to go back and someone is going to tell me it's all a joke. A terrible joke that nobody will think is funny but at least it's not real. I don't want to live in a world where this is real." My emotions caught in my throat. That part wasn't pretend. That was all real. I didn't want to be here doing this any more than she did.

"Did Perez tell you what they think happened?" Whitney asked.

"That they think one of us killed Kiersten?" Brooke looked straight at her when she said it. It was a direct hit.

Whitney's facade crumbled for a second, and she looked surprised. She hadn't expected that answer from her any more than I had. Didn't guilty people usually try to avoid talking about the crime or the investigation? Whitney gave a weird, strangled laugh. "Yeah. That. That's what we wanted to talk about." She made another strange sound, and her face looked funny, like she didn't know how to arrange it. "When she told me, I was like—no way, there's no way someone would hurt Kiersten on purpose. It had to be an accident."

"I told her the same thing," Brooke said without missing a beat.

Is that what she'd said, or had she pointed the finger back at one of us? Whitney cast me a quick sideways glance. She was thinking the same thing. Awkward tension hung in the air. What were we supposed to say now?

"So, how's the whole sobriety thing going?" Whitney asked with absolutely no tact.

"What do you mean?" Brooke asked, instantly offended, and I couldn't blame her. It wasn't exactly her business, especially coming from Whitney. If there were anyone voted Most Likely to Join Brooke at Her AA Meetings, Whit would get all the votes.

Whitney didn't care that she'd upset her, though, or that she wasn't in any position to question someone else's sobriety. She shrugged. "Exactly what I asked. You were wasted at the Griffins', and I was wondering if you were wasted that night at Kiersten's."

"Maybe if you were sober yourself, you'd remember," Brooke shot back without skipping a beat.

That's when I knew the conversation was over. Whit's drinking was off limits. I'd tried that once. Only once. Never again.

Whitney narrowed her eyes to slits. "I'm not the one—"

I jumped up from the couch and held my arms out like I was physically separating them in the living room. "You know what? Let's just all take a minute and relax. This is a super-stressful situation, and none of us know what we're doing."

But Brooke wasn't paying attention to me. She was staring right back at Whitney and spoke it at her instead of me, so there was no mistaking who she was directing her response toward. "Oh, she knows exactly what she's doing."

CHAPTER NINETEEN

NOW

WHITNEY

"Mrs. Gilmore, there's someone here for you," our nanny, Grace, called out from downstairs.

I'd just stepped out of the shower, so I hadn't heard anyone at the door. Who was here? I wasn't expecting anyone. I wasn't seeing clients, and Jade and I weren't meeting until later this afternoon. We had to debrief after yesterday's spoiled confrontation with Brooke. I went to look at my phone to see who it was, but I'd left that downstairs. Shoot.

"Coming!" I called back as I threw my hair into a wet bun and slipped on one of my favorite T-shirts.

I hurried downstairs. Detective Perez and another officer I'd never seen before stood at the entry at the bottom of my stairs. I stopped in my tracks on the third step. What were they doing at my house? I quickly recovered my composure.

"Hi, Whitney," Detective Perez piped up immediately. She pointed to the guy standing next to her. "This is one of my colleagues, Frank. We were in the neighborhood and had a couple of follow-up questions, so we just thought we'd stop by."

"Sure. No problem." I turned to Grace hovering in their shadows. "Can you bring us some tea in the living room?"

"Absolutely," she said and hurried away while we headed into the living room.

I motioned to the furniture scattered around the room. "Please, have a seat. Grace is getting us tea, but can I get you anything other than that?"

They shook their heads in unison. The last thing I wanted to do was sit, but I'd look like a total weirdo if I paced while they talked, so I reluctantly grabbed a seat on one of the chairs. I waited for them to talk. I wasn't going first.

We sat in silence while the seconds dragged, but I wasn't falling for their tricks. Doing that thing where you kept silent long enough so the other person started talking. Most people just started rambling because they couldn't stand the silence. You could tell a lot about a person from what they rambled about when they were uncomfortable. I was no dummy. I waited them out. Looking as awkward as they did as we just stared at each other from across the coffee table. Finally, Perez broke the silence.

"I've really appreciated how helpful you've been in the investigation. Your information has pointed us in the direction of some pretty promising leads," she said. Frank sat next to her, bobbing his head in agreement.

I folded my hands in my lap. "Thank you."

"We've been talking to some of your former business associates." Her voice trailed off.

That's it? That was all she was going to give me? Which associates? And what had they said? But the look in her eye told me she was toying with me, being intentionally vague to see how I'd respond. What I'd do. What I'd ask for. And she'd use all that information to form an opinion about my role. Make judgments about who I was as a person. I might've grown up with a trust fund and gone to private school, but gaming people was the same whether you'd lived on the streets or gone to all the best schools. She was going to have to lead the way on this one.

"That's nice," I said with a pleasant smile.

Her face remained stuck in its position, but she blinked a few times really quickly. A natural tell. She hadn't been expecting that from me. Now there was no mistaking that she was here to mess with me. That I was no longer on her side of the investigation. Which meant I couldn't trust her anymore. You couldn't trust someone that thought you were a criminal. Especially one that thought you were a murderer.

It was Frank who broke the silence this time. Had she given him a signal? Had they talked about their strategy before they sat in my living room?

"What is it that you do again?" he asked as if he didn't already know. He probably had a head full of all my important details. A detailed fact sheet.

"I own a talent agency." My heart sped up. I always knew this day was coming. Not like this. Not under these circumstances, but I knew it'd come. Eventually.

"What kind of a talent agency?" he asked.

I did my best to keep my face pleasant and agreeable. "Oh, you know. The usual LA talent agency. We've got lots of actresses and actors, musicians, some big writers. Oh, and we also represent a couple of big people on TikTok. Can you believe viral people on TikTok need representation now? You'd be surprised."

Perez leaned forward in her seat. "There's some other unique talent at your agency, too, isn't there?"

I swallowed hard. *Here we go.*

"I'm not sure what you mean by that," I said, even though I did. I knew exactly what she meant.

"Oh, come on, Whitney." She cocked her head to the side. "Don't play me like that. You know what I'm talking about."

I shook my head. I couldn't give in that easily. I still didn't know exactly what she knew, and until I did, I wasn't budging.

"Why don't you tell me about Jasmine? Or how about little Lolita? Let's talk about your relationship with them."

My resolution to maintain secrecy crumbled immediately. Like a house of cards that had just been waiting to get blown down. "They're clients of mine," I said softly.

No use denying it. Once you peeled back the layers of my life, the rest was easily exposed. The best way to hide was in plain sight. That's what I'd always done. I'd been here all along. All anyone had to do was look.

"Do they call you their pimp?" she asked next.

"It's not like that," I snapped at her even though I hadn't meant to. "I take really good care of my employees."

She snorted. "Spoken like a true pimp. That's what they all say. If I had a penny—"

I cut her off. "Here's the deal. I take good care of every single person that works for me. It's a mutual work agreement." And it was. Sixty-five/thirty-five. Of course I got the higher cut because I did all the work matching people and managing schedules. The level of secrecy and discreetness required went above and beyond what they had to do as escorts. Not to mention, I took the bigger fall if we ever ended up here.

"It's a genius idea. I'll give you that." She nodded at me, looking genuinely impressed. "You open a talent agency and lead all the young hopefuls to you like sheep to slaughter. They have no idea what they're actually signing up for at the time. But I bet you meet them here, don't you? Bring them into your beautiful home." She motioned to the space around her. The $18,000 custom-made couch. The handcrafted chandeliers from a small villa outside Rome. It had taken over six months to arrive. All the sun shining in from the massive windows, making everything sparkle like diamonds. "Which, by the way, this place is absolutely gorgeous. Stunning, really. Business must be going really well." Perez smiled at me, and I wanted to slap the smile off her face. She didn't know me. She didn't know anything about me.

"Listen, you can look down your nose all snotty and judgmental at me all you want, but it's a situation where everyone wins. Yes, I have a talent agency. A reputable one that's constantly filling leads within the industry. But I also have a husband who gambles away our money as fast as I can make it. I worked hard to build this life, and I wasn't going to give it up just because my husband has a problem. I had to do something."

"Some people would just get a divorce."

Some people murdered their spouses to get out of bad situations too. I wasn't doing that either.

"I love Colin." I shook my head. "I know that makes me sound like a desperate, pathetic woman, but honestly, it's just the truth. I love being his wife. I love our family. The life we're building together. All those things. His gambling was destroying our lives. Every single part of it, and he wasn't going to stop until we were in shambles. So, I took matters into my own hands." I was on a roll now, and I wouldn't stop or apologize for what I'd done. "I run a legitimate business that satisfies a demand. Wealthy businesspeople are always going to want dates when they're in this city. That's not going away, and since I'm already in the industry, I have access to high-end clientele because of those connections. It puts me in a unique position, and I took advantage of the opportunity. Simple as that." I cocked my head to the side. "Come on. You know how it goes. All the young kids coming here to get famous. Convinced they're going to walk down the street and get discovered, but it doesn't take them long to learn the harsh realities of what life in LA is really like. That this city will eat you alive and spit you out like you're nothing." I locked eyes with her. She'd been here almost twelve years. She knew exactly what I was talking about. Most people couldn't even afford to live by themselves. Apartments in the city filled with people struggling to pay bills and eat. Doing auditions during the day and running a side hustle at night. That was the norm. Most people didn't last two years before they went home. It'd only gotten worse since the pandemic. She knew the stats.

"So you exploit their weaknesses?"

"Are you kidding me?" I shrieked. "I keep them from making worse choices. I recognize the ones that are really struggling. I mean, they're pretty easy to spot—living in one-bedroom apartments with six other people, can't pay their bills, barely affording to eat. The young hopefuls never understand how this city works until they're here. If you're living in an apartment by yourself, you're doing well. But most of them don't do well. Lots of them start doing porn, even though every person always swears they won't. It starts small with a private Instagram, and before you know it, they've been lured onto someone's live cam, and it's a quick downward slide from there. That's where I come in."

"You're the better alternative to porn?" She snorted.

"Absolutely," I said, crossing my arms on my chest. And I was proud of it. I didn't steal from them, and I made sure they were safe at all times. They had choices. They were the ones in control. They didn't have to do anything they didn't want to do. You could still say no in porn, too, not like it wasn't an option. Except if you said no there, you were out of a job. It didn't work the same way in my business. People tried to pretend like we were the same, but we were two totally different businesses.

Frank raised his eyebrows. "You're trying to tell me that your girls don't have sex with their clients on their dates?"

"Absolutely not." I crossed my arms on my chest. "They're escorts. Not prostitutes."

"Then why isn't anyone licensed?" he asked, exposing the elephant in the room.

"Because otherwise they couldn't have sex on their dates, and Mrs. Gilmore would have to pay taxes on all that income," Perez answered for me, and she wasn't wrong. In a state where operating an escort business was legal, there wasn't any reason not to be certified unless you had something to hide or were trying to avoid taxes. Unfortunately, I fit into both, and she knew it as well as I did. There was no sense trying to keep it from her. She was too smart for that. Besides, maybe if I was just honest and up front about things, she'd let me out of the thousands of dollars in fines she could slap me with for all the laws I'd broken.

"What happens on their dates is strictly confidential and one hundred percent up to them. Clients are told up front that sex is not guaranteed. Some of them actually just like the chase. And you'd be surprised. There are a few men that just want a pretty face next to them for the pictures and nothing more. Like they're renting a model for the night to make sure they look good in the pictures. It lets them control their image. Not even kidding."

"Must be rough." Frank laughed.

"So that's where your real money comes from, then? The escorts?" There's no amusement on Perez's face.

"Agency commissions can't compete with what men will pay to be with an attractive woman for the night with no strings attached, so to answer your question—yes. The business has served me well." And I wouldn't apologize for it. Even now.

"And in your business, I would imagine that might bring you into contact with some unsavory characters?" she asked next.

"Yes, it does. Occasionally. But it doesn't bring me into contact with any more unsavory and unsafe characters than women face every single day. We're surrounded by predators."

She gave me a knowing nod, but she wasn't letting me off the hook. "Have you had any incidents with anyone at work?"

I stiffened, realizing where she was going. The possibility that my job was related to this never crossed my mind. Not once. "You think someone I work with had something to do with hurting Kiersten?"

"This is an open and active investigation, so we're pursuing all leads. Now can you tell me about any troubles you've had with any of your escort clients?"

"There are always guys that get too rough with them."

"What's your definition of too rough? Have any of them ever been assaulted?"

I shook my head. "I work very hard at keeping my escorts safe. It's important to me. That's why they trust me. They come to me if anyone crosses the line, and there's been plenty of times where clients have grabbed them too hard or tried to get them to do something they weren't comfortable with. As soon as they come and tell me about it, that person is removed from the agency's list. Their access is denied, and they never get it back. Period."

"That must make some of the men you serve very unhappy when that occurs."

I shrugged and tossed my hair over my shoulders. "Maybe for a minute, but they just move on to the next agency. But if one of them acts out with me, they almost always repeat the behavior somewhere else, and there's definitely some people that have been blacklisted from all the agencies in the city."

"Anyone particularly mad?"

I shook my head. "Not about that, but one of our clients did get ahold of Devin's personal cell phone number a few months ago, and that didn't go well. All the escorts have work phones and personal phones. We stress the importance of never giving out their personal numbers, and since the girls are just as concerned about their safety, we don't usually have any issues."

"What exactly happened?"

"His name was Allen Grigsby, and he gave her the creeps on their third date, so she decided she didn't want him as a client anymore. Happens all the time. Like I said, the women are in charge of everything, and once they say no, that's it. Anyway, he wasn't happy about that at all, and for weeks, he incessantly called me, trying to get me to change my mind, but I wouldn't budge. I told you, their safety is always the most important thing to me. Anyway, we still don't know how, but he figured out who her grandmother was, and he called her posing as a student loan adjuster. Said that Devin had received payment from a student loan forgiveness program, and he was trying to reach her to give her the money. Her grandmother handed over Devin's number without a second thought, and once he had her number, that was it. He called her thirty to forty times a day. It was ridiculous. And he was constantly sending her pictures." I rearranged my face so she knew exactly what type of pictures I meant. "They were pretty bad. There was one that looked like he might be masturbating outside her window, and she was terrified he was following her too. That he'd somehow figured out a way to track her through her phone number. I was never sure about that, but the pictures were disturbing enough for me to make her go to the police with them."

Her head perked up immediately. "Did she file a report?"

I nodded.

"Do you have the number?"

I shook my head. "I didn't follow up on any of it. She filed a report, and he left her alone after that. I'm not sure she ever even had to go to court. I haven't thought about it until just now."

"Can you give me her name? Should be super easy to find the file."

"My escorts are strictly confidential. I can't do that."

She raised her eyebrows at me. "This is a murder investigation for your best friend—in case I need to remind you. And I can get the information without your help or your consent. All I have to do is get a warrant, but that takes time. Time away from your best friend's murder investigation that I'm only trying to solve." She looked at me like I was a bad child. "And really, I don't want to have to pull this card, but you're aware that all of this is illegal? Do you know what I could charge you with?"

"I was hoping we could avoid that small detail," I joked. She didn't look amused. Not even slightly.

"I'm not playing with you, Whitney. I know you've spent your life in a big, huge bubble of white privilege, but all that's about to end. I'm going to lay out how things are going to work for you moving forward. If I decide to come after you—and believe me, that's not something you want me to do—the first thing I'm doing is going through your list of escorts to see if there are any minors." She was all business. Any semblance we'd had in the past of being friendly was gone.

"All of my escorts are adults." I folded my arms across my chest. "Every single one is background checked."

"Really? Come on. You think if I dig, I'm not going to find one girl that created a different identity? Gave you a made-up name? Fake social security number? How many minors do you have working for you? That's where I'm starting. Do you know what happens to people that sex traffic minors? You know how they treat them in jail?" She had me backed in a corner. Right where she wanted me.

I swallowed hard. I'd looked it up. Done my research before I ever decided to dip my toes in this business. I knew the risks. Two to ten.

"Here's what we're going to do. Frank here"—she pointed to him in case I'd forgotten he was standing there next to her—"is about to call the rest of our forensic crew to your house. Once they're here, you're going to take him and his team through every room here, you understand me?" She didn't give me a chance to answer before continuing. "And then you're going to give them access to all of the computers and turn over every single one of your business records." She put *business* in air quotes and wore a disgusted look when she said it. "Sound good to you?"

The taste of fear filled my throat. This was the part where I said I wanted an attorney. I should've said it a long time ago. Probably the moment they showed up in my living room, but this was about Kiersten. I'd go to jail for her if it meant we could find her killer. I swallowed the fear and looked into Perez's face. "You can have whatever you need."

CHAPTER TWENTY

NOW

BROOKE

I hovered outside Abby's door, scared to breathe in case she heard me. I didn't want her to know I was creeping around spying on her. She came home after work tonight. Home! For the first time in over a month, she came home when she was done with work.

I'd almost fallen over when she walked in the door, it'd taken me by that much surprise. Shocked me speechless. I'd steadied myself on the kitchen counter.

"Hey, you," she said like it wasn't a big deal. As if she hadn't spent the last two months trying to stay away from our house as much as possible. It was like she was afraid if she spent too much time within these walls with us, she'd remember how much she used to love our life. Might even remember how much she used to love me. And she did use to love me. I didn't care what anyone said.

She came into the kitchen and stood next to the table.

"Can you just give me a second? Julian spit up all over my shirt." I didn't give her a chance to respond or look at me any closer. If she did, she'd see that I was a mess. I hadn't showered or brushed my teeth in three days. Not even to go to Whitney's this afternoon. I didn't want to make it look too obvious, though, so I raced upstairs and threw off the old T-shirt as fast as I could. I chucked it into the bathroom.

I brushed my teeth, then quickly washed my face and put deodorant on. Did a fast pit sniff. Not as bad as I expected. I didn't have time to brush the gnarled mess out of my hair or get the crusty baby puke off, so I threw it in a messy bun. I gave myself one last glance in the mirror before hurrying back downstairs.

Be cool, Brooke. Be cool. I gave myself the pep talk over and over again on my way into the kitchen. I couldn't mess up this opportunity. This was huge.

She was standing in the kitchen, making herself tea like she'd done hundreds of times in the past. I just stared at her back while she went through the familiar motions. The tiny spoon from our trip to Sweden. The natural honey. Her favorite mug.

"Julian sleeping?" she asked, turning around.

I nodded. "He got really worn out after his Gymboree class and was fussy most of the afternoon, so I put him down early."

"Is that super-nosy mom still there?"

"She is." I smiled, grateful she remembered. Claire was our favorite mom to make fun of after every class. The woman had no social skills.

"How are you doing?" Her voice was soft. Her eyes kind. She hadn't been open to me in months. I fought back tears, turning around quickly so she couldn't see them and I could pull myself back together before facing her again.

I leaned back against the counter. "It's been really hard."

"I can't imagine what it must've been like that night."

I mentally stumbled backward. She was talking about the night at Kiersten's. I thought she was talking about us. I nodded quickly. "It was pretty awful. I wish you would've been there. You would've done better than me and Natasha. Everyone was totally freaking out."

"I heard you were the one that tried to save her?"

I gave a short laugh. "I just jumped in the water. I had no idea what I was doing."

The whole thing was etched in my memory in a way I'd never forget. The terror. The fear. The frantic desperation of trying to breathe air into her lungs, life into her body. Feeling somehow responsible for her death.

"Was she . . . was she dead when you got to her in the water?" I appreciated the gentle way she asked the questions. Not in the harsh interrogative way of Detective Perez.

I shrugged my shoulders. Thinking about it made me feel weak, or maybe being with her was going to my head. The intoxication of being in her presence—really being in her presence where she's giving me her energy. I took a seat at the stool underneath the island.

"Natasha was tangled around her and doing more damage than she was really helping her. Mostly, I just focused on trying to get the two of them unstuck. Natasha was flailing around like she was drowning even though it was only like four feet of water."

"It was in the shallow end of the pool?"

"That's where she was floating," I said. I shifted in my seat. "Is this really what you want to talk about?"

It was a good entry point, but I wanted to get to us. That was the good stuff. Guilt flooded me instantly. Our friend had died, and I should be focused on that, but so had our marriage, and unlike Kiersten, it had a chance at being resuscitated.

She shrugged. "I just . . . I just . . ." She cleared her throat and started again. This was hard for her, and I appreciated her trying. I'd be as patient as she needed me to be. "I want you to know that no matter what, I'm here for you. You can talk to me about what happened that night. You can talk to me about anything."

I didn't want to talk. I wanted to leap across the kitchen and throw myself in her arms. I wanted to break down sobbing and have her hold me while I cried out all the pain of these last four months. To hear her tell me she was sorry. That she hadn't meant it. How she loved me still.

But I stayed in my seat. If I moved too quickly, it would spook her. She spooked easy. Instead, I gave her a small smile and looked away so she couldn't see into my eyes. Just in case she still knew how to read what was written on my soul. "Thanks, that was kind of you."

Everything felt awkward and strained. She looked just as uncomfortable as I felt, but we had to start somewhere. That's how new beginnings started.

CHAPTER
TWENTY-ONE

NOW

JADE

Whitney was already at Pan Pacific Park when I pulled up. She had Asher strapped in his stroller and Nikes on her feet. Her sunglasses hid her eyes, but I didn't need to see them to know she was on a mission. That'd been crystal clear when she called me thirty minutes ago and told me to meet her here without telling me why. She hurried over to us as Lily jumped out of the car and I unstrapped Iris from her seat.

"Mommy, can I go play?" Lily asked, pointing to the playground equipment filled with other kids scampering up and down it.

"Sure, but just for a few minutes while Mommy gets Iris ready and I talk to Ms. Whitney, okay?" She was already skipping off to the swings before I finished the sentence.

"Hey, thanks for meeting me," Whitney said, out of breath from the way over. She'd practically run to us. She held out a Starbucks cup.

"Thanks," I said, taking it from her and putting it in the stroller's cup holder. I buckled Iris in, hoping she'd stay asleep. We'd been up all night again with her stupid tooth. I breathed a sigh of relief when she didn't stir.

"You're never going to guess who showed up at my house," Whitney blurted, wasting no time getting started. "Perez."

"Detective Perez? She came to your house?" I hadn't heard anything from her since our last interview down at the station.

Whitney nodded vigorously. "Yes, and I was totally shocked. Just like you. I didn't even know they could do that. Just show up at your house any time they wanted and whenever they wanted."

"They're police officers. They can pretty much do what they want. What'd she say? Are they coming to all our houses?" Anxiety flooded my body. I didn't want them at mine. I didn't want them anywhere near my family.

"I don't know. I have no idea what they're up to, but I'll tell you this much. Today was the first time I felt like we weren't on the same team. She came at me totally different, and I didn't like it. I didn't like it at all." She jiggled her legs. Nervous energy radiated from her. There was more. She wasn't telling me everything. Her eyes darted around the park. She looked at her tennis shoes while she spoke the next part in a whispered confession. "They know about the business."

Everything stilled. Got bigger. Then smaller. Louder. Then quiet.

"What?" I asked. No.

She nodded reluctantly, like it was the last thing she wanted to be telling me about at the moment. "They do."

"Ohmigod. Ohmigod. What if they? What if . . . I can't . . ."

"It messed me up too." Whitney grabbed my arm. "Come on. Let's go sit on one of the benches over by Lily for a second."

I followed her to the bench like I was in a trance. When I'd said yes to her business proposition six months ago, it was because the likelihood of anyone ever finding out was slim to none. Whitney had been operating her escort service on top of her talent agency for almost four years completely undetected. She had it down to a science. And besides, I trusted her. She knew my secrets. The truth about my life.

Besides Ryan and his family, Whitney was the only one who knew what we were hiding. We were poor. Dirt poor. Like could-barely-afford-groceries-or-to-put-gas-in-the-car poor. Ryan's parents were the wealthy ones. His dad was a refugee from Iran, and he'd built an entire commercial construction company from the ground up. He'd designed all the major buildings on the south side. He was the rags-to-riches dream that America used to be famous for. He told the story proudly. So did Ryan.

We didn't have a mortgage. The beautiful home we lived in was a wedding gift from his parents. But I avoided having anyone over to the house because the insides didn't match the outside, and when we did, no guests ever went upstairs.

"You're like the total opposite of Midwest people," Colleen said once while we were out shopping. She spent her early childhood on a dairy farm in Minnesota. "They have all these creepy unfinished basements that you never go in unless there's a storm or that kids only go down on a dare, but you're like the California version. Nobody gets to go upstairs." She poked me in the side. "Is that where you keep all your dead bodies?"

It wasn't dead bodies hidden upstairs, but it was IKEA furniture. Dressers and bookshelves I'd picked up at garage sales and Goodwill. A few items I'd even found on the side of the road and thrown into my car as fast as I could before someone saw me. That's how I'd decorated our home over the years. We only let people into the parts of the house that were finished. The ones that looked pretty and nice.

Our downstairs was meticulously designed. His parents had felt bad for the state of affairs after we'd moved in to such a beautiful house after we got married. They didn't like the idea of us living in a big empty house without furniture. No things. That was also the last time Ryan's dad ever gave him a job at his company. They'd given us money, and they'd given him a job. That was the final time.

If we had to pay the mortgage, we'd be homeless. I never would've told Whitney. Never. I didn't want anyone to know that's how we lived. But she'd stumbled on me when I was having a breakdown. She'd spotted me in the Goodwill parking lot sobbing. Literally sobbing my eyes out. I'd been at the counter yet another time and had my card declined. There were no more cards left. I didn't know what I was going to do. How I was going to go on. And then suddenly, a knock at my car window that almost sent me soaring through the roof.

Whitney's face in my window. Banging on it. "Are you okay? Jade, what's going on? Are you okay?"

What was she doing dropping off donations all the way in Pasadena? That didn't make any sense. I made a point never to do any of my thrift-store shopping in places where someone might see me. Always made sure I was at least ten miles away.

I couldn't roll down the window. I didn't even know why. I just sat there frozen and staring straight ahead. She banged again. "Please, honey. What's happening? Are you okay? Do you want me to get someone? Should I call Ryan?" She started digging in her purse, trying to find her phone after I still didn't answer. "I'm calling Ryan."

I rolled down the window and screamed, "No!" Except I hadn't meant to scream. I'd wanted to speak in a regular voice. Or whisper. What I really wanted was to disappear. For a sinkhole to open up in the parking lot and take me into the dark matter.

She stopped. "Okay, okay, honey. I don't have to do anything that you don't want me to do."

I started sobbing again. I couldn't help it, and I couldn't stop it.

She didn't try to reach into the car and hug me, and I appreciated that. The hug would've felt too humiliating. I'd literally been wailing seconds ago. Full-on mental breakdown, and she'd seen it. I might as well be sitting in the car with dirty underwear.

"Can I get in the car?" she asked.

I nodded, refusing to look at her, still quietly crying. She walked around and got in on the other side. I didn't know how long we sat there, unmoving and unspeaking. I just stared straight ahead, and she held the space for me. It was one of the most intimate moments of my life.

"We're broke," I said finally. She'd already seen me a mess. What did anything else matter now? She'd never see me as the person she'd seen me as before anyway.

"What happened? Did Ryan get involved in a bad investment?" Her eyes filled with concern.

"God, I wish it was that simple, but it's not." I'd never had a simple life. Not like she had. But I tried not to be too jealous. My jealousy had almost destroyed me once.

"Okay, so like when you say broke, like how bad is it? You have to take out another mortgage? The kids have to go to public school?" She wrinkled her nose at the idea. "Or like you just can't go anywhere or do anything extravagant for the next year?"

I gave a wrangled snort. It was a combination of a sob and a laugh. It sent snot flying.

"Ohmigod, that's so gross!" Whitney yelled as it splattered on the dashboard. She quickly slapped her hand over her mouth. "I'm sorry. I'm so sorry. Really. It's fine," she said, motioning to the dashboard while she tried not to look at it. "That's totally okay."

This time my sound was all laughter. I opened the diaper bag sitting in the center and pulled out one of Iris's burp cloths. I wiped my eyes with it, avoiding any potential spit-up, and blew my nose hard into it. I let out a deep sigh after I was done.

"It's bad. Like really bad. We have no money."

"Like it's all gone?" She looked stricken. That was the most all-American fear you could have—losing it all.

"It's all gone, but we didn't have anything to begin with. Ryan has never had money of his own because he can't keep a job, but I didn't realize that until after we were already married. I feel like a complete and total idiot. You know what I mean? It's like on top of everything else, I'm utterly humiliated and ashamed. It was there all along right under-neath my nose. It wasn't like he was hiding it, but I just never thought to ask questions, you know? And it all seemed so legit. Nobody treated him like they treat us now. I guess they wanted him to have a wife?" I shrugged. I really didn't know. His family had been so wonderful in the beginning. "They've all pretty much turned their backs on him now, but back when we first started dating? His family was so much a part of our early dating lives. We hung out together all the time. Went out to dinner. Shows. Movies. All of it, but that was just because they were completely checking me out, you know? To make sure I wasn't just after his money. Because he looked like he had money. He lived in an amazing penthouse suite above Wilshire. Like half a floor was his."

"Ohmigod, I remember that place," she exclaimed, smacking my arm. "He hosted a Super Bowl party there once. I went with Colin, and I was bored to death, but I remember that apartment. It was so amazing. I loved all the leather, especially the couch. And those windows?"

I nodded vigorously. "Right?" This was helpful. So much more helpful than I thought it'd be. I just thought I'd be ashamed, but since I'd been stripped raw, none of that really mattered now anyway. "And he drove a black Jag. He took me to all the best restaurants. The guy wined and dined me first-class-style. Turns out, his parents were funding all that. They always were, but he made me believe he was working, and I trusted him. When he said he was going to the office, that's where I thought he went. And it's not like he didn't have an office. He had two. One downtown and one in our house. How many did he need? I never thought to turn all investigative and see if he was actually working."

"Who does that? I've never followed Colin to his job. For all I know, maybe he doesn't go to the office either. Maybe he works out all day long or goes to the movie theater and sleeps. He could be a total loser, and I'd have no idea. Ohmigod." She clapped her hand over her mouth again. "I'm not good at these things. I'm just not. I never say the right thing. I didn't mean Ryan's a loser."

I started laughing again and laid my head against her shoulder. "No, seriously, really. It's okay. He is a loser."

And I'd dumped it all in the car. Told her everything. She'd been keeping the secret ever since. I'd been so worried that she told Kiersten, but she never did. She kept my secret. Whitney was really good at keeping secrets.

It was why I trusted her when she told me nobody would ever find out what we were doing. I'd never planned on this.

"What am I going to do?" I asked, turning to look at her as she guzzled her coffee. She had fancy lawyers to protect her. I had no one.

"I don't think anything is going to come of it, but I had to tell you because even though I didn't give Perez your name, I had to turn over all my files this afternoon. Your name is on all the paperwork . . . I'm sorry." She gave me a second to let it all sink in before continuing. Accounting and math had never been Whitney's strong suit, and it'd been one of the things sucking up so much of her time, so she'd gladly handed it over to me. It'd freed up so much time for her to work on the things she was good at, like getting more clients. Even though I met with clients sometimes, the biggest part of my job was handling all the paperwork and administration stuff. "Honestly, I'm just crossing my fingers that none of our clients had anything to do with hurting Kiersten. I don't know how I'll live with myself if that's the case."

Of course that's where her head was at, but not mine. What if they searched all the records? All roads led back to me. My name was on everything. I would be the fall guy on this if they decided to do something with it. Didn't she see that?

But she didn't. She was still going on and on about her guilt over the business being linked to Kiersten's death. And I cared about that, too, sure, but what would they find if they took their time on this? That's what I was afraid of, but she didn't care about that because she didn't have anything to lose. I had everything. Our playing fields weren't equal. They never had been. I wasn't even sure we were playing the same game.

CHAPTER TWENTY-TWO

NOW

WHITNEY

Jade had still been shell shocked when we left the park, and I wish she could've stayed longer, but she wanted to get home before Ryan got back from his parents'.

"I'm going to have to tell Ryan." She just kept shaking her head and saying it over and over again, but honestly, I didn't see what the big deal was. Dude hasn't worked a solid job in six years. They were almost bankrupt, and they have a kid with cancer undergoing really expensive treatment right now, so he didn't leave her with a lot of options. She didn't even try to pretend like she wasn't a little ticked off at me, and I couldn't blame her. I'd taken her down with me without her permission, but it's not like I really had a choice.

She'd get over it. She had to. We were in this together.

Lily looked good tonight, though. She'd been so sickly last time I saw her, but she had some color in her cheeks and she played on the playground without resting the entire time we were there. Jade got her a new wig that looks absolutely adorable. A red pageboy. That's the only thing about her cancer that's tolerable. Lily gets to pick a different wig whenever she goes out. It's like playing dress-up for her, and Jade's approached it that way since day one.

That's the whole reason she's in this with me. She never would've agreed to the arrangement if it hadn't been for the experimental drug treatment she so desperately needed for Lily. After her breakdown in the Goodwill parking lot, Jade and I started spending more time together, and it wasn't long before I learned how many burdens she'd been carrying alone. Finding out their family was broke was one thing. Finding out Lily had a rare form of childhood cancer was another. Despite all the wealth they were surrounded by, the two of them were too proud to ask for help.

Could you imagine? Your baby had cancer and you didn't ask everyone you knew to help? It made no sense to me, but she was adamant. As adamant as she'd been about not telling anyone they were broke.

"You can't tell anyone. Not yet. Not until I'm ready," she'd pleaded with me, but she didn't need to. I'd do anything she told me to. I didn't pretend to understand what it was like to be going through what she was. "The moment everyone knows, they'll treat her like she's dying. I don't want people to treat her like she's dying. She's sick, and she's going to the doctor to get better. And she will get better. That's how we're approaching this with her. It's the only way I can do it. I just—"

She hadn't been able to get any further. I didn't make her. All I did was say the same thing I always said to her in these tough moments: "I'm so sorry you're going through this."

I'd used the same line the day she revealed the most devastating news.

"I have to tell you something, but you have to promise not to tell anyone else," she'd said while we were watching the kids play at the Giggles N' Hugs playground. She'd just sent Lily scampering back to the bounce house after losing her shoe, and her eyes misted as she watched her dance around inside it.

"Your secrets are safe with me," I said, giving her an encouraging smile. She needed all the support she could get.

"You know how I couldn't meet everyone here last week?" I nodded. There was a Tuesday-morning playgroup that had a standing open invitation. She'd canceled at the last minute because she said Lily had a doctor's appointment. "I wasn't taking her to her regular pediatrician. I had an appointment with a specialist because of that weird rash that we can't get to go away, and she ran some blood work. It's bad."

And then she'd crumpled. Right in her seat. That's when I knew it was serious. Jade was the only one who wasn't a first-time mom, so she almost always stayed calm when the rest of us were freaking out. She was our voice of reason with the kids. If she was upset, especially this upset, then it had to be bad.

"Honey, what is it? What happened?" I asked, putting my arms around her as she sat hunched over and crying quietly into her hands. It was a few more minutes before she could speak.

"It's cancer." It was almost a whisper. "Lily has cancer."

She'd said the words no parent ever wanted to hear, and I'd been trying to help her ever since. That's all I ever wanted to do. I didn't think we'd ever end up here.

My phone vibrated in my pocket, and I pulled it out. Normally, I'd ignore it since it was an unknown number on my personal line, but there was too much going on.

"Whitney?" I recognized Perez's voice immediately. "Do you have a minute to talk?"

"Sure," I said, instantly regretting that I'd picked up. I liked to prepare myself for her. "What's up?"

No way this was about my records. It'd only been four hours since they left my house, and my records were a complicated system. Nothing about them was straightforward. I'd made them that way on purpose to give myself time for something like this. Everything was written and recorded in shorthand code. It'd taken forever to teach it to Jade.

"We turned up some interesting information today when we looked into Allen Grigsby's background. Except I'm pretty sure his legal name is Dustin Miller. I'm texting you a picture of him now. Can you see if that's Allen?"

The alert popped up on my screen. I tapped on the picture. His hair was slightly shorter, and there were more wrinkles around his eyes, but there was no mistaking it was Allen Grigsby.

"That's him."

"Turns out, he's got a history filled with domestic violence charges against women and did four years for attempting to murder his second wife." She said it with such an ominous tone, but I wasn't the least bit surprised. Men like him were all the same. Except it dawned on me as she continued that there had to be something more—something bigger—or she never would've called me.

"Is he . . . is he somehow related to Kiersten?"

"We're not sure, but that's what we're trying to find out because he's the worst thing we've been able to connect to her. I'll let you know." She ended the call without saying goodbye. I sank to the floor in my living room. Her words ricocheted inside me. If I was responsible for leading a predator to Kiersten, I'd never forgive myself.

CHAPTER
TWENTY-THREE
THEN
WHITNEY

I took one last look in the mirror before I pulled open the door to meet Jade. She held the baby in one arm, and Lily clung to her other one. Lily's body was slightly hidden behind Jade's legs. Her chicken elbows poking out. She was so tiny already. The sixth percentile for height. The third for weight. Always had been. She had eating issues when she was young and ended up having to go to a specialized clinic to get it worked on. She'd never really caught up. And now this?

Jade looked frazzled, but she always looked frazzled these days. How could she not be? I held back from giving her a big hug even though I wanted to, but sometimes hugs made it harder for her when she was trying so hard to be brave and strong.

"Here, let me take her," I said, grabbing Iris from her. It felt strange holding someone's baby when mine was gone, but I promised Jade I'd help her, and I meant it. She had so much on her plate. I still couldn't believe she'd been carrying around all those secrets with her for so many years. Stuff like that would eat your insides. No wonder she had irritable bowel syndrome.

Grace had taken Asher to the park. They'd been there all morning. It was a good thing because otherwise I'd have two babies. One was hard enough. Asher kept me up half the night, and I needed a break. I'd just woken up from my nap when Jade called. She was frantic. Lily had her first treatment today, and the babysitter canceled at the last minute.

"Of course. Bring her over. Asher's at the park with Grace, so I've got free baby hands," I'd said as I quickly jumped out of bed and hurried downstairs to make an espresso. I couldn't believe I'd thrown myself together so quickly.

How's she doing? I mouthed to Jade as she stood in the entryway. When she told me about Lily's cancer diagnosis, she said the hardest part for Lily was all the needle pokes. Lily was terrified of needles, and her phobia had only grown worse. Jade said she was forced to hold her down, and it was the most traumatic thing she'd ever been through. Last time they'd given her kiddie Xanax. Who knew there was such a thing?

Not good, she mouthed back.

I gave her an apologetic smile, wishing I could do something more for her than watch Iris. And then, it hit me. Almost like I'd smacked into an actual wall.

I couldn't take the pain of any of this away. I couldn't make Lily any less afraid of shots or Jade's lazy husband go to work. But I had a way to alleviate the financial burden this was taking on their already-battered finances. A way for Lily to get the experimental treatment that her regular insurance wouldn't cover. Jade needed room to breathe, and I had air.

Could I trust her? I looked at her as she gave Iris a quick peck on the cheek and set her bag down on the entryway bench. Was it worth risking everything to help her?

I gave her a hug and sent her on her way, assuring her that we'd be fine. And we would be. Worst-case scenario, I'd call Grace. She was my savior. I called her with anything related to Asher. She was the oldest of nine children and raised six of her own. Fourteen grandchildren and counting. She took better care of my lovely baby than I did. I had no shame about it either. We all have our strengths.

All I could think about the entire time Jade was gone was how I held the solution to her biggest problem. Business was booming. I turned away people all the time. It'd been that way for the last two years. It'd always just been me and my girls. A very small circle of trust. That's why it worked.

Most of the initial client meetings were at my house. And no matter what, I interviewed all the women at my house when I hired them. Letting them inside my house was a risky move, but it was necessary if I wanted them to trust me. For them to see that I was taking risks too. But it was even more than that. Letting someone inside your home was intimate. It was a quick peek at who you were behind closed doors. No matter how hard we tried to pretend like we presented our authentic selves to the outside world, we all knew that wasn't true.

So, I invited them into my home. To see me. So I could see them. And together we could determine if we were a good fit. I had the entire system down to a science.

If I worked with someone I trusted and who could help me juggle some of the business responsibilities, I could probably manage twice as many escorts, which meant twice as many clients. If that was the case, I could pay off our second mortgage within a year. Not that this was about me. Truly, she needed the favor, but it would benefit me too. I wasn't going to pretend like it didn't.

I went back and forth all afternoon. Up until recently, I hadn't known Jade that well. I'd been distracted the night we went over her application and essay. Kiersten insisted on essays for the moms' club like they were applying to college. Everyone else thought it was ridiculous, but no one had fought her on it because you couldn't fight her on something she was organizing.

But then Jade came back home with Lily this afternoon, and I made up my mind the moment I saw their faces. I opened the door to find them both with swollen red eyes like they'd been crying all afternoon, and nothing else mattered except helping them any way that I could.

"Hey," I said, opening the door wider, "do you want to come in for a second? I think I might have a way to help you."

CHAPTER TWENTY-FOUR

NOW

BROOKE

Kiersten's memorial service had been beautiful. Breathtaking, really. Tommy was supposed to give her eulogy, but he was too upset to speak. According to all the hushed whispers, people were worried about him and he wasn't doing well. Of course he wasn't. Who would be?

Everyone passed around Rinley like touching her got them closer to touching Kiersten. I hadn't known where to sit. It wasn't like a wedding. We were all on the bride's side. The video photomontage made every person in the place cry. Except for me.

I wasn't sure what was wrong with me. How could you go to a ceremony like that? See all those pictures. The ones of Kiersten as a baby being held by her parents next to the ones of her holding Rinley the same way when she was a baby. They showed all kinds of juxtapositions of Rinley's life overlapped with hers while they played a song about being in the arms of an angel. Kiersten could've been a total stranger to a person, and there was no way you'd be able to sit through that service without shedding a tear, but I didn't cry. Not a single tear.

Maybe I've cried all my tears. Was that possible? When Abby first declared it was over between us, I was afraid that I'd never stop crying. And then when I did, when I finally found a way to get it under control, the smallest thing could set me off and send me spiraling all over again.

I turned to look for Abby, but she'd slipped away in the crowd. She'd sat next to me during the service. If anything had brought me close to weeping, it was that moment. It wasn't even just that she did it—even though that alone would've made me beam—it was how she did it. She didn't ask if it was okay or act like she needed my permission. She slid in next to me like that's where she belonged, like it went without saying. I spent the first ten minutes of the service trying to focus on what the rabbi was saying and not on the heat of her body next to mine. That occasionally her thigh would brush against mine.

I'd never been so acutely aware of the circle of life. The death of one great love had reawakened the birth of another. Of course we hadn't spoken about it yet. We were still tiptoeing around it. Being cautious and gentle with each other. Living like roommates, but she was still at home, and she'd come out of her room. Three nights in a row.

I slowly moved my way alongside the wall, trying to look as inconspicuous as possible so no one would notice me and talk to me. Small talk at memorials was about the worst you could get. Nothing was more uncomfortable. People should just be quiet. Sometimes not talking was okay.

But Abby always knew exactly what to say and how to be in any given social situation. That's why she was so amazing at her job. She could walk down Rodeo Drive or Skid Row with the same level of confidence. Be anywhere or anyone she needed to be. And she'd been all around the world with lots of different people. I turned the corner and spotted her with Taylor.

Just as I was about to make my presence known, something held me back. I stopped. Waited. Listening.

Don't do this, Brooke, I told myself, but I never listened to that voice. I pressed in farther, getting as close as I could without them knowing I was there.

". . . she's been acting just as weird as she's been acting for months, so I don't know how to answer that," Abby said in a hurried whisper. "She's anxious and jumpy all the time. Like you can see she's shaky on the inside, but she's trying to keep it together on the outside, you know? And she walks around half the time with that strange dazed look in her eyes? Like what's that about?"

"Yes! I know exactly what you mean," Taylor gushed, getting excited. "They said she was acting like a total zombie when she was over at Whitney's. They couldn't get anything out of her. Has she said anything about it? Anything?"

Abby shook her head. "Not anything that we don't already know, but honestly, we don't talk about it all that much."

Taylor balked. "How do you not talk about something like that?"

"It's not like I haven't tried—I have—but she really doesn't want to go there. She just wants to talk about us. It's awkward, you know? Like I have to pretend like everything's fine. Like I'm not just there to make sure my kid is safe."

She kept talking, but I couldn't hear anything else she said after that. That's why she came home? To keep Julian safe? From me? She thinks she has to keep Julian safe from me? For a second, I couldn't feel my body. Part of me wanted to storm out there and confront her. Get up in her face with what I'd just overheard. But I held myself back.

I took a few deep breaths instead. Forcing myself to calm down and focus.

She'd gotten caught up in the investigation. Of course she had. It was impossible not to. Detective Perez probably put all kinds of things in her head about me, just like she'd put in everybody else's. And Abby was right. We hadn't talked about it. Not since we briefly touched on it the first night she came back home. We didn't talk about our relationship either. We were still tiptoeing around each other in the house. I'd been telling myself that all that would come in time. I just needed to give things time.

I had to focus on what was important. Abby was back home. That was the most important thing. Sure, so maybe she wasn't back home because she was reconsidering leaving me. But that didn't mean she wouldn't get there eventually. My heart pounded, and my head throbbed as I leaned against the wall.

It was okay. It was going to be okay.

She was back, and that was all that mattered. If I confronted her right now about what I'd heard, she might go away and never come back. That's exactly what I didn't want.

I heard them leave and head back to the other people in the party.

I took a few more minutes to gather myself together before joining them.

"Hey," Abby said when she saw me approaching.

I gave her a wide smile. This didn't change anything. I'd just work harder. All we needed was time. We just needed more time.

CHAPTER TWENTY-FIVE

NOW

BROOKE

I woke slowly. How long had I been asleep? Julian didn't wake me up once to eat after his midnight feeding. He'd slept through the entire night? Really? I sat straight up in bed.

If he started sleeping through the night, my life would be so much easier. Lots of people could live off relatively little sleep, but I wasn't one of those people. I never had been. I needed my sleep as a kid and needed it even more now. But having Julian had changed all that.

From the very beginning, he'd never slept more than two hours at a time, and since he was exclusively breastfed, I was responsible for all his nighttime feedings. He still refused to take a bottle no matter how hard I tried, and we'd tried everything, but nothing worked. After a while, Abby hadn't even bothered. It was the biggest reason he was always with me—he couldn't eat if he wasn't.

What were the two of them doing this morning? He had to be starved, but I listened for the sound of him crying and didn't hear anything.

I rubbed my eyes and slipped out of bed. I grabbed my phone on the nightstand and saw that it was almost nine o'clock. I'd slept for almost nine hours. Wow. I hadn't slept that late since before he was born. I got up and hurried downstairs. Now that I was up, I just wanted to be near them both. This was how we'd always talked about it being—taking turns letting the other one sleep in.

I walked into the kitchen expecting to find them, but they weren't in there. The room was untouched from the night before. Even our dirty plates were in the sink. The coffee maker wasn't turned on. There was no way she'd gotten up and started her day without coffee. She must've left to get some, but I opened the drawer and there were plenty of pods, so where had she gone?

I walked into the living room and down the hallway, popping my head into Abby's bedroom again just in case I'd missed them the first time, but they weren't in there. I hurried down the hallway to Julian's bedroom, across from mine.

"Abby?"

They weren't in his bedroom either.

But they weren't the only ones gone. So were some of his favorite things. His blanket. His stuffed panda. His special pacifier—the nighttime nook. Sirens went off inside my body. He couldn't sleep at night without his blanket or his special nook, and we'd made it a rule that they didn't leave the house. We had fake second ones for emergencies and vacations. I whipped open the top dresser drawer. His favorite teddy bear pajamas were gone. Lots of his clothes too. Everything swirled in front of me, then stilled.

This wasn't happening. It couldn't be happening. There had to be an explanation.

I raced back into my bedroom and grabbed my phone off the nightstand. I called Abby, but her phone went straight to voice mail. I ended the call and quickly tapped out a text:

Hey! Just got up and nobody's here. Where you at?

I stared at the screen, waiting for the text to say *read*. But it didn't. The seconds dragged as it stayed on delivered. I called her back. Voice mail again. Another message. Then another.

"Hey, Abby. Just trying to get ahold of you. Wondering where you and the baby are. Can you call me when you get a chance?"

I paced the living room. I was overreacting. Being paranoid. Just because she'd packed his clothes and some of his favorite things didn't mean anything. That's what I kept trying to tell myself, but it wasn't working.

Maybe she'd gone to her mom's. I pulled up Martha's number. She didn't pick up. I just kept texting Abby because I didn't know what else to do.

Answer me.

What are you doing? What's going on?

Abby answer your damn phone.

You can't just disappear with Julian and not tell me where you're going.

Except that's exactly what she'd done. It'd been over an hour. What should I do? Call the police and tell them my wife had kidnapped our child. My head spun. I called my best friend. She answered on the second ring.

"Ohmigod, Erika, Abby took Julian. She took Julian, and she won't bring him back," I cried as soon as she picked up. I'd never needed her more than I did at this moment, but she was on the East Coast. "I keep calling and texting her, but she won't answer. She's ignoring me completely, and she's got him."

"What? What are you talking about?" I could hear the sound of worry in her voice.

"Abby took Julian, and she won't bring him back," I repeated myself. "I don't know what I'm going to do. Ohmigod, what am I going to do? I thought I knew her. I thought I knew exactly who she was, but I don't. I don't have any idea who she is. Who the hell is this person? Who does this? I'm his mom. You can't just—"

"Slow down. Slow down," she interrupted me. "What do you mean Abby took Julian?"

"I mean she took him. I got up this morning, and they're not here. Her car is gone, and she's taken a bunch of his stuff with them." I was back in the living room, pacing while I talked. Flipping open the curtains and hoping any minute her car would pull into the driveway.

"Okay, well maybe they went out for the day, so she packed him a lot of stuff. I've seen you guys go out with that kid. He needs a lot of stuff," she joked, trying to calm me down and lighten the mood, but I knew I was right. Something was wrong. Terribly wrong.

"They're not on some day trip. She took his blanket and his nook. Everything he needs to sleep at night. She wouldn't take that unless she was trying to get him to sleep at night somewhere else." I shook my head. Her words hadn't touched my panic.

"Okay, okay." She thought fast on the other end. "That still doesn't mean something awful is happening. She might be taking him somewhere for the night to give you a break. Maybe she's going to call any second and tell you that she booked you a room at the Four Seasons or she left with him so you could have the entire house to yourself for the weekend. You know, like a staycation."

I burst out laughing at the ridiculousness of her suggestions. The old Abby might've done one of those things, but not whoever she'd turned into. This person that'd taken over her body was a stranger, and she didn't care about me at all. Just as I started spiraling, I heard the sound of her car in the driveway.

"Ohmigod, she's here! She's back!" I screamed. "I'll call you later."

I didn't wait for a response. I ended the call and raced outside just as Abby was walking up the sidewalk.

"Where's Julian?" I asked, sprinting past her and straight to the car. The car seat in the back was empty. I whipped around to face her and screamed, "Where is he?"

She stood in front of me with her hands on her hips, and I wanted to throttle her. She'd stripped me of everything, and now she'd taken my baby.

"He's fine, Brooke. Relax," she said, holding her hands out in a peaceful gesture.

"Relax?" I screeched. "You want me to relax? I woke up, and my child is gone. Gone. And his mom won't answer the phone to tell me where he's at. Now where the hell is my baby?"

I got right up in her face. My heart pounded. She stepped back slowly.

"Settle down, okay? Just take a breath."

"I swear to God if you tell me to settle down again, I'm going to hurt you!" I'd never said anything like that in my life, but I meant it. I would tear her to shreds with my bare hands if she didn't give me my baby.

"He's with Whitney."

I stumbled backward, stunned. "He's with Whitney?"

She nodded.

"Why is he with Whitney?"

"Because that's where I went when I left. She's going to watch him while I go apartment shopping."

"Apartment?" This was all happening too fast. I fumbled behind myself for the car and leaned against it. Something solid. Something steady to ground me. To hold on to.

Her voice was flat and devoid of all emotion. "It's not safe for Julian to be here with you, so I'm taking him with me until we can get you some help and figure this whole thing out."

My veins felt like they were going to burst with anger. "What are you talking about?" I asked through gritted teeth.

She put her hands up in front of her face as my pulse pounded in my forehead. "Listen, Brooke, I'm just not comfortable having you around him until we know what happened to Kiersten."

"How can you do this to me?" All hope I held of us getting back together vanished in that moment. So did my feelings for her. Gone that quickly. I didn't want to be anywhere near someone who could take another woman's baby. That was heartless.

"How could I do that to you? Protect our son from you? From someone who is so unhinged that she hurt our friend?"

"Are you serious? Are you really serious right now? You can't honestly think I had something to do with hurting Kiersten, do you?" What was wrong with the world? How did we get here? The questions fought for space as my insides spun along with my surroundings. I felt so dizzy, like I might throw up.

There was no hesitation on her part. Not a second to think about it. "Honey, look at you." But she didn't say it in a way like she cared. She said it like she was patronizing me—like she felt sorry for me, and I wanted to throttle her.

Just like I wanted to do again as she flipped her hair back and said, "How you responded the other night was disturbing, and that's not the first time you've acted like that."

I leaped forward and got right up in her space again. "Are you kidding me?" I pointed my finger at her. "The way I responded the other night had everything to do with feeling betrayed by you again and had

147

absolutely nothing to do with Kiersten. Nothing. Are you kidding me?" I took a step closer to her. My breath came hard and fast.

It was true. I'd lost it on her when we got home from Kiersten's memorial two nights ago. I'd kept it together throughout the entire gathering. Somehow managed to act like everything was okay. To tell myself that even though she was back home to keep an eye on me and not because she really wanted to be with me, it was a small step in the right direction. Back in our home. With us.

And I'd never brought up that part. Still hadn't. I'd swallowed that truth like nasty medicine and forced myself to keep it down. But I'd gone ballistic when I'd walked in on her FaceTiming Liza as she was putting Julian down for the night. They were reading him a book together.

"You told me to take a bath and you'd put him to bed," I fumed at her.

She muted her call and turned to me. "That's exactly what I'm doing."

"With her!" I'd screamed and slammed the door hard, sending Julian into a crying fit that lasted for twenty minutes. She'd been furious when she came back downstairs after she got him calmed down.

"You can't go around acting like that, Brooke. It's not okay!"

"I'll tell you what's not okay." I circled the island and cornered her in the kitchen. "Telling me you're going to put our son to bed and then hanging out with your little girlfriend."

"I didn't hang out with my girlfriend," she snapped back. "I did exactly what I said I was going to do—I put our son to bed, and yes, I did it with my girlfriend because, guess what, Brooke? She's going to be in his life."

I narrowed my eyes to slits. "I don't even know who you are anymore. You're a liar. And a monster. And a—"

"I'm a monster? Because I decided to take care of myself and put my needs first? Because this marriage didn't work for me? That makes me a monster?" She was breathing just as hard as I was. "You act like this isn't hard on me. I'm going through the same thing."

"Going through the same thing? Are you fuckin' kidding me? The same thing? I'm sorry. My entire world fell out from underneath me in a second. Gone. Destroyed. Just like that. You don't get to compare our experiences to each other." I smashed against her. My face inches from hers. "Do you know what you did? You walked out of our home and into the arms of another woman. Do you know she's posting stuff already? Already? Your little AbbyandLiza4eva TikTok? You seem to be getting along just fine."

She hung her head. "I know. I told her not to. I told her to wait and give it more time, but"—she shrugged—"I can't control what another person does. I'm sorry. And she's young, you know? Everyone young is into TikTok."

"Just how young is your little miss Liza Jane?"

"Brooke, don't be like that."

"Me?" I let out a laugh. "Be like that? Right. How is it that you'd like me to be?"

"I don't know. Less hostile," she said with the most casual shrug.

And then I shoved her.

I just did it. Before I even knew what was happening. One minute I was talking to her, and in the next, shoving her as hard as I could. It caught her off guard, and she stumbled backward. She quickly recovered her balance, but she looked horrified.

"I'm so sorry." I reached for her, but she jerked away.

She held her arms up. "Don't touch me right now. Just don't."

"Abby, please, I didn't mean to do that. I don't know what I was thinking. I didn't mean to." I grasped and clawed at her, but she recoiled from me again.

She'd turned on her heels and walked away. The next morning, she pretended like it never happened, so I didn't bring it up. But clearly, she hadn't forgotten about it.

I loosened my grip on her shirt and slowly stepped back. "I'm sorry, okay? I'm sorry." I wasn't sorry, but I'd do anything to get my baby back. I might've lost her, but she couldn't take him too. "Just please bring Julian back. You can leave. Go." I pointed to the street. "Do whatever you want with whoever you want, but please, leave my baby out of it."

"He's my baby too." She smoothed down her shirt and tucked her hair behind her ears. "And I'll do whatever I have to do to protect him from you."

CHAPTER TWENTY-SIX

NOW

JADE

"Damn," Ryan exclaimed in the middle of an episode of the Jeffrey Dahmer documentary on Netflix. But it wasn't about the show. His eyes were glued to his phone.

"What?" I asked.

"Apparently, Abby took Julian from Brooke because she thinks Brooke had something to do with hurting Kiersten, so she's super worried about leaving the baby with her. This shit is wild," he said with an amused grin plastered on his face.

"How do you know that? What's happening?" I asked, scooting down to the other side of the couch to be next to him. I'd been sitting on the other end with my insides being gnawed with worry half the night. Just like I'd been ever since Whitney told me the police knew about our business.

He showed me his phone. It was paused on an Instagram video. "Because Brooke is going nuts on Instagram. She keeps going live with all these play-by-plays, making it sound like Abby actually kidnapped Julian. That's how she's treating it. She's even got all their text messages screenshotted." He pressed play while he talked, and Brooke's wild-eyed face opened up on his screen.

She was midrant. "And she can't do this to me. You can't do that to a parent. You can't just take their kid and rip them away from their home. From their mother. No contact. No way to get ahold of them. She's keeping him from me. Look at this." She waves wildly at the screenshots behind her, scrolling through their texts while she's talking and walking. There are tons of them on repeat scroll:

Bring Julian back home.

You can't take him from me.

This is kidnapping.

I'm calling the cops.

I can't believe you did this.

You think I'm crazy? You're fucking psycho!!!

She'd been going live and posting videos for the last three hours. All of them were just as manic. Like she was some rogue reporter. It was disturbing.

"Where is she?" I asked. "Can you tell?" I gave him the phone.

He swiped to another video and zoomed in. "I'm pretty sure she's at her house." He moved it around, panning in and out. "Looks like their backyard. She does a lot upstairs too. Keeps going in and out of Julian's bedroom. Showing the empty crib." He shuddered and handed the phone back to me, but I didn't want it. I'd seen enough.

"I can't believe Abby did that." I shook my head. Taking a baby away from their mother when you didn't really know what happened was pretty awful.

"Can you blame her?" Ryan asked, surprising me by taking her side.

"Is that what you'd do?" I asked.

"Take the kids if I thought you killed your friend?" I nodded, and he smiled back. "Nah. I'd probably help you hide the body," he said, laughing. I smacked his thigh.

"You're terrible." But I couldn't help laughing with him because he probably would.

I grabbed my phone and texted Whitney. I hated to celebrate someone else's misfortune, but maybe this would work in our favor. The police had to be following all our social media accounts, and there was no way they were missing this.

Did you see that Abby took the baby and Brooke's freaking out about it on ig?

She's here with me.

Brooke????

☺ no. Abby.

Abby's there? W u? And the baby??

Yep.

Omg.

Come over.

I liked the message and quickly tucked my phone back in my pocket. "I'm going over to Whitney's."

"I thought we were going to watch a movie tonight?" he asked, looking hurt. "It's Tuesday night."

"I think we can make an exception for date night on this one." His recent motivation to be the world's most involved dad had also renewed his drive to be the world's best husband. He was attentive and engaged in that totally present way you have when you're first dating. It was what I'd been trying to rekindle for years until finally giving up. But in the last few days, he'd done everything I'd been nagging at him to do forever. Kiersten's death gave him one of those dramatic moments that made him realize how precious life was. He'd been getting up every morning with a "seize the day" mentality that I'd never seen from him in all our years together. It was sweet. "Maybe we can do date night next week when our friends aren't dying and going crazy, okay?" I joked, giving him a quick peck on the cheek before racing out the door.

CHAPTER
TWENTY-SEVEN

NOW

WHITNEY

I was still stunned Abby was here. She'd shown up at my door this morning in tears, holding Julian's diaper bag and a bunch of his stuff.

"I didn't know where else to go with the baby," she'd said, and I'd ushered her inside without a second thought. "I just can't have him there with her. It makes me too nervous."

She sat on the couch desperately trying to get Julian to take a bottle, like she'd been doing most of the day, but she was having the worst time. He was screaming and writhing against her. His face scrunched and angry red.

"I don't know how you can exclusively breastfeed a baby. What are you supposed to do?" I said, wishing there was something I could do to help her. He'd been screaming for the last hour, and he wasn't calming down at all. I felt so bad for her. And the baby. Poor thing.

"Exactly." Her face was lined with frustration. "Have you ever met a baby that didn't take a bottle?"

"I've heard of it happening, but not with anyone I know." He was working himself up into an even bigger fit again. Growing more and more frustrated the longer he went without eating. I heard the door, and it wasn't long before Jade walked in looking flushed. She'd made it in less than fifteen minutes. Traffic must've been super light.

"What's going on?" She directed her question at me. Abby was too focused on trying to keep it together while Julian went into full meltdown mode again.

"We're just trying to get Julian to eat, but not having any luck," I said. "They weren't lying when they said he refused to take a bottle."

"What are we going to do if he won't eat?" Abby asked, glancing up. She looked like she was going to cry. I'd never seen her cry before. She probably did at the funeral, but I hadn't been around to see it. "I just thought if he went without it long enough, that he'd have no choice but to do it."

"He'll eat. He has to eat. Your natural instincts have to kick in eventually. It's not like he's going to let himself starve to death," I said with way more confidence than I felt. She'd been here since this morning, and he still hadn't eaten. Six hours was a long time for a baby to go without food.

"He still doesn't take a bottle?" Jade asked in disbelief.

"Nope," Abby said, practically yelling to talk above Julian's cries.

"One of us could feed him," Jade said with a casual shrug.

"You can definitely try," Abby said, handing her the bottle. I'd already tried a bunch of times. He didn't want to take it from me any more than he wanted to take it from her. He'd only screamed louder.

Jade shook her head. "That's not what I meant." She looked at each of us, but neither of us was following her. She pointed at me, then herself. "We're breastfeeding, so one of us could totally feed him."

Abby looked shocked, and I burst out laughing immediately.

"I'm serious. Women used to do it all the time. What do you think old-school wet nurses used to do?" She shrugged like it wasn't a big deal, and if it'd been coming from Taylor, it wouldn't have seemed like it was, but something so nontraditional from Jade was unexpected.

Abby looked at me, but all I could do was giggle. "Technically, I guess you could." Abby spoke slowly, clearly considering Jade's proposition, which was probably becoming more and more attractive by the second as Julian wailed in her arms. He was to the point where there was nothing you could do for him except let him cry. He only wanted one thing. Abby turned to me expectantly.

"Me?" I grimaced. I grabbed my boobs protectively. "It just . . . I don't know . . . it feels so weird. I don't know if I can."

"I'll do it," Jade piped up.

Abby looked at me, then back at her. Jade shrugged. "I really don't think it's that big of a deal."

"Okay," Abby said, still speaking slowly like she wasn't entirely convinced it was a good idea, but the possibility of ending Julian's piercing cries was too attractive to resist. She handed him over to Jade. I started laughing again.

"I'm sorry," I said, covering my mouth. "I don't know why I think this is so funny, but I just do. It feels super tribal, you know? Like we're cavewoman sisters or something."

Jade laughed and rolled her eyes as she pulled her shirt up.

"Do you think he'll go for it? Do they know the difference?" Abby asked.

"What if you can't get a letdown because it's not your baby?" I asked at the same time.

The three of us stared in fascination as she unclipped her nursing bra and brought Julian to her chest. He still wailed, trying to thrust himself away from her, but she cradled him against herself tightly. And then he froze. As if he suddenly smelled the milk inside her. He turned his head and scrambled to latch on to her nipple as fast as he could.

"Ohmigod. Ohmigod!" Abby clapped while I bounced on the couch beside her.

"That's amazing! This is amazing," I squealed. "What does it feel like?"

Jade smiled. "It feels exactly the same but different." This time she giggled. "I don't know how to describe it. Like the letdown is totally the same, for sure, but his tongue on my nipple is different. It's like slightly rougher or something, and his rhythm isn't the same. Feels kind of like dancing with someone else, you know?"

"I wonder if Iris will be able to tell when you feed her," Abby said, her face a mixture of relief and happiness.

I giggled beside her. "Right? What if you get home and Iris smells him on you?"

"Ohmigod, like I cheated on her." Jade burst into laughter, and for a second, that's all we could do. And it felt good. We needed it. Like a fresh breath of air after we'd been shoved underwater for too long.

Our laughter finally subsided, and we slipped into silence, watching Julian nurse. No one wanted to move or speak. The moment was too magical, and nobody wanted to ruin it. Talking about murder was going to have to wait. We couldn't do that now. Not after we'd just watched our friend nurse another woman's baby. Jade was always so full of surprises.

CHAPTER TWENTY-EIGHT

THEN

JADE

I hurried through the kitchen. Wiping off the countertops for a second time. Not because they were dirty, but because it soothed my mind. Calmed my racing thoughts. Cleaning had that effect on me. Always had.

Saying I would do this was one thing. Agreeing to it when Whitney proposed it to me on her $18,000 leather couch was entirely different from actually doing it. What would I do if Ryan found out?

That'd ruin everything. He'd never be able to keep his mouth shut. All he'd be able to think about was how the escorts could be his daughters. He'd see Lily's and Iris's faces in every one of theirs. That was the problem. You couldn't do that.

These weren't little girls. They were full-grown women who were making a responsible choice. One that was theirs to make. That's what I'd been telling myself all week, ever since Whitney met me at the park and told me she had my first client to interview.

"You ready?" she asked with a grin. She'd been so excited to finally have a business partner. She told me she'd been so nervous to ask me but hadn't realized how isolated she'd felt with it until she had someone to be in it with her. I couldn't imagine anyone knew what she really did. She was a successful talent agent for sure, but this was what paid her bills.

Just like it'd pay mine. I'd been on the fence, but when she told me how much money I could make every week, and considering how badly we needed it, I couldn't pass it up. Besides, I said I'd do whatever it took for our family, and sometimes that meant extreme measures.

She'd handed me a glass of wine that afternoon even though I'd declined it at first. "I hate drinking alone, especially during the day," she'd said with a strange smile. "But trust me, you're going to need a drink for this conversation."

I'd taken the glass from her with my curiosity piqued. She took a big drink and wiped her lips after she finished. Her lips stained even darker red.

"Okay, so it's been breaking my heart that you're going through all this with Lily. I just can't imagine how hard it is." Her eyes filled with tears. She held Asher in her arms. He'd come back while I was away with Lily. No question she was thinking about how she'd feel if her son had cancer. Every parent did when you told them. She struggled to talk. "I'd love to help you financially. I—"

I interrupted her immediately. "Absolutely not, Whit. That isn't why I told you about any of this." Ryan would be mortified if he even suspected she knew our financial situation. What our life was really like. It was his most carefully guarded secret, and he'd probably do anything to protect it. I shook my head again at her just so she knew how serious I was about my refusal. "We're not taking your money."

I got up and started gathering my things to leave. It wasn't that I was insulted. Just embarrassed. I hated this. Everything about it.

She grabbed my arm. "No, don't go, Jade. That's not what I'm talking about. That's not what I mean." She stood and put her arms gently on my shoulders. "I'm not trying to give you money, but I do have a way for you to earn it on your own if you'd like."

I'd stopped in my tracks. Slowed down. Listened to her. Given her a chance to explain herself and lay out the details of her business.

If I'd kept going and left like I had intended, I wouldn't be here. Doing this. Everything would be different. I wouldn't even know about her business. It was such an easy secret to keep tucked away neatly in the Hollywood Hills, where locals were used to seeing expensive cars and important people. Everyone minded their own business, hidden from their neighbors behind tall privacy fences and hedges. Carefully guarded by armed security patrol.

Keeping a low profile was going to be a bit more challenging for me. Not because we didn't live in the land of huge homes and expensive everything, too, but there hadn't been much traffic going in and out of my house these past couple of years. It had grown harder and harder to keep the secret, so keeping everyone away made it easier.

Coupled with the fact that I lived in the valley and had very nosy neighbors. Everyone knew everyone else's routines, especially since COVID, when we'd spent so much time locked in our repetitive daily cycle. Long after the rest of the world had gone back to semiregular functioning. We all walked down the chalked-up sidewalks. Rode bikes in the middle of the street. The neighbors would notice if I suddenly started having people over all the time. What was I going to tell them? That I'd suddenly turned into the world's largest social butterfly? And what was I going to do if, God forbid, one of them happened to pay a surprise visit while one of the clients was here?

All week I'd told myself I was going to back out. Tell Whitney I'd changed my mind. That it was too risky for me. Felt too wrong.

"I really appreciate how supportive you've been over these past few weeks and how much you've helped me. Seriously." I'd rehearsed it in the mirror more than once, trying to get it right. I didn't want to appear ungrateful or like I thought I was better than her. It wasn't about morality. I'd give her a smile and then let her know: "I have absolutely no judgment for what you do, and I think it's incredible that you've found a way to support your family on your own, but I don't think it's going to work for me."

No matter how I said it—even if I stressed that I wasn't being judgmental—it still sounded like I was. What if she got mad? I'd seen Whit mad before. She was vicious. Before I spiraled any further, my new phone buzzed. She'd set me up with everything I needed. A new phone. A computer. A new password. Everything I needed to keep my new job a secret.

"Don't give them personal information about yourself. Who you really are," she'd said when she sat me down to give the play-by-play instructions like I was going into a football game.

I'd given her a strange look and raised my eyebrows. "They're just going to google the address anyway. That'll point them straight to us."

She shook her head. "No, because from the very beginning, you let them know the home is rented."

"Please, like they're going to believe that."

She cocked her head. "You thought people around here just rented out their houses for commercials?" She looked at me with a mischievous glint in her eye. Amused by my naivete about all of it. "They rent them for just as much porn as they do HGTV and sex parties."

"Sex parties are a real thing?" I asked in disbelief. We always pretended like we lived where the real *Eyes Wide Shut* went down, but it was only supposed to be a joke.

"Oh girl." Whitney laughed. "You really have no idea what goes on in this city, do you?"

I didn't, but I was about to have my first taste because Maura was outside my front door. I smoothed down my shirt one more time and threw my shoulders back. Love required sacrifice. Pushing yourself to new limits. It wasn't always easy, but you did it.

"You can do this. You got this," I said out loud as I hurried to the door.

CHAPTER TWENTY-NINE

NOW

BROOKE

I sat parked a few houses down from Whitney's gate. All the lights were on in the house. The entire place was lit like they were having a party. Everyone was there. I'd been out here long enough to watch all their cars pull up. Still surprised Abby ended up here instead of Liza's. That's where I expected her to spend the night, but Whitney posted something about Kiersten on Instagram tonight, and I spotted Abby's bag in the background. I'd whipped my car around and headed straight here. I'd been here ever since.

And now they were too. Every single one of them. Whitney. Jade. Abby. My baby. All their stupid husbands. Even Colleen and Taylor. I guess we were no longer the six. They'd become the five. Five against one.

I'd never hated them more than I did at this moment. Every single one of them.

I glanced at the brown paper bag in the back seat. The one holding the cheap bottle of whiskey I'd picked up on my way over. I wasn't going to drink it, but there was something comforting about its presence. Just having it there felt like having your old teddy bear stashed in the closet during a sleepover. Not that you'd take it out and use it. But it was there if you needed it. That was enough.

And I needed something because I had no one supporting me through this. Erika had been texting me constantly, but that wasn't the same. She wasn't physically here, and sometimes you needed a person to actually be there for you. This was one of those times. But she was gone. Off vacationing in some cheap all-inclusive resort. Which made me question if my choice in women extended to friendships, too, because who doesn't show up for their best friend when they needed them?

I shoved the thoughts aside and returned to staring at Whitney's house. How could they all just sit there together knowing they'd taken a baby away from his mother? You couldn't do that. Not without warning. Not without reason.

Except that was the thing. They thought they had a perfectly valid reason. If they were all in the house with her, then it meant they agreed with her. I'd known everyone was always on her side. That was obvious. But this was an entirely different level.

They all think I'm a murderer.

I couldn't get the thought out of my head. People I knew and cared about. That I'd spent time with. Traveled with. Spent hours of my life with believed I was capable of violence. Horrific violence. Abby had never acted like there was any possibility it was an accident. There were lots of ways Kiersten could've gotten a gash on the back of her head, but they'd jumped straight to I'd done it on purpose. I couldn't think of anything more awful.

That wasn't the most ridiculous part, though. The one piece of the scenario that nobody saw or thought to ask about. But it was so glaringly obvious to me. Why would I want to kill Kiersten? Every murder has a motive, and what could mine possibly be? She'd never been anything but nice to me. We'd never had any kind of an issue. We had no history outside the moms' club. I'd only been in Los Angeles seven years, so we'd never run in similar circles like some of the others.

I could understand how the others might turn on me. Even though I didn't like it, I could still understand why they felt that way. They didn't know me all that well or anyone in my family. The finger was easiest to point at the outsider, but I wasn't an outsider with Abby.

She was my wife. My best friend. The person who was supposed to know and love me more than anyone else in this world. The one closest to me. People always said that about their spouses, but we were the real deal. We'd sat through hundreds of hours of therapy together before we ever became a couple. Baring and exposing our souls in a way that's only possible in those type of intense inpatient settings. We knew each other's psyches, and she thought I was capable of hurting another person.

And that hit me hard.

Which was the most ironic part. I hadn't done it. Despite what they thought, I wasn't the one that hurt Kiersten. Which meant one of them did. They were all in there trying to hide from me, but the real villain sat among them. What a great place to hide.

CHAPTER THIRTY

NOW

WHITNEY

I whipped open the police station door. At least they called and asked me to come down instead of just showing up at my house like last time. It had been all kinds of chaos since Brooke called the police and reported Abby for kidnapping. I better not be in trouble for letting her stay at my house. I expected her to go to Liza's, but she told me they were taking some space from each other last night.

I hurried through the reception area and down the hallway. The same one I'd been in just eight days ago, but that seemed like a lifetime ago already. The fact that it'd been over a week without Kiersten seemed unreal. I'd lived more than a week of my life without her. How? The familiar sobs rose, and I shoved them down as I headed for Perez's office. Not now.

Her office was easy to find since I'd been here before, and I quickly took the elevator to the third floor. The same receptionist sat at the desk, and she recognized me immediately even though I was still wearing my sunglasses.

"Hi, Mrs. Gilmore, just go on back." She motioned to the door to her right that led to all their offices.

"Thank you," I called out as I hurried down the hallway. I was already running five minutes late.

Perez looked up from her desk as I entered the room, and motioned for me to shut the door behind myself. Her desk was as meticulously arranged as before. Everything was in its place, and part of me wanted to cock her pen to the side just to see if it would irritate her. Was she one of those people? I took a seat and gave her a smile.

"Thanks for coming in again," she said, giving me one in return.

"Of course," I said, folding my hands on my lap. "I'll do anything to help."

"Including taking in your friend's ex-wife and their kidnapped baby?" she asked, making sure we didn't bring that elephant into the room with us. At first, I couldn't tell if she was joking, but then she broke into a slightly amused grin. "Now that's an interesting development I didn't see coming, and one of the reasons I don't touch domestic situations."

"Can you really blame Abby?" I kept forgetting Perez didn't have kids, so she didn't understand what it was like. How once the mama-bear instinct kicked in, there was nothing you could do to stop it. And Abby's mama-bear instinct hadn't just kicked in—it'd throttled her.

"She seems pretty convinced that her wife hurt Kiersten." Perez stated the obvious. She had a habit of doing that.

"She's more than convinced. She's like a hundred percent on it."

"And you agree with her?"

I raised my eyebrows at her. Why was she playing dumb? We'd had this conversation before. The first time she told me the case had moved from an accidental drowning to homicide. "I was the one who told you to look at her, remember?"

She nodded like I was refreshing her memory, but she'd slipped into a different game—I didn't know which one we were playing anymore. "Right. You did. So, you agree with Abby?"

"There's really no other logical explanation. She's our best guess." I'd only grown more confident watching her very public meltdown. She was going live on IG every hour, at least—sometimes twice—with ranting updates about their situation. She acted like Abby had ripped Julian away from her and taken him out of the country or something. In reality, he was only a few blocks away from her house with people she knew and loved caring for him.

All her videos this morning were disturbing. She'd gotten her face right up into the camera, too, making it distorted and huge. "They think I hurt Kiersten McCann. That's why. But what happened to a fair trial? What happened to innocent until proven guilty?" She got even closer to the camera, making her face even larger. You could see right up her nostrils to the stringy snot. "You know what? You know what? There's no basis to it. Know why? Know why?" Her eyes were wild and manic. Just like all the comments said:

She seems like she's in the throes of a manic episode.

I hope you get some help.

Poor thing. This is mental illness folks.

With all the hashtags. #gethelp #mentalhealthawareness #thereshope

I shifted my attention back to Perez. "You don't?"

"See, that's the thing. Brooke is just a bit too obvious for me, you know? I don't go for the most obvious. The one everyone's pointing their finger at. Unless it's the husband." She laughed and gave me another grin. "Then, I'm going straight at him, and I'm usually not wrong. I don't like being wrong." She paused for a second, making sure that I was following. Oh, I was. I was hanging on her every word. Because if she didn't think it was Brooke, then she thought it was somebody else, and I couldn't imagine whose name would come out of her mouth. "You're right about Brooke. Everyone is. She's having a really hard time. Divorce is one of the top three stressors, and she's definitely struggling going through it. All of this doesn't help. She showed up here demanding I get Julian back."

"She did?"

"Of course. And who wouldn't? She knows Abby took him because of the case, and since I'm working the case, she assumed I'd have some jurisdiction over it, but family matters and custody disputes have nothing to do with my job. Ultimately, that's what's happening with those two. A nasty custody dispute. I think people need to be more concerned about Brooke's current mental health than whatever happened before."

It was hard not to agree. She was more out of control and irrational than she'd ever been. But if Brooke didn't do it, then who did? She was the only person that made sense.

"Interestingly, we turned over some surprising leads when we started looking into Supermodels LLC." She gave me a pointed glance as she shifted the attention away from Brooke. There was no mistaking she'd done her homework. My LLC was buried deep. "I find it interesting that you never said anything about Jamar King."

"That creep?" I hadn't left him out on purpose. He'd slipped my mind.

"Yes, that creep. You know, the one that one of your security guys beat up?"

"Look." I leaned across the desk. "I know this looks bad, but I didn't intentionally not tell you about him. He was over four years ago. It was very early in the business. I would've handled things totally different now if I had any other choice, but I was so nervous and scared at the time. Honestly, I didn't intentionally leave him out. He never even occurred to me. What could he possibly want all these years later?"

"Can you tell me what happened with him?"

"Jamar was one of my first clients. He passed all the background checks, and I met him in person three times before I ever set him up with a date." Back in those days, I met every client multiple times before letting them anywhere near one of my escorts. I was still just as cautious, but I'd learned to recognize the signs early on, and my entire process had gotten so streamlined over the years. "Anyway, he was from Dallas and only here every few months. He was open about being married. Some are. Some aren't. We don't care either way. That's none of my business." She narrowed her face with disdain. And I got it. She's one of those women who think there's something wrong with women using their bodies for profit. That being in charge of themselves was somehow lesser than the life she'd made for herself. The respect she'd gained in her field. She didn't have any respect for my girls, and she definitely didn't have any respect for me. The small amount she might've had at the beginning of this investigation was gone. Didn't matter to me. I didn't need her to like me to have her find Kiersten's killer. "He started stalking her. He followed her home after their second date, unbeknownst to her."

She raised her eyebrows. "That doesn't happen more often? What stops any of the men from following the women?"

"You assume all of our clients are men." It wasn't necessary and added nothing to the conversation or the investigation, but I just enjoyed surprising her. She liked thinking she had the upper hand. She looked down at me. Like she was smarter. Better. And shocking her worked. She blinked a few times and quickly rubbed underneath her nose. That was her tell.

"Women use your services too?"

"Plenty of them. You'd be surprised how many women like spending their business weekends with other women." I gave her a smug grin. I couldn't help myself. Hopefully, it'd take her down a few notches.

"To each their own, I guess." She shrugged. "Anyway, back to Jamar. What happened with him?"

"We have all sorts of protocols and procedures in place to make sure things like this don't happen. Starting with meeting in public places. The client has to arrive first, that helps ensure it. Even so, we plan on things like them being late. So, we always tell them twenty minutes before the time we give the girls and add an additional ten minutes just to be safe. It's the same when it comes to leaving. The client has to leave first. We have security at every site. But there's always a certain amount of risk involved. Every one of our clients knows that. We make that clear from the beginning. We do our best, but we can't one hundred percent ensure their safety. All of them are aware of that."

"So, what happened?" she prompted a third time. Her voice was tinged with impatience.

"He followed her to her job. Her actual real job. You know how it is here. Everybody's got more than one job to survive. Her real job happened to be an elementary schoolteacher." Perez was immediately shocked, and I'd been, too, after I'd found out. She was our only schoolteacher. Jasmine didn't need the money. She had a steady job as a second-grade teacher and worked as a server three nights a week at Laurel Hardware. She did it because she liked it. It made her feel powerful, and it was so different from her traditional life. "She marketed herself as the sexy schoolteacher, and she loved it. She's one of my oldest workers and still books the most clients. I think it's safe to say that fetish has been around forever and it's not going anywhere. Anyway, it wasn't hard to figure anything out as soon as he had a name, and he was all over her. Social media. Her job. Showing up where she went. She ended up filing charges, but there wasn't anything they could do because he'd never threatened her in any way. All he'd done was follow her around, and there weren't any laws against that."

"How'd you get him to stop?" she asked like she didn't already know.

Was I really safe? Everything about my business was illegal, including the tax evasion, but I was never trying to hide the money from the

IRS—just Colin. But none of that mattered now, and I'd tell Perez anything she needed if it meant finding out who hurt Kiersten. I'd go to jail, pay any amount of fine, lose all my money, whatever it took to bring her justice. "The police didn't do anything about it. As soon as they found out what she did, they looked down their noses at both of us and acted like we were too trashy to help or keep safe. That's when I decided to hire my own security squad to handle things and take care of people when they got out of line. One of my security officers had a talk with Jamar and set him straight pretty fast. We never had a problem with him afterward."

She pulled out a piece of paper from the folder on her desk and pushed it toward me. "Is this Jamar?"

I leaned over and took him in. His basketball-size head. Big swollen neck. He was a farm boy from the Midwest who'd been on steroids since he was in high school. He hadn't changed in four years. If anything, he looked younger like he had work done. "That's him." I moved the photo back across the table to Perez.

"Guess who was at Kiersten's that night?"

"Jamar? Jamar was there that night? Are you kidding me?" She nodded at me. I grabbed the picture and looked at it again. Just to make sure. "I can't believe he was there that night. What was he doing?"

"I was hoping you might be able to help me with that. Turns out, he was one of the caterers. He was one of the chefs."

My head swirled and then stilled. I felt so dizzy. Ohmigod. If I led a predator to our party and I was the reason Kiersten wasn't alive anymore, I wasn't sure I could live with myself.

"We're bringing him in for questioning this afternoon, but we wanted to talk with you first. We were hoping you might be able to give us something on him. Something that would help us get to know him. Anything you can think of that might somehow be related to the case. Did he ever meet Kiersten?" I shook my head. "Did Kiersten know about your other business?"

"I already told you that we told each other everything."

"So, she knew?" she pressed, unwilling to let me off the hook.

"Yes, she knew." She'd known since the beginning. But just because she knew about it didn't mean she necessarily agreed with me about it. We weren't the same person, even though we were about as close as you could get. She wasn't a fan, and that only increased after she had a little girl. "It was something we didn't talk about much, but she knew."

"The two of you told each other everything?"

"We did." It hurt to talk about it. Who would I tell all my secrets to now? Finding out who hurt her was the fuel keeping me moving and giving me enough energy to get out of bed every morning because if I let the magnitude of the loss get near me, I wasn't sure I'd ever be okay again.

"It's funny you say that because she didn't know about a big part of your life. The part of your life that was in trouble. The one that's the reason you do what you do in the first place."

My stomach dropped. Then twisted.

Shit.

She opened her bag and pulled out an iPad. She scrolled while she talked like she was looking for something important. "One of the things about having a husband that's not a suspect is that they're the most coop-erative people you could ever hope for in an investigation." She was build-ing up to something. She had me. She knew it. Whatever it was. It was written all over her face. All I wanted to do was run out of the room.

GO. Run, my insides screamed at me. Instead, I sat perfectly still in the chair with my hands neatly folded in my lap and my legs crossed.

"Tommy gave us Kiersten's cell phone and the password. He gave us everything we could need to look into her life. He has nothing to hide. Not to mention he wasn't there."

"Just because he wasn't there doesn't mean he didn't have anything to do with it," I fired back. Not that I believed for a second that Tommy had anything to do with hurting Kiersten. He wouldn't hurt her any more than I would. Except Perez didn't know that. As far as she knew, we could've easily hurt the person we loved. People did it all the time, and in any violent crime, it was almost always someone close to the victim.

She brushed me off with an annoyed look. "He's not even on our list of people of interest anymore." The way she said it made it clear that even though he wasn't on it, there were plenty of other people that were. Had I made the list? Was that what this was about? She thought I had something to do with hurting her?

I shifted back in my chair. It'd never occurred to me that she thought I might actually have hurt Kiersten. She'd implied it in the beginning of the investigation, but I'd never taken her seriously. Suddenly, I reversed in my head, racing through all the things I'd disclosed that could be used against me. Stuff she could twist and turn into something sinister. I sat up straighter.

Jesus. Where'd I fall on the list? What if I was number one?

It was hot in here. Too hot to breathe. Were my cheeks flushed?

She just sat there letting the silence marinate. Finally, she spoke. "I find it really interesting that she didn't know anything about Colin's gambling problem." She cleared her throat and looked down to read something from the screen, "'How are things with Colin? I can't believe he's been clean for a year again.'" She stopped and looked up at me. She knew. Of course she knew. Everyone knew. It wasn't hard to find. "And you say"—she dropped her voice lower—"'Yeah, I can't believe it either.' You have like six different excited and happy emojis and then, 'I didn't want to make a big deal of it, you know? But maybe we should all go out to dinner to celebrate?'" She stopped again. "Did you all go out to dinner?" I didn't want to tell her the truth. I wanted to shake my head, but I didn't know what she knew. Who she'd been talking to, and it wasn't hard to find out the truth. I'd never tried to hide his tracks even though he kept it up. He had no idea I knew he wasn't clean. I'd never said anything to him about those receipts all those years ago. I hadn't said anything to him or anyone else. That's how I'd lived my life for the past couple of years.

And honestly?

It'd been wonderful. Denial was a lovely place. Pretend something didn't exist, and it didn't. My plan had worked. I never thought about his gambling. It didn't consume my every waking thought and eat me up with worry. I didn't check up on his stuff. I just assumed that he was. Every day. I didn't go through all his accounts to see how much money he'd spent or what precarious edge our finances were balancing on. I figured that we were bankrupt. I figured there were new credit cards. Ones he'd probably even used our child's social security number to get. I remembered when I first heard all those things the other addicts did in therapy. The lengths they went to get money. One of them set their home on fire.

Insanity. That's what I'd thought then in my naivete. Until a year later, he crashed the car into a tree to collect the insurance money. Faked an injury on top of it so that he'd get extra money for psychological and emotional suffering. I hated the way Perez was looking at me right now. Like she felt sorry for me. I didn't want her pity anywhere near me.

"You have no idea what it's like to live with someone intent on destroying themselves. Do you know I've always struggled to see Colin's gambling as an actual addiction?" I nodded at her. "I have. I just do, but there are definitely some things that are the same. I can see the reasons why they classify it that way. For example, they have all these sayings. Weird sayings and slogans that the recovery community lives by like they're some sort of weird cult. Anyway, doesn't matter. One of them is that 'How do you know if an addict is lying?'" This time I was the one to be silent while I waited for her to speak. She finally shrugged. Not amused. But it wasn't a joke. "'Their lips are moving.' And that's the thing. Somewhere along the line, and I don't even know when it happened—honestly, I couldn't even tell you—but I realized my husband was a liar. Like a compulsive liar. He lied about everything, even things he didn't need to. Do you know his grandmother was the closest person to him? She lived with them for most of his childhood. He was devastated when she died. And one time when I thought he'd relapsed again, I confronted him about it. Do you know what he did? He looked me dead in the eyes. The most earnest expression. Desperation. And he swore on his grandmother's grave that he wasn't."

He'd grabbed my arms and turned me around that night. "Whit, listen to me. Please, don't go. Don't be mad. I don't know what's happening. I don't know where that card came from, but I swear, I'm not using. Please." He sounded like he was going to cry again. I hated seeing him cry. Desperation and pleading washed over him.

"You're really not gambling again?" I searched his eyes for clues.

He shook his head. He gripped both my arms so tight and got down on one knee just like he'd done when he proposed. "I swear on my grandma's grave that I'm not gambling."

Except he was.

I tried explaining that to Perez. "Here's the deal. I don't think my husband's a psychopath. He's actually one of the most incredible fathers I've ever met, and he's super funny. He makes everyone laugh. No one makes me laugh like he does. But he has a problem, and he lies about it. He lies about everything when it comes to gambling. He was never going to tell me the truth. He was always going to hide it. And I didn't want to leave. Not because I'm pathetic. You have to understand that the rest of our life functions perfectly. I like our life. I hate that part. So, I just decided to let it go. Bury my head in the sand about it. And you know what? It's worked. These last two years have been some of the best of my life." I couldn't imagine what it would've been like to go through pregnancy and all this early-motherhood stuff if I was still hooked into monitoring his gambling. There was no way. All the anxiety. The fights. The lies. The emotional roller coaster. I didn't have to do any of it because I'd gotten off the ride. And once I got off, once I took that first step off, I didn't want back on.

Perez cocked her head. "Funny part is how hard you're working to point us at Brooke, but the closer we look at Brooke, the cleaner she looks. Not to mention that she used the bathroom in the baby's room, so the nanny cam has her on camera. Both leaving and entering. I don't know what she ate, but she was in there a long time. Long enough to be tucked away on a toilet during the time we know Kiersten must've died. Kiersten was alive when Brooke went into that bathroom and likely dead by the time she came out. We've had to expand our reach. We've had to look at other people who might have shady pasts."

"And me?" I pointed to myself. "Because my husband's addicted to gambling and I ignore it? That makes me hurt my best friend?" I was livid. I'd never been so insulted. I was through with her. Done.

"We didn't just talk about Julian when Brooke came to visit me. We talked about the case, too, and she told us things weren't always what they seemed in your marriage. It's not just that your husband's addicted to gambling. Sounds like he has a bit of a wandering eye too." She said it with a smirk. Like the two of them shared a secret. Like I was one of those women with a husband whom everyone knew was a cheater. They were the only ones that didn't know their husbands were cheating. While everyone else did and felt sorry for them but never bothered to tell them? Just secretly talked about them behind their back? No, I wasn't one of those women.

I gave her a coy smile. She really thought she was so smart. And she probably was. Book smart. She had the Ivy degrees lining her office wall to prove it. I'd do the same if I had them, but I had something she didn't have in all her years of training. Street smarts with rich people. She'd been raised by her books, but I'd been raised with them, and they were wolves.

"Oh, you mean the fact that Kiersten and I shared each other's husbands?"

She snapped back. Quickly readjusted her face, but it was too late. There was no mistaking I'd surprised her. I couldn't hold back my smile. No use pretending we weren't playing a game at this point.

"We weren't sister wives or swingers. Nothing like that." I gave a casual shrug. People had been speculating about it for years. They always wondered. The way we traveled in a foursome. We'd been taking trips together that way for years. Our husbands were best friends. We were best friends. We lived in a state full of swingers and every other imaginable kind of lifestyle there could be. There weren't many boundaries where we came from, and the ones that existed were very loose. "Everyone's fantasies about it were probably much sexier than the reality of it."

"Care to expound?" she asked, trying to regain her composure, her dominance, but she was struggling. She'd taken that last hit hard.

"It was our idea, first of all, not the husbands'. I'm sure they talked about it. You know what disgusting pigs men can be." I smiled at her. I liked being the one in charge. "But sharing each other's partner didn't start with our husbands. We started doing it in college. We had different reasons for doing it then. Back then, it was just for fun. Once we got married, it was more to keep them than anything."

Her shock had turned to judgment, but I didn't care. Let her judge me all she wanted. We were happy. I was really happy. Up until eight days ago, my life had worked perfectly. I'd created it, and I loved it. If you'd asked me one thing that was lacking, I wouldn't have had an answer. Now my entire world had been turned upside down, and it was easy for her to sit on the outside and judge it, but we'd all agreed on the rules. That's why it worked. There wasn't any dishonesty between us.

"Really?" She raised her eyebrows. "From what I hear, it wasn't just Kiersten who got a taste of your husband."

I wanted to wipe the smug look off her face. "Oh, you mean Camille?"

God, she was beautiful. One of the most beautiful women I'd ever seen. She was from the Middle East, and she had this thick, sultry voice that was one of the sexiest I'd ever heard. Like you just wanted her to whisper nasty things in your ear.

"You knew about her?"

I tilted my head back and laughed. "I picked her."

This time she looked horrified. I laughed again, which only made me look more like an evil villain, but I wasn't. I wanted to keep my husband happy, and I wanted to keep him married to me. It was that simple. And he came with needs. Ones I didn't have time for, and why shouldn't we both be happy?

Truth was, it was kind of a turn-on listening to Camille describe the things they did together. She told me everything, even sent me pictures. Part of the deal was that she report back all the details of their relationship. Kiersten had looked at me the same way Detective Perez was looking at me when I'd told her the plan about Camille.

"Are you sure about that? I mean, I don't need to tell you this, but there are SO many things that can go wrong with that scenario," she'd said as we made our second lap around the track. We were back to power walking three miles every night on the track behind the high school.

"Totally. I've thought it through. He's so needy lately. I can't even tell you. Taking these hormones to get pregnant has literally drained my sex drive. Like I have none. Zero, zilch, nada." I took a second to catch my breath. I was struggling, but she wasn't even winded. She probably walked in the morning, too, when she wasn't with me. "I feel like the world's most horrible wife, but I don't even want him to touch me, and I feel bad. He shouldn't have to go through that."

"You treat him like a child," she said, but I ignored her because she wasn't any better with Tommy. She still packed his lunch for work every day and folded his laundry like his mom taught her back when they first got married.

"I just want him to be happy. That's all." I'd shrugged. It all sounded very 1950s housewife, but I didn't care. I got to make up my own rules.

I pulled my attention from the memory and back into the moment with Perez. "I paid her extra on the side, and she needed the money, so she took it. It's not like she had sex with him. I had a strict no-intercourse policy. Mostly it was just blow jobs."

"Wow. Okay." She let out a slow deep breath. Detectives weren't like therapists. They didn't try to be nonjudgmental and impartial with the information you gave them. Her disapproval and disdain were written all over her face. It was stamped on every one of her features.

I flipped my hair over my shoulders. "Can we get back to trying to figure out who killed my best friend?"

"That's what I'm trying to do." Her chin was set. Whatever ounce of respect I might've had from her was gone. She glanced down at her notes, then back up at me. "What had the two of you been arguing about lately?"

"Me and Kiersten?" She gave me a clipped nod. "We hadn't been arguing."

"That's not what we've heard."

"What have you heard?" She was baiting me, but I couldn't help myself. Who said something?

"Just that you and Kiersten hadn't been getting along. Apparently, there was a bit of trouble in paradise," she said, sounding old enough to be my mom.

I narrowed my eyes to slits. She couldn't just throw something like that out there and not tell me who'd said it. But then I remembered she had Kiersten's phone. She might've read through all our texts too. "We've been friends since we were six years old, and we're pretty much sisters, so guess what? We fight like sisters too. There's stuff each of us does that gets on the other's nerves."

She shook her head. "I think there was a bit more to it than that. Seems like you were fighting about one thing, uh, not thing—a person." My heart shrank. She'd read our texts. That was the only place we talked about what was really going on between us. "Sounds like Kiersten was jealous of how much time you'd been spending with Jade."

"You know how women can get. When it comes to friendships, sometimes I don't think we ever grow up past fourth grade, you know? Like she's my best friend, so you can't play with her? That's pretty much what was going on between me and Kiersten."

"Your husband seems to think it was more than just a little bit of jealousy between the two of you. He—"

"My husband?" I cut her off.

"Yes, your husband, Colin," she said, not batting an eye. "He said you guys had been fighting and arguing a lot. In fact, he even told me she stopped by the house a few weeks ago, and he overheard the two of you yelling upstairs. He said she left crying and you didn't come downstairs for the rest of the night. That doesn't sound like a small argument about jealousy to me."

Everything reeled. My head spun. I felt like I was going to be sick. Not about the argument, but that Colin had talked to Detective Perez without telling me. I didn't even care all that much that they'd talked to him. They could ask him all the questions they wanted because I had nothing to hide. The upsetting part was that he'd never said a word to me about being at the police station. He didn't tell me they'd called him. He didn't tell me he'd gone, and he certainly didn't tell me what they'd talked about.

His lies. His secrets. All that was supposed to be about gambling. Ever since the day I made the decision not to tell Kiersten about Colin's continued gambling, it was as if that part of him existed in a different dimension from the one we lived in together. A separate life in a parallel universe on the other side of the sliding glass doors of our real life. What if all it'd ever been was a kaleidoscope of mirrors? Like light reflecting off multiple windows? He couldn't lie to me about other things. That's not how this worked. That's not why we did things this way.

If he hadn't told me about meeting with the police, what else hadn't he told me? And why was Detective Perez looking at me like that?

CHAPTER THIRTY-ONE

NOW

BROOKE

I'd been sitting on my front steps for over twenty minutes. I couldn't make myself go into an empty house again. I just couldn't do it. This couldn't be happening. How could you do this to a person?

I spent all afternoon with Children and Family Services downtown. The last place on earth I ever thought I'd be. Turned out, I was going to have to fight to get my own child back even though I'd done nothing wrong to get him taken away in the first place. None of that mattered. It didn't matter that I have a spotless record, with not so much as a speeding ticket on it for eight years. Nobody cared. Every person looked at me like I'd done something wrong the moment I explained my wife had taken my child. They all assumed there was a good reason. There was no innocent until proven guilty in this. Nobody took a child away from their parent without a reason.

Except she did.

So, I called the police and reported Julian missing. Told them she'd kidnapped him. That's what started this in the first place. They'd come to the house to take the report, but they'd quickly put their pens away.

"Ma'am, I'm really sorry you're having to go through this, and it seems pretty awful, but this is a domestic situation, and we can't do anything about it at the moment," the short one with the black spiky hair and wire-framed glasses explained for the second time.

"What do you mean you can't do anything about it? You absolutely can do something about it, and you will. You can march straight across town to where she's staying—and I know exactly where she's staying—and get my baby back. You can bring him back home to me. That's what you can do." I did my best not to yell. It wasn't working. "You can arrest her. That's an option too. I—"

His partner raised his hand to stop me. "Your wife hasn't broken any laws. Technically, all she's done is take your son to a friend's house without asking your permission."

"She's done more than that. Are you kidding me? She's refusing to bring him back. You should see the things she's saying about me." I grabbed my phone from my pocket and pulled up our text chain. I handed him the phone. "Look. You'll see exactly what I'm talking about." He refused to take the phone. He raised both hands in the air, making a peaceful gesture.

"Ma'am, again, I'm sorry me and my partner can't do more for you, but this isn't a police matter. This is a marital dispute, and police don't get involved in marital disputes. Now, I'm not saying there's not something wrong going on there, but we don't have any laws that have been broken. Unless she's threatening to hurt the baby. Is she threatening to hurt the baby?"

"Yes!" I blurted it out without thinking. She hadn't, but he didn't know that, and I'd say whatever I needed to if it meant holding Julian against my chest tonight.

His partner stepped forward. Up until this point, he'd been the quiet one. "If you could pull up those texts and show us those, that'd be great."

"I . . . uh . . . I just . . . there weren't any text messages. She just . . . that's what she told me." I was a terrible liar. The worst.

It was no surprise that they didn't believe me. They'd given me a card for the Department of Children and Family Services. They'd promised to call and let them know about my situation. Said they were the ones that would be able to help me.

Detective Perez hadn't been helpful at all either. She made it clear from the moment I walked into her office that she wasn't interested in helping me.

"You can't just barge in here like that," she'd said, jumping up from her chair after I'd made a mad dash from the waiting room without checking in. The police officers were right behind me. The ones the receptionist had called when I blew right past her and went straight for the hallway leading to Detective Perez.

"You're responsible for all of this, and you're going to help me make this better," I practically screamed at her. Maybe I did. I could've. I'd screamed at the gas station attendant when I couldn't get the pump to work on the way over here. I didn't mean to. I just couldn't keep it together.

One of the officers moved like he was going to grab me and pull me out of the room, but Detective Perez stopped him. "It's okay," she said, motioning for him to go and leave me with her. "I need to talk to her anyway."

She spent the entire time trying to get me to sit down, but I was too keyed up for that. Not after I'd just gone by Whitney's again and couldn't get past the front gate. They changed the code. We'd all had Whitney's gate code since the first playdate she hosted at her house. They were trying to keep me as far away as possible. Physically locking me up. I couldn't even get to her front door. You couldn't just strip away a woman's rights. There had to be a law against it.

"They can't keep me away from my baby." That's all I'd said over and over again in Detective Perez's office. I hadn't wanted to cry, but I'd turned into a blubbering idiot. That's what happened whenever I talked about it.

Detective Perez was the one who set me up with a Children and Family Services advocate. She said they'd help me. I didn't know how going to court to get my baby to come home was going to help me, but I'd do anything to get him back. The house was so empty and lonely without him. I had no purpose. Like there was this huge void inside me with no way to fill it. I felt bad for every time I'd ever gotten mad about his crying or not sleeping when he was supposed to. For every annoyed look. Every time I raised my voice. Had a bad thought about him. I took it all back. I just kept pleading with the universe to bring him back to me. Give me another chance. Last night I got down on my knees to pray, and I didn't even believe in God.

Losing Abby had felt like the worst thing that could've happened to me, but it didn't feel anything like being stripped away from my baby. He was a part of me. It physically hurt not to be close to him. And my breasts burned. Still on a schedule with a baby I couldn't feed.

My blood pressure rose. All my feelings toward Abby had turned into venomous rage. How dare she? How dare she do this? And how dare they help her with it? They all deserved to be punished. Every single one of them, and I was going to be sure it happened. They weren't getting away with this.

I'd already started it today when I met with Detective Perez. I told her every single little dirty secret I've ever heard whispered about them. Every one. All their secrets. And I hoped their secrets destroyed all their lives the same way they'd destroyed mine.

CHAPTER
THIRTY-TWO

NOW

WHITNEY

Colin's socks were scattered at my feet. I'd taken them out of his drawer and pulled them apart one by one. This used to be my life, and I was so glad it wasn't now. I couldn't remember the last time I'd checked on him like this.

All the old memories of going through his stuff flashed through me in quick snippets. After finding out he lost our Lake Arrowhead house, I obsessively checked on him every single day. Multiple times a day. Dug through everything he wore, searched through his laundry, went through his nightstand. Anywhere he might've stashed evidence. I smelled things. Licked things. Went through the trash. Even the trash in the bathroom behind the toilet. That was one of my ultimate lows.

I felt humiliated and embarrassed on top of everything else. Utterly mortified that I could be so stupid. That's how I felt. Besides the betrayal, I just felt really dumb. All those feelings rose to the surface as I went through his stuff again now. Something I swore I was done with.

His backpacks were empty. He had multiple ones. One for the gym. One for his snowboard gear, and one for hiking. All with numerous pockets. They were some of his favorite spots to hide phones. All of them were empty.

I went to the laundry room and pulled everything out of the washing machine, just like I used to do a couple of times a week. God, were we really here again? This felt so horrible. It's what I'd avoided most these past few years. All these feelings. I shoved them down. I needed to focus. Were there any parts of him that were real, or were they all just made up? I hadn't seen him since I left Perez's office. What was I going to do when I saw him? Did I confront him? Of course I'd confront him. I had to say something.

Except he'd just lie.

But why? Why would he keep talking to Perez a secret? Had she planted a seed in his head about me? Made him suspicious? Did he actually think I had something to do with it? I shook my head. There was no way. But then why was he there? And why hadn't he told me about it?

I moved into the glorified man cave he called his office. There wasn't any work that actually happened in here. Just lots of football games and golf on the TV the size of a small theater that he'd spent way too much money on. I came up just as empty handed in his office as I did in the other rooms.

I headed upstairs and back to my office. I opened my laptop and combed through our joint bank accounts. It'd been so long since I'd been in them, I didn't even know the passwords anymore and had to reset them. I wondered how he thought we made ends meet every month. Didn't he ever wonder how we kept making it? All the questions I never allowed myself to think were unlocked. There wasn't anything suspicious in any of our accounts, but that didn't mean anything. He only went into our accounts as a last resort because he knew I looked at them. For all he knew, I probably still did, but we hadn't checked in about our finances in a long time even though it used to be one of our weekly requirements. Credit cards were his favorite poison. That's where you'd find what was really going on.

I logged on to our lifestyle app. I'd never used it. I didn't even know if his was active on his phone. I didn't follow him. I used to be obsessed with all the tracking apps. They'd just started coming out, and I was almost as addicted to those dopamine hits from knowing where he was as he was to the tables. I shuddered to think what my life would be like if I still lived like this.

No matter what, my life was never going to be the same after this. The magnitude of the loss threatened to swallow me into its darkness, but I fought to stay present. This was the only thing propelling me forward. Finding out who killed Kiersten. It was impossible not to be consumed by it when you were considered one of the suspects.

That's what today was about, and since I hadn't done anything to hurt Kiersten, even if nobody else believed me, it meant I also knew that whoever had was still out there.

Was Perez right? Was there any way the dots could connect this back to Colin? He was out with Tommy that night, but did that matter? Was there any chance someone thought Kiersten was me? That they were coming for me and not for her? I'd never considered the possibility, but it wasn't that far fetched, especially if you didn't know us. We looked alike, and people were always mistaking us for sisters. One year we'd even gone to a Halloween party dressed as twins, and there'd been people that hadn't been able to tell us apart. Was that where Perez was going today? Is that why she was asking me about Colin? All the specifics? Was she actually worried about me like she'd said?

"Be careful out there. Sometimes we don't always know our friends as well as we think we do." That's what she'd said when I left her office this afternoon, and I hadn't been able to shake it.

Julian cried from downstairs. His cry was so different from Asher's. Funny how you could recognize the sound of your baby over anyone else's. I hurried downstairs to grab him from the Pack 'n Play in the living room. Abby was in one of the upstairs offices on a Zoom call, and I'd promised to keep an eye on him until she was finished.

She'd found an apartment for the two of them in Silver Lake, but couldn't move in for another week. I didn't mind having her here, and it made things easier for her. She already had all the baby gear she needed, and now that Julian was finally taking a bottle, all our lives had gotten so much easier.

Jade had been the one to teach him. Brooke was one of those people who acted like formula was poison, so Abby was doing her best to honor her wishes despite what Brooke said on social media. So far, we'd been able to keep Julian supplied with breast milk by giving him ours.

Natasha and Taylor gladly jumped in to help, and between the four of us, we already had half the freezer full. Taylor suggested getting some milk from Brooke, but Abby hadn't been back to the house, and she wouldn't go. Not even for breast milk. She was afraid Brooke would confront her on camera, and she didn't want to deal with any of that mess, so we'd all been donating ours. Pumping what we could in between our own feedings. Taylor had brought over her bags last night, and we'd all been shocked.

"Ohmigod," Abby had said, taking in all the frozen bags. They filled two coolers. "How much do you produce?"

She giggled. "I told you I'm like a cow. I'm thinking even after I'm done having babies that I should just keep on nursing, you know? I could sell this stuff. And it's good stuff too. A hundred percent vegan," she joked.

We'd all started joking about who Julian was going to look like as if our DNA was in the milk. Strangely, the last few days taking care of Julian had banded us together. It made losing Kiersten the teensiest bit less sad. We were doing something. Something good, and we needed that right now. All of us.

CHAPTER THIRTY-THREE

NOW

WHITNEY

I couldn't imagine what I would've done if the tracking apps had been this good when I was following Colin everywhere. I would've lost my mind. There was so much more technology available now. High-tech stuff too. I'd hacked into his phone and set up a spying app. It would download all his data. Send it straight to me. I never would've known such a thing existed if I hadn't seen it on *Dateline* twice. Women who'd followed their husbands. They'd followed them the same way I've started following mine.

I never said anything when he got home from work last night. As hard as it was, I didn't ask him if he'd gone to see Perez. He acted like everything was fine—well, not fine, because my best friend was gone, but he'd been loving and attentive all night. He'd taken Asher from me the minute he walked through the door and only brought him to me when it was time for him to nurse or when I asked to snuggle him.

I hadn't gone to Abby's suite to watch trashy TV with her like I'd been doing every night since she arrived. I lied about having a headache. Instead, I'd gone over and over what it meant and what I should do about Colin going to see Perez and not telling me about it. We told each other every exciting thing that happened during our day, and being interviewed by a detective certainly qualified as important news to share. Not to mention, out of the ordinary. I couldn't shake that there was a reason. And not a good one. Eventually, I'd texted my chief security officer and asked if he could help set up the app. He always took care of me no questions asked, and he'd done just that this time around. He'd done it all without even having to touch Colin's phone.

"I'm sorry, boss," he'd said because it'd only taken minutes for flirty exchanges to start between Colin and someone with a 323 area code. You couldn't see backward in their text chain, only forward, but that didn't matter. It was clear they were hooking up:

Hey love! How's Tuesday?

Hi beautiful 🌱☀️ I hope you have an amazing day. Can't wait to see you tonight 😌

He sent her a funny TikTok parenting video at nine. She responded with her own funny one.

A selfie waving at her with a cute grin halfway through this morning. Then Jade's face.

Wait. What?

My phone must be glitching. I got out of my texts and closed all my apps. Then I opened up the spy app again.

It was still there. A selfie. Jade with fish lips. Sexy eyes.

And then he responded with a picture of his leg and a fire emoji.

My insides sank. The picture seemed bizarre if you didn't know Jade was obsessed with calf muscles. She thought they were the sexiest part of a man's body, but you'd only know that if you were one of her closest friends or her boyfriend since that's not something you made well known, otherwise you looked like you had some strange fetish.

There was no way. It couldn't be. That's what I kept saying to myself over and over again as I copied the phone number and pasted it into my contacts search bar. I dropped the phone like it would burn me: the results matched Jade's information in my contact list.

I'd imagined lots of tragic things happening in my life. It wasn't like I was naive about the world, but never in my wildest imagination had I ever expected Jade to hook up with my husband. And they weren't just hooking up. Their texts reeked of a relationship. A feelings one.

I bent over and picked up my phone. This didn't make sense. None of this made sense.

They went back and forth. All through their morning. Cute emojis. Constantly checking in. All those things you did when you were really into someone. People gave you their attention when they were interested in you, and they had each other's completely.

I could've said or done something. I had lots of ideas. Take screenshots of their exchanges and create my own hysterical-wife reel like Brooke was doing. Put the three of us on a group text together and just totally mess with them. See how uncomfortable I could make them. Toy with them for days until I drove them mad. I mentally smashed out individual texts and FaceTimes to each of them like hundreds of times. Alternating between angry and devastated. The same way that my emotions swung.

But ultimately? I just watched it play out like a movie in front of me and did nothing. At around noon, I decided to send Colin a text just to see what he'd say. I couldn't help myself.

Hi hon how's your morning?

It took him almost an hour to respond. Not because he was away from his phone and couldn't. Oh no. He responded plenty of times to Jade while I waited for something to me. When it finally arrived, I got the usual:

Good babe. U?

For a second, I wanted to text back *miss you* like Jade sent after almost every one of their exchanges, but I stopped. I never said I missed him unless I was out of town or he was away. That'd only lead to something else, and it didn't feel right to confront him. Not yet. Instead, I took screenshots of their texts and made a quick video detailing what was happening. The only thing I knew about the legalities of divorce was that documentation was important. I didn't know where any of this was going, but I was protecting myself from day one just in case. I downloaded everything to the cloud and then changed all my passwords to things he'd never guess.

He didn't go to his office after lunch. He went to the gym, and I felt like backhanding myself. I missed the most obvious sign of an affair—he suddenly looked amazing. He'd dropped the twenty pounds of sympathy pregnancy weight he'd gained and was in the same shape he was in college. One of the first pictures Kiersten had shown me was him at the gym working out next to Tommy. They were both wearing skintight tank tops. How could I have missed the most obvious sign? He was just as cut now as he had been then.

I grabbed my keys and headed to the gym. My heart sped up as soon as I pulled into the parking lot, terrified that he'd see me. Ask me what I was doing there, and I wasn't nearly as good of a liar as him, especially not in person. What would I say? What was I doing here? I didn't know. How was I supposed to react when my best friend died and I just found out my husband was having an affair with one of my closest friends? I'd say I was doing pretty well, all things considered.

I opened the door and slowly got out of the car. Was I going to go inside? What would I say to him? I crept through the rows of cars, trying to keep my head down so no one could see me even though I wasn't doing anything wrong. My eyes furtively scanned the lot for Jade's minivan. Hers was impossible to miss. The **I USED TO BE COOL** bumper sticker on the back was a dead giveaway. I didn't see it anywhere, and I wasn't ready to go in yet, though. Did I really want to make a scene in front of all those people? The thought of being that woman filled me with dread. I slowly turned around and headed back to my car just as Jade pulled into the parking lot. She was headed right toward my row.

Shit.

If I wasn't ready to confront my husband about their affair, I sure as hell wasn't about to confront her. I dropped down and crouched in between two cars. What would I do if she saw me? I never went to the gym with Colin. She'd know something was up immediately. My heart pounded.

Jade's having an affair with my husband.

I couldn't wrap my brain around it even though it was the truth.

If there was anyone who understood sex and love could be separate, it was me. Christ, I'd seen him sleep with my best friend. But this? Whatever was happening between them? Going to the gym and wherever they planned to go next—lunch. Sex. Then back to each of their respective spouses as usual. That was sociopathic. To come home to a family and children. Act as if nothing was wrong. Especially during this. My best friend just died. They should both be ashamed of themselves.

How could either of them look me in the eye? But that's what they'd do. Colin when he came home for dinner tonight and Jade when we met to debrief about Brooke. Yesterday already felt so far away.

Jade parked and headed inside. Part of me wanted to chase after her. I pictured myself grabbing her long black hair and pulling her back. Snapping her neck. Punching her in the face. Not so much for sleeping with my husband but for lying to me. How long had it been going on? I should storm in there and confront them both.

And then what?

Scream at them? Act like the crazy scorned wife, as would be expected of me now?

Did the others know? Colleen? Taylor? Even Brooke? The thought of everyone knowing filled me with so much humiliation and shame it made me feel dizzy. But if they knew, then Kiersten would've known too. She would've told me. She would've been all over that. So it still must be a secret.

At least nobody knew. There was that. A small shred of my dignity still left. I felt disoriented, like I'd just stood up after a really turbulent flight.

I took three deep breaths. I had to think. Use my head. I didn't get where I was today by allowing my emotions to control me. There was only one thing I knew for sure—they weren't getting away with this.

CHAPTER THIRTY-FOUR

THEN

JADE

How could Ryan just stand over there and act like everything was fine? Like we hadn't just been screaming our heads off at each other in the car the entire drive over. How did I always end up apologizing or feeling like I'd done something wrong when he was the one screwing up? That's how it'd started out this morning, and we'd been at it that long. Pretty much since our eyes opened. So many of our days were like this. Constantly at each other.

But seriously.

How many times could he get a job and lose it? Like he'd literally been given jobs his entire life. And not just any kind of jobs. Good jobs. Silver spoon ones.

DreamWorks had been his first real job in years. One where he made a decent wage. One I could proudly let my friends know about and didn't have to pretend like it wasn't another multilevel marketing scam. He'd only been at DreamWorks nine months before COVID hit.

He'd started struggling in all the usual ways—missing work, calling in sick, only doing things half-assed—when the pandemic struck. I'd been grateful at first because I thought it'd give him a much-needed break. A chance to decompress and refocus again. I couldn't have been more wrong.

Unlike some instances when working at home went wonderfully and people proved how capable they were of doing it, he was the reason we had the stereotypes about people not being productive when they worked from home. He turned into the biggest bum. He could barely get off the couch. It made me furious. How hard was it to show up on time for Zoom meetings?

"You act like this is my fault," he screamed at me earlier today. The argument had started over another maxed-out credit card bill. We'd spiraled into the same madness. It never mattered what we argued about. It always brought us back here. "They laid off half the company. Almost forty of us, Jade. You act like I was the only one. Give me a break."

"Guess what, Ryan? Half of the people at the company still work there. They didn't put people's names into a hat and randomly draw them out. They kept the people they wanted to keep. The ones that were the hard workers. The good ones. The ones that did their jobs."

I'd given him so many breaks. I was out of them. I didn't have another one to give.

I was going to have to quit therapy. That's what made me furious. I was already two payments behind, and there was no way she'd let me miss another one. My therapist was the only person helping me through all this. The one keeping my head above the surface long enough to breathe. The only person that knew everything. Who I could be completely honest with about all my feelings. Everything I was going through. How much I really didn't like my husband. That I'd lost all respect for him and didn't know if I'd ever get it back. Could you be with someone you had no respect for? Married to them? I wasn't sure I could.

Right now, I couldn't even stand to look at him. I flipped around and stormed across the Duttos' backyard over to the food on the patio. They'd gone all out for their son Elliott's birthday. They'd catered chicken tacos, and they were the best ones in West Hollywood. I'd already had two, but oh well, I could eat my pain. Wouldn't be the first time.

Colin was filling up a plate in front of me.

"Hey," he said, turning around and giving me a lazy grin.

"Hey," I said before turning back around to order. "Two chicken, please."

"These are amazing," Colin said as he took a huge bite. "I've already been up here once."

"Same," I said, giving the staff a thankful nod as the caterer handed me my own plate. Colin and I hadn't had many conversations, and I barely knew him because Ryan wasn't part of the husband crew. Colin and Tommy were friends as close as Kiersten and Whitney. They hung out together all the time, and in the past couple of years, Colleen's and Taylor's husbands, along with a couple of the others, had started joining them. They worked out. Played golf. Sometimes they went to concerts. In the beginning, they asked Ryan to go. It wasn't like they'd intentionally left him out. He excluded himself. He'd told them no or flaked at the last minute so many times that eventually they stopped asking him.

"We've been to one of these every weekend for the last two months," Colin said, motioning to all the toddlers tumbling out of a huge bounce house shaped like a pink dragon. You could hear their happy squeals and shrieks from where we stood. Interspersed with the cries because every two seconds someone got hurt or threw a fit. "I had no idea becoming a parent meant you'd be invited to every birthday party on the planet. I wasn't prepared for all this."

"People don't even wait for you to have kids. They start inviting you the moment you're pregnant, and then it just doesn't stop," I said, digging into my taco.

"Right?" he said, giving me a big smile. "Who knew there was this whole world of character-themed birthday parties and performances happening right under our noses all these years?"

I smiled back. "And it's LA, so everyone is constantly trying to outdo everyone else. This just gets wilder and wilder."

"Can you imagine how many of these we're going to be at before they even get to kindergarten? I'm not sure how many more I can take." He shook his head. "Don't get me wrong—I love a good *Little Mermaid*–themed party. Last week we were at one with actual mermaids swimming around in the pool, and my brother's kids from New York were here and thought it was the most amazing thing they'd ever seen."

"I like the magic guy. You seen him yet?" I asked, taking another bite of my tacos. Lily was almost four, so we'd been at this for years. I'd seen some of them twice.

"The guy that pulls the bunny out of the toy fire truck?"

"Not that one. Seen him too. He's pretty great, but I'm talking about the one that swallows flaming swords?"

"Nope, haven't seen him yet, but sounds impressive." He laughed.

"Oh, just wait, you will. Give it time."

"Then, once you're there, you have to go through the same conversations every time with every person, you know? How old is she? Does she sleep? What about attachment parenting? Do you cosleep?"

"Right? Are you breastfeeding?" I quickly blushed when I realized they probably weren't asking him that, but he didn't miss a beat or maybe he wanted to make sure I wasn't embarrassed.

"Oh, they ask me too. I've seen more women's boobs in the last year than I did in college."

I practically spit out my food. It was the last thing I expected him to say and so incredibly inappropriate too. People just didn't say things like that anymore, but all I could do was laugh and try to pretend like I wasn't still half-choking.

"My favorite is the screen time questions. Like, uh, I have no idea if I'm going to let him be on screens. I'm just trying to get through the day." He threw his hands up. "I haven't thought as far as potty training."

I laughed again. It felt good to laugh. Really good. And he was so gorgeous. One of those stripped-all-your-thoughts-from-your-head-when-they-looked-at-you kind of gorgeous. Big green eyes with gold specks in them that were mesmerizing. The most incredible smile. He was one of the few people in LA that didn't have perfect teeth. He had this half-crooked grin. The fact that he wasn't perfect, didn't have the perfect face, made him more attractive instead of less.

He was one of those guys that walked into every room as if he'd already conquered it. Smooth. Like he didn't have a care in the world. As if the world would just open at his feet. Because that's what it'd always done for him. You didn't expect anything less than that when that's all you'd ever known.

If we were meeting at a bar or a club, he wouldn't have picked me. And if he happened to turn his attention my way, I'd be stumbling over my words. But it was different now. We were on a different playing field. We lived in a different world, and none of the regular social rules applied.

He turned back to the table. "You want a beer?" he asked as he grabbed himself one from the fridge next to the bar and threw his plate in the trash.

"Sure," I said, taking it from him even though I hated beer. I twisted the cap and held my drink out to him. "Cheers," I said, clinking my bottle against his.

"You come here often?" he asked, holding his bottle against his lips before taking a sip.

I burst out laughing. "Okay, so you really have become a domesticated man. Is that really how you used to pick up women?"

He laughed back. His eyes almost had a twinkle when he smiled. Like something clicked. He shrugged. "I've been out of practice for a while. Gimme a break."

"Okay, so let's pretend." I straightened up, pulled my shirt down, and tucked my hair behind my ears. I gave him my sexiest smile. "Let's pretend you're meeting me for the first time. Give me your best shot."

He burst out laughing again. "Okay. Okay, gimme a second. Let me get myself together." He turned around like he was giving himself a pep talk and straightening his face. When he turned back around, the look on his face almost knocked me off my feet.

"Hey," he said, moving in close, leaning into me but without actually touching me. "I noticed you standing there all by yourself and thought you might like some company. Can I stand next to you if I promise to be nice?" His eyes twinkled. So did his smile.

My stomach flipped. His smell was intoxicating. I felt myself blushing. I couldn't remember the last time a man had made me blush. "I don't care if you're mean. You can treat me however you want."

My boldness shocked me completely.

"Well, look at you, Mrs. Porter. Full of all kinds of surprises." He gave me another one of his charming grins. It had been a long time since someone smiled at me like that. And if I was the cheating kind, I might've done something about it. But I wasn't.

CHAPTER THIRTY-FIVE

NOW

BROOKE

"Your Honor, there's an active murder investigation in which Mrs. Lyons is a suspect, and until she's been ruled out, my client wants to make sure her child is safe," Abby's lawyer interrupted from the other side of the table. She'd brought a lawyer. Jeff. I recognized him as one of her work colleagues.

That was okay. I'd brought mine too. If she thought I was going to take this one like I'd taken her leaving me, she had another thing coming. She didn't get to just destroy my life. I haven't done anything wrong. But she'd turned everyone against me.

"Has she been named a person of interest in the case?" Judge Goldberg peered at him from the head of the table, looking just like Judge Judy. What was the point of sending her all the depositions beforehand if she wasn't going to read them? All this was clearly laid out.

"No, Your Honor. She has not been," my attorney, Gill, interrupted before Abby's could. "Unfortunately, my client was at an event where a terrible accident occurred—"

"Your Honor"—Jeff jumped back in—"it wasn't just a terrible accident. It was a murder. There is an active police investigation into the death of Kiersten McCann."

"I understand that," she said sternly. "Please, Counsel"—she motioned to Gill—"continue."

Gill continued without looking smug, but we'd scored a point. Judge Goldberg clearly didn't like to be interrupted. "They've brought in everyone who attended the event that night for questioning, and my client hasn't been questioned any more than the other women who were there. In fact"—he paused, taking a moment to scan his notes—"she's definitely not the one that's been called in the most. The one they've called in the most"—another dramatic pause, but I knew exactly where this was going—"is actually Whitney Gilmore. Police have questioned her more than anyone else on the list of attendees. Shoot, even the husband." He pretended to be surprised by that one, but I was responsible for that juicy bit. I'd been keeping track of everything since day one. "Brooke's been interviewed twice, like most of the other women at the event. But Whitney?" He held up four fingers to emphasize the point. "Four times. Five if you count the time the investigators came to her house."

Judge Goldberg shifted her attention to Jeff, but I kept my eyes locked on Abby. Who did she think she was playing with? She refused to look at me just like she refused to answer any of my texts or phone calls. That didn't matter. Whenever she looked up, I'd be here. When she tried to go to sleep, I'd be there too. When she tried to leave our kid with her friends so she could go to work, I'd be there. I wasn't going anywhere.

I'd been following all of them for the last two days. Ever since they took my baby. Those women were as guilty as she was, working with her to keep him away from me. I despised them. Vile women with disgusting secrets while they cast judgment on others. While they destroyed my life as if it meant nothing.

"Is that true?" Judge Goldberg asked Jeff.

"I'm unaware of how many times Whitney was interviewed by the police."

"But you *are* aware of how many times Brooke was interviewed by the police?" He nodded his agreement. "And according to you, her being interviewed by the police is one of the main reasons, if not the primary reason, that your client is concerned about leaving their child with Mrs. Lyons, correct?" Another nod from Jeff. This one more reluctant. "How are you aware of that information?"

"My client has been in touch with Brooke this entire time."

Gill joined in. "If I may speak, Your Honor?" She motioned her approval for him to speak. "Here's the thing you really need to know: Abby Blackman is staying with Whitney Gilmore. Right now. And remember, we're here in this room today because Abby was so concerned about her baby living in the same house with a potential murder suspect that she took the child away from his mother." He gestured while he talked, growing more animated as he went on. "And fine, you know what? Part of me understands that. I'm a parent myself." He patted his chest to emphasize the point. "If I thought my partner might've killed a friend of mine, I'd have a hard time letting my kid be around them. I get it." He put his hands up again. "But see, this is where that becomes a problem because the house Mrs. Blackman took the child to was Whitney Gilmore's. Another woman that's also a potential suspect in the same investigation. In fact, one that's been questioned even more times than the victim's spouse. The woman your client claims she's so afraid of. If the number of police visits is the determining factor Mrs. Gilmore uses in deciding whether or not someone is a viable suspect in a crime, well." He shifted his eyes to Abby for a second before returning them to Judge Goldberg. "Whitney would definitely rank higher on the suspect list and pose a much greater threat than Brooke based on her very own criteria. Yet, Abby continues to stay there without a problem." He gave a nonchalant shrug, but there was nothing casual about what he'd said or where he was going.

Jeff squirmed in his seat. He looked flustered. That's because he wasn't prepared for something like this. Of course he wasn't. He might be the best attorney at Abby's firm, but he didn't practice any type of family law.

I'd done my homework and gone for the biggest pit bull family law attorney I could find on such short notice. It hadn't been easy, but one of my old colleagues from Dartmouth had a connection and put me in touch with him. Gill's retainer was astronomical, but I didn't care. I'd do whatever it took.

I wanted my baby. Just give me my baby.

I wanted to reach across the table and shake Abby until she promised to bring him back. Where had she left him while she was here? I didn't even know where he was. In all his life, I'd never not known where he was or who he was with. This wasn't fair.

"Yes, it's been convenient for my client to stay with Mrs. Gilmore because they have babies around the same age and Whitney's like family," he said, but he spoke too soon, and Judge Goldberg interrupted.

"More like family than her wife?" she asked.

I wanted to jump up and squeal. Give her a high five. See. This was what I'd meant all along. You couldn't just do this to another person. You couldn't rip a woman's child away from their mother. It was inhumane. Beyond cruel.

Judge Goldberg turned to me for the first time since we'd done introductions when we came into the room. Gill had given me very strict orders beforehand:

Only speak when she's directing a question specifically toward you. Other than that, stay quiet no matter how hard that is.

Only answer the questions she asks. Don't give up any extra information. Stick to the facts.

I rehearsed his instructions while Judge Goldberg continued, "Mrs. Lyons, I've seen some of the videos you've posted on social media, and I have some concerns about your mental health."

All the air got sucked out of the room. I didn't like the way she was looking at me. She wasn't looking at me the same way she looked at Abby. I didn't know what to say, but I had to say something. Which ones had she seen? She'd acted like she wasn't familiar with the case, but clearly she was if she'd watched any of my videos.

"I've just been trying to draw attention to what's happening. I thought maybe someone might've had a similar experience and they could help me. Point me in the right direction for resources. I just wanted help, and no one was listening to me, so I had to do something." I stumbled over my words. That's really what I was doing. All I wanted was someone to pay attention to me. Give me my baby back.

"Have you ever been diagnosed with a mental illness?"

"Your Honor," Gill interrupted. "We're here to get my client's child returned to his mother and set up some form of temporary custody order so this doesn't happen again. I'd like to point out that her wife hasn't expressed any concerns with Mrs. Lyons's mental health. Her only concern is that she's been interviewed by police in a murder investigation. That's all."

Judge Goldberg's face was stern. "That may indeed be what you're most concerned with and what brought you into this room, but now you're in my room and in front of me. I don't care what your clients are worried about at this moment. I'm concerned with the state of your client's mental health." She turned to me. Her face wasn't any less stern. "Mrs. Lyons, do you have a history of mental illness?"

"No." I shook my head hard to emphasize the point. "Never." It wasn't a mental illness to do everything you could to get your child back after they'd been stolen. And that's what Abby had done. I didn't care how they sugarcoated it or what they called it. She took my child from my home without my consent and was purposely keeping him away from me. Unacceptable. I didn't need any family law judge to tell me that, and if she couldn't see that's what was going on here, then she wasn't very good at her job.

She laid both her hands on the table. "Here's what I'm going to do." Her eyes still hadn't left mine. "I'm going to order that you be evaluated by one of our court-appointed psychologists within the next seventy-two hours. Just to make sure there aren't any safety concerns there. And then once that's taken care of, we'll meet back here to create the child-custody arrangement."

I nodded. That seemed reasonable. If this was happening—if we were really splitting up, and I was pretty sure we were—then there were going to be lots of evaluations. There was no coming back from something like this. All those legal processes with the court were going to happen whether I wanted them to or not. I would just take them one step at a time.

"So, until that's complete, Julian will stay with Abby?" Jeff asked.

Judge Goldberg nodded. "Yes, but she must allow Brooke to visit once a day. I'll write that into the order."

Everything screeched to a halt in my brain. "What are you saying? Are you saying Abby just gets to keep Julian? He's not coming home?"

"Just for the next three days. This is only temporary. Whenever an emergency custody hearing happens, the outcome of any one of these is that I have to award temporary custody to someone. There has to be an official order on paper."

"Then give him to me!" I shouted. Gill put his hand on my leg to shush me.

Judge Goldberg shook her head. "I'm sorry, but I can't do that. Not until I'm certain you're not experiencing a mental health crisis. We have to be sure the child will be safe. That's how these things work. I don't make the rules. I just make sure they're followed."

We'd stepped into the ring with the attorneys and judges. We couldn't step back out now. That wasn't how these kinds of things worked. Once you were in, you couldn't just leave without jumping through their hoops. My parental rights had been stripped away from me in an instant, and there was nothing I could do about it.

"Safety concerns?" I cut her off before she could go on. "With my mental health? There's nothing wrong with me. How do you expect me to react?"

"No child should be taken away from their mother, and I understand how incredibly painful this must be for you."

"Your Honor, assessing my client's mental health is outside the scope of this meeting," Gill interjected.

"Exactly." She nodded. "Then we agree. That's why I ordered an evaluation."

"Understandable. But please permit the child to be returned home or at least shared custody while she undergoes the evaluation."

She shook her head. "I'm sorry, but I can't do that. Have you seen the videos?"

"I have, Your Honor."

"Good, then you know that a forty-one-year-old woman parading her issues on social media in such a fashion is an immediate red flag. That's just the beginning of my concerns. Second, you can see the time stamp on all of them, and from the looks, she posts twenty-four hours a day, which leads me to believe she's not sleeping. Her speech is pressured and all over the place. Her thoughts don't connect, even though she thinks they do. They're tangential. She sounds irrational and paranoid. Do I need to go on? You've seen the videos." She gave my lawyer her most pointed look yet.

It took every ounce of willpower to keep myself in my seat. How was a person supposed to act when their child was taken away from them, their friend just died, and their wife left them for a younger woman? Of course I was upset. Who wouldn't be? The constant insinuation that I was this hysterical, crazy woman was making me feel crazy.

And the more I said that I wasn't only made me look crazier. There was no way to win. I'd never felt so powerless or trapped.

I turned my gaze back to Abby. How dare she do this to me? All the love I'd felt for her turned into a cold ball of hate. I'd never wanted to hurt another person in my life. Not once. But I wanted to lay my hands on her. Grab her by the shoulders and just shake her. That's all I could picture as Judge Goldberg went on.

"As soon as the psychologist signs off on the evaluation and can assure me there are no concerns, then we'll proceed to the next step. See if we can't get the two of these women to agree to a fair and equal custody arrangement while they're going through the divorce." She'd shifted into talking in the third person about us as if we both weren't sitting there. "Hopefully, they can see that despite their differences, there's a child involved in this situation, and maybe they'll be mature enough to put their own feelings aside and work out an agreement that's in the best interest of their child."

"My client is more than willing to do that. That's been her primary concern all along. Making sure her baby is with both parents. She realizes the importance of the child having both caregivers present. Stability. Consistency. Those are all the things my client is prepared and ready to provide."

"Great," Judge Goldberg said, slapping the folder shut like it was over that quickly. "I'll have someone from my office connect with you about the evaluation, and we'll be back in here together in a few days." She shifted her eyes from the attorneys and gave both Abby and me a clipped nod.

"That's it?" I asked. Gill put his hand on my knee. "That's just it? I still don't have my baby? I have to prove I'm not crazy? How did this become about me and my mental health?" Gill squeezed my knee to tell me to shut up, but I couldn't. This was so incredibly unfair. "How can you do that? This isn't about me. It's not about me. I didn't do anything wrong." He squeezed my leg harder. I wanted to stop. I knew that I should. That every word coming out of my mouth—my desperation, my pleading—only made me sound more unstable. Like everything they were saying about me was true. But I couldn't stop. Without warning, I burst into tears.

"I'm sorry, Your Honor, you can imagine how difficult this is for my client," Gill said, jumping in as the sobs took over. I tried to speak through my tears, but this time he squeezed my thigh hard enough to leave a mark. I needed to calm down.

I kept my mouth shut, but my insides raged on. This was so unfair. I'd never felt so trapped. So powerless and alone.

And it was all Abby's fault.

CHAPTER THIRTY-SIX

NOW

WHITNEY

I opened the door, and Jade stood there with a big grateful smile on her face. The same smile she wore every time she dropped Iris with me while she took Lily to her chemotherapy appointments. What kind of a sick monster did that? She and Colin had been texting all morning about meeting up at their spot. I kept waiting for them to say how Lily fit into their plans, but they never did. Eventually, I stopped reading because their texts made me sick. He kept telling her how proud he was of her. How he couldn't believe how well she was handling things on her own.

I bet that's how she'd lured Colin to herself too. Gave him the same sob story she gave me about how she lived every day in terror of losing Lily, but that Ryan was in complete denial of what was going on, so she had to fight the battle alone.

"It's like he wants to pretend it's not even happening. He won't go to her doctor's appointments with me. Not since the first one when she got diagnosed. He always comes up with an excuse for why he can't go. How am I supposed to do this on my own? I can't do it without his help," she'd said one night after she called me upset and crying again because she'd tried to bring it up when they went out to dinner, but he'd refused to talk about it then too. Her therapist had suggested date nights as a way of getting him out of the house and away from the girls. She thought that might help him open up about his feelings. But he stayed a closed door.

"You know what, Jade, it's not okay." I spoke slowly and purposefully, hoping it'd help her calm down. "He definitely needs to be there for the two of you, but he's probably just in shock, you know? Everyone processes trauma differently. And some people just shut down, but I bet if you give him time, he'll come around. Just give him time to process it in his own way." I wasn't the only one who told her that. We all did. At least the ones who knew. Only a few of the others in our moms' group knew about Lily's cancer. You couldn't keep something like that a secret from everyone.

But Ryan hadn't changed or gotten any more involved. It turned all of us against him. I couldn't stand being around him, and I was totally bitchy whenever we interacted. She might have to be nice to him, but I didn't have to be polite. You couldn't help but be angry at him and want to help Jade.

That's how it had to have started between Colin and her. There was no way he'd just decided to have an affair with one of my closest friends after all these years. No way. She probably went to him to talk about everything she was going through, and he would've listened because Colin was a great listener. He was also a huge sucker for a damsel in distress. He loved to be the hero. And she probably needed one.

Still.

It didn't make me hate either of them any less in the moment. I wanted to say to her, *How can you just stand there and hand me your baby while you're about to go meet my husband?* But instead, I plastered a fake smile on my face, too, and reached out my hands. "Here, let me take the baby. It's so good to see you."

She handed Iris over to me, and Iris greeted me with a goopy, toothless smile. She gnawed at her fist, and drool soaked the front of her onesie. "She's teething," Jade said, but she didn't need to. "So, she might be a little cranky. Sorry." She gave me an apologetic shrug.

"No worries," I said, bringing Iris against myself. I wasn't afraid of a little baby goo. I gave Jade another big smile.

I couldn't believe I was doing this. Is this how the two of them felt every day? Just playing a character? A role? I couldn't believe how easy it was to pretend. Here I was smiling and chatting with her like she wasn't about to go sleep with my husband. Like she wasn't the one he'd said *I love you* to last night and meant it.

And after everything I'd done.

I was the only reason we had this roof over our heads. The cars parked in the driveway. That we could even afford to send Asher to preschool or have Grace's help. I was responsible for everything even though he liked to pretend he was the one keeping us afloat. Giving us this wonderful life.

He hadn't given me anything in a long time, and while I was busy being heartbroken and trying to figure out a way to fix things and make them better for us, he'd been falling in love with another woman. That's all I was doing. That's the reason I worked so hard. Why I did what I did. The sacrifices that I had to make. Every mother had to make them. We always had to choose.

Men didn't have the same burden, so how could he know? How could I expect him to understand? No man really could. They got points just for sticking around and not leaving. Their bar for parenthood was set so low, you could step over it. Ours was impossible to reach, and there was no way to win no matter what you did.

And I'd felt so bad about keeping secrets from him. Wrecked. Torn up. I'd lost so many nights' sleep over everything. Racked with guilt and remorse. Constantly second-guessing and doubting myself. Every decision I'd made.

Meanwhile, he'd been screwing around.

I was furious.

So how was I smiling like I didn't have a care in the world?

And she was too.

I'd trusted her. That was the other part. I'd trusted her as my business partner. I'd promised to keep her secrets if she kept mine.

It wasn't just about her sleeping with my husband. I'd been married long enough to know that sometimes sex was just sex. Sometimes that's all you wanted. But she was my friend. Her betrayal hurt almost as much as his. We'd promised to help each other get through this. Do whatever we had to do to save our families. Spare our children. We had to take care of them if our husbands couldn't.

She'd taken down her walls, and I'd taken down mine. How long had it been going on? Since the very beginning? For a second, my breath caught in the back of my throat.

The sob.

The cry.

The sadness.

The rage.

All the wrongness.

The loss.

All the feelings. They flooded me. Like a real wall I'd run into, and for a second, my facade almost crumbled. I didn't have it in me. I couldn't do this. I'd lost too much. Who cared? What did it matter?

But it did. And I couldn't shake the feeling that somehow it was all connected to Kiersten. So, I sucked my emotions back inside. Forced the tears to go away and kept my voice steady.

"Take all the time you need today," I said in the sweetest voice I could muster. "She'll be fine with me."

"Thanks so much, Whit. Really." She beamed with what I'd always assumed was gratitude, but maybe it was lust. She could barely wait to run out the door and jump into bed with Colin. What was she going to do with Lily?

"Just go." I waved her out the door before I broke down and confessed everything. Told her all that I knew, but I kept it in check just long enough for her to go. I bounced Iris on my hip and waved to Jade from the window.

I shut the door and collapsed in tears, but I didn't leave myself there. I let myself have the release, then quickly pulled myself together. I hurried out to the garage to install the other car seat. I'd gotten it delivered yesterday. I was so afraid it'd arrive when Colin was home, and he'd wonder why I'd gotten Asher another car seat when the one he was in functioned just fine. I had a story ready but never had to use it since the seat arrived shortly after lunch.

Iris's car seat was easier to install than Asher's, and I had them strapped tight in their seats in no time. Thankfully, Asher was a deep sleeper, and he didn't even budge when I carried him from the crib into the car. I didn't know what I was going to do if Jade spotted us, but I couldn't waste time worrying about that. I'd deal with it if it happened, but I wanted to catch the two of them together and bust them that way. I'd practiced my speech all morning.

She'd only been gone seven minutes, so it wasn't going to be hard to catch her. Besides, I knew where she was going. Wilson Barrio Children's Cancer Center. The fourth floor. I'd picked her up from there after one of Lily's treatments before. Lily had thrown up all over my back seat, and Jade had been so embarrassed that day. I'd promised her it was fine. Swore Colin had thrown up more than once back there.

I didn't see her when I pulled in, but the parking lot was small. I didn't care about following her inside to Lily's appointment. I cared about where she went afterward. That's when I was going to confront them with all the kids and film the entire thing. How could she take her daughter and meet with another woman's husband? People had no decency left.

I'll meet you after my appointment.

That'd been her last text to him twenty-two minutes ago.

I spotted her minivan in the parking lot almost immediately. I went around the corner and parked far enough away that I could still see her but she couldn't see me, and I waited for them to come out. Her treatments usually took two hours. If he walked into her appointment with her, I wasn't sure I'd be able to sit in the car. What if he did? Could he be that bold?

She had to have used the cancer story. She would have melted his heart with it the same way she'd melted mine. And the most messed-up part about it was that in some ways, I understood her terrible choice. Your kid having cancer gave you a free pass to act out. No, not a free one. More of a get-out-of-jail-free card. Who wouldn't lose their mind if their kid had cancer? I had no clue what I'd do. Absolutely none.

But Colin had no excuse. God, I bet he loved being needed. He was such a sick little man that way. They all were.

I sat up straighter and forced myself to stay alert. The elevator opened. Jade and Lily stepped out. Wait. It hadn't even been an hour yet.

They held hands and skipped along next to each other through the parking lot. Lily was in big pink flip-flops. The kind they give you when you get a pedicure. All I could think about was the last text Jade sent me yesterday when we talked about me babysitting today:

Might be a bit longer tomorrow. Have to stop and get Lily's rx
after her appt and they always take 4ever!!

What was happening? What was going on? I strapped Asher to
myself and threw Iris in the stroller. I raced toward the elevator and
took it all the way up to the fourth floor. I was out of breath as I hurried
down the hallway, scanning for pediatric oncology. It was the last turn
before radiology. I hurried up to the receptionist's desk and tapped on
her plexiglass guard. "Excuse me?"

She looked up. A petite mousy thing. Cute freckles sprinkled on
her nose. "Can I help you?"

I pulled my wallet out of my purse while I bounced Asher. "The
woman who was just here with her little girl left her wallet in the waiting room."

"The woman with the little girl?" She looked confused.

"Yes, the little girl about four years old. She's like this tall." I put
my arm up to my waist. "Maybe a little taller. Has blonde hair. Had
the *Frozen* backpack?"

"Pretty sure she wasn't here." She shook her head. "I think you
should leave the wallet with security downstairs. There are lots of other
offices. Somebody will turn up for it."

I tried to be patient. Stay kind. "She was here, and I'm sure it was
hers. We were sitting next to each other waiting for our kids to finish
with their treatments. Both our kids have cancer." The lie rolled off my
tongue without even thinking about it, but I had no idea what I was
doing. I hadn't thought any of this through. Other than finding out
what was really going on.

"What are you here for?" she asked.

"My son has cancer too." I spoke as fast as I could before she asked
who he was and tried to look him up. I'd just have to run out of here
if she did. My heart pounded. "Her name is Jade, and we've been here
together a few times before. I meant to give it to her when she came

out, but I was in the bathroom, and somehow, I missed her. Could you call or text her and let her know she left it?"

"Sure," she said, tilting her head to the computer. "I'll pull up her chart. She's probably frantic. What's the patient's name?"

"Lily Porter."

She quickly typed. "Hmm . . . I'm not seeing anyone with that name."

"Maybe it's under her mom's name—Jade Porter?"

"No, we don't have anyone by that name either." She stopped typing. "What'd you say your name was again?"

"I'm Sarah." I flushed, instantly hot. I quickly looked away from her. "Oh, you know what? Why don't I run out and see if I can catch her in the parking lot?" I turned and bolted before she had a chance to say anything to me.

Why wasn't Lily in her system? This was the place. I'd even picked them up from here once. There were only two pediatric cancer centers, and the other one was all the way across town. It'd take forty-five minutes to get there. No way that's where she went.

Had she faked the cancer diagnosis to get to my husband? To get to me?

I put my hand over my mouth. What if the entire conversation in the parking lot that day had been bullshit? What if she'd been playing me this whole time? Playing him the same way? What would he do if I told him she was a phony and a fake?

I pulled out of the lot slowly. It couldn't be. Nobody was that sick. But she barely told anyone about the cancer. And those of us she told, she asked us to keep it a secret. Said it was private, and I thought nothing of it. Some people loved the attention having sick kids brought them. They plastered their faces all over social media. Those videos with sick kids had millions of followers, but she wasn't that type. She never posted anything about Lily being sick or any of her treatments. None of that seemed odd to me because I would've been the same way. I shied away from anything personal on social media.

Jade had shaved Lily's head. For Chrissake, she'd shaved her own kid's head. Who did that? And what'd she say to Lily about it? There was no way she wasn't telling her something. That was child abuse. Right there. They should be doing an emergency hearing for an order of protection on her and not Brooke.

Colin needed to know who his girlfriend really was. The person he was throwing away his marriage for. This changed everything.

CHAPTER
THIRTY-SEVEN
THEN
JADE

I twisted my hands anxiously on my lap. What was I doing? What was I thinking? We hadn't crossed over any lines yet. Not technically. All we'd been doing was texting. I'd been shocked to get Colin's text after the birthday party since I didn't give him my number. I told myself he'd asked Whitney for it, so that's why it was fine that we were talking. She must've known about this because how else would he get my number? And if she was okay with it, then I was okay with it. Besides, we were just talking.

Hey u. I had a lot of fun at the party today.

I'd stared at the text forever, trying to decide what to say. We'd flirted by the food table for another five minutes before a group of toddlers swarmed us and put an end to it. There'd been no mistake we were flirting, and it'd put me in the best mood for the rest of the party. Talking to Colin felt so good, and it'd been so innocent. Like nerdy middle schoolers.

So were our texts.

He asked me how my day was every day, and it was so nice to have someone care about what was happening to me and how I felt about things. It wasn't like Ryan didn't, but Ryan asked out of obligation and habit rather than a genuine desire to know how it'd gone. We slipped little innocent flirts into the texts. More and more, I found myself waiting for the vibration of a text alert. It just felt good. Nothing had actually happened between us. But then he'd asked if I wanted to meet him for lunch, and I'd said yes.

But nothing had even happened yet. *We're just having lunch,* I told myself. *There's nothing wrong with having lunch with a friend.*

Except this was a line. A very distinct line.

And I knew I'd crossed it as soon as he sauntered into the restaurant. The magnetic pull toward him was so strong. It almost dragged me from my seat when he walked through the door. He gave me a huge grin the moment he spotted me, and all my insides turned to mush.

I stood to greet him, and he planted a quick peck on my cheek like he'd been doing since the first time we met, but the air was electric between us. He slid into a seat on the other side of the table and gave me another smile.

"It's so good to see you," he said.

"You too," I said in a voice I hadn't heard myself use in a long time. That's what happened when passion went out of your life. Passion drained the rest of your life energy from you.

He locked eyes with me. We didn't speak. The energy hovering between us over the table. In that moment, we both knew what we were doing here. What we'd come for. And there was still time to stop it. Nothing had to happen. We didn't have to cross any real lines.

An innocent flirtation was nothing. Nobody got divorced over innocent flirtations. And while emotional affairs definitely didn't feel good for the other person, I'd never bought the idea of an emotional affair qualifying as real cheating anyway. Getting your emotional needs met by someone else didn't mean you were being unfaithful. That's all this was. This could just be that.

Which need was I fulfilling for him?

"Can I get you both anything to start with? Water? Coffee?" Our server interrupted our moment, and I pulled myself away from Colin's penetrating stare. I wanted him to penetrate me. The thought came unbidden. Hard and fast, just like I wanted him.

"I'll have a water," I said with my cheeks burning. Could he read my thoughts? Was he having the same ones?

For a minute, I pictured us in the bathroom—me bent over the sink, him behind me—then quickly banished the images. I'd just gone too long without sex. This was what happened when you didn't get laid. But I didn't want my husband. I wanted him. More than I'd wanted anyone in a long time. Maybe ever.

I needed to get out of here. Now.

I jumped up like I'd been burned. My knee hit the table, making it wobble. "I'm sorry." The server gave me a bewildered look, then turned her attention back to Colin. She was still waiting for him to order. "I'm so sorry. I have to go. I can't do this." My voice shook.

I threw my napkin on the table and bolted out of the restaurant as fast as I could. I didn't give him a chance to stop me or turn around. I practically ran through the parking lot, obsessively unlocking my car on the way there. *Please don't follow me. Please don't follow me,* I chanted as I ran.

I jumped into the car and slammed the door. I scanned the parking lot to see if he was there and breathed a sigh of relief that it was empty. I tried to slow my heart. That was too close. Entirely too close.

What was I going to do when I saw him the next time? And I was going to see him again because our mom circle was intertwined in so many different ways. There was no escaping him. But I had to escape this. This would get me in trouble. So much trouble.

CHAPTER THIRTY-EIGHT

NOW

WHITNEY

I called the clinic when I got home and pretended to be Jade. The receptionist said the same thing she'd said to my face—she'd never heard of Lily or Jade Porter. I still couldn't believe it. What was happening?

I texted Colin and asked him to come home. He'd been at the park with Jade. That's where they'd gone after leaving the clinic. I followed them there. They sat on the bench while Lily played on the swings. It looked like the most natural scene in the world. And even though it seemed brazen and bold to just be out in public like that, they never crossed over any lines. They looked like two regular parents hanging out at the park with their kid. You'd never know anything different. She was probably filling his head full of fake cancer-parent woes.

I was done with the lies. Every single sick, twisted one. They'd eaten away at every part of our lives. Nothing had gone untouched. If we stood a chance at surviving this, and I wasn't sure it was possible, then we had to be totally honest. I couldn't lose my best friend and my husband in the same two-week period. I wouldn't survive that. How did you go on after you'd lost the two most important people in your life? Just the thought of it made me want to stick my head in the oven.

So, we'd talk and work things out. We had to. This couldn't be how this ended. It just couldn't. I couldn't help but let out a bitter laugh as I watched Colin's progress coming home on my tracking app.

This.

This was exactly how Brooke had felt when she lost Abby. Losing someone you loved turned you into a crazy person, but you didn't know that unless you'd actually experienced it. She'd been here. She knew. And I'd been a horrible friend about it. Absolutely terrible to her. I didn't have a clue what it felt like to have your world ripped away from you in an instant. My insides swirled. Karma was indeed a bitch.

Colin made it home in less than ten minutes. His face was lined with concern and his eyes full of worry.

"Are you okay?" he asked, cupping my face with both hands and peering into my eyes. There wasn't an ounce of guilt in his expression. It took my breath away, especially since I knew he'd just come from meeting Jade.

"I'm not." I forced the tremble out of my voice. "We need to talk."

"Okay, okay, sure. Whatever you need, babe. We can talk about anything," he said, putting his hand on my lower back. "Do you want to go into the living room? The kitchen?"

It was code. Our code. The one all married couples had when they'd been together more than a few years. When we fought about money or other things related to the house—the business part of running our household—we did it in the kitchen. We used to have kitchen meetings all the time. We didn't have them now. Our intimate conversations. The even harder ones. The *peel back your soul and share yourself* happened in the living room.

"Let's go to my office," I said. What we had to talk about didn't fit in either of those rooms. And I wanted to be in my office surrounded by all the things that made me feel safe. He was no longer on that list.

My response took him by surprise, and he coughed nervously, but he kept his hand on my back as he led me through the living room and into my office. We called it my office, but it was really my separate bedroom. We each had one. I had a couch big enough to sleep on. Sometimes I did. The picture of Kiersten and me on my wedding day was in a beautiful frame on my desk. I couldn't imagine what she'd say about all this. I wanted to flip the frame around so she didn't have to watch what was about to go down. There was nothing in the world Kiersten hated more than cheating.

He thought this had something to do with her. He had no idea where this was going. I could tell by the look in his eye and the way he carried himself. If he had any clue this was remotely related to him, all his defensive posture would be up. This would take him by total surprise.

"I know about Jade," I blurted out. I just wanted it to happen. Slice the wound open, and let it bleed. We could bleed the poison out of our marriage. We had to.

He put his hands on the couch like he needed to steady himself. "I don't know what you're talking about, Whitney. I'm—"

I held my hand up. "Please stop. Just stop, Colin. Don't even try to lie about it, please. Can you just spare me that part?"

"There's nothing to know about Jade, Whitney. I swear. There's nothing going on there." He shook his head wildly.

I'd been prepared for his lies. Ready for the denial. I almost laughed at how predictable he was. How his face looked identical to how it had all those years ago when I held the credit card invoices behind my back while he looked in my eyes and told me he wasn't gambling. There was something seriously wrong with him. Something you couldn't fix. I held up my phone for him to see. My screen mirrored his.

His brow furrowed. "I didn't . . . I mean . . . how did . . ."

I shook my head. "Colin, just stop. Please. We need to talk. Just get everything in the open. Everything that's happened. Can you just be real with me? For one second, just be real?"

"I *am* being real," he shouted like he was insulted.

"Stop lying!" I screamed back at him. I couldn't stand the lies. They were everywhere. I didn't know who anyone was. Who I could trust. "I feel like I'm going to lose my mind if someone doesn't start telling me the truth."

He wouldn't stop shaking his head. "Well, I don't know what to tell you, but I'm telling you the truth."

I slapped my phone on his leg and pointed at the texts. "That's your number, Colin. Right there. That's you."

He swiped my phone off his leg and jumped up. "Are you serious right now? You've got some weird tracking spyware on my phone? Are you kidding me? I can't believe you."

I jumped up and squared off. "You can't believe me?" I pointed at his chest. "You don't get to be mad. You're the one having an affair."

"You don't get to tell me what to do. Not anymore," he spat at me.

"I just want to know why." My voice shook. A combination of rage and sadness. "How could you have an affair? Like an actual affair with another person behind my back? Why? Why would you do that to me? To us?"

"You don't know why?" In all our decades of marriage, I'd never seen him look at me the way he was now. Pure disgust. But that's all his eyes held. "You don't love me. You never have."

I stepped back. That was the last thing I ever expected him to say. "I don't love you? What are you talking about? How dare you make this about me?"

"You should've married Kiersten. I'm not kidding. I know we joke about it all the time, but it's the truth. She's your person. Always has been. Not me."

I reached for him, but he stepped back like he wanted to get as far away from me as possible. "What are you talking about, Colin? That's not true."

"Yes, it is. You know who you call when you're having a bad day? Kiersten. Or when you've got great news you can't wait to share? Kiersten. How many times have you gone away on a weekend because you desperately needed alone time with her? We carved that time into our marriage because that's how important it was to you, and I wanted to honor what was important to you. And guess what, Whit? When you came back from your weekends with her? Your quality time? Because your love language is affection and quality time?" He narrowed his eyes to slits. This had been festering. He'd been having this conversation with himself for years. "You were better. It wasn't the spa or the green smoothies. It was her. It was always her."

"But I love you, Colin. I've loved you from the moment I met you." I grabbed his arm, but he quickly jerked it away. How'd I miss this?

"Yes, you have," he said. "And do you want to know why?" His body vibrated with anger. Anger I had no idea had been simmering underneath the surface. How long had he hated me? Days? Weeks? Months? Years?

I felt sick.

"The reason we got along so well is because Kiersten handpicked me. She filled out your entire profile on PartneredUp. Every part. She went through your matches like they were job applicants. She was your own personal matchmaker. You told me that yourself. But do you know what else she did? Do you know what she told me?" He gave me a pointed look and a smug grin because he knew something about her I didn't. "She set herself up as the administrator on that account so everything had to go through her first before you saw it. She didn't even let you see the men you matched with that she didn't think were a good fit for you. Did you know that? She prescreened everyone for you."

I didn't know all that. I hadn't wanted to get on the app to begin with. Tinder was just getting started, and I hated the idea of it, but she assured me it wasn't anything like it. It was for people like us. Educated. Proper. Privileged. Wealthy wife material. With similar men looking for similar things. Everyone's profile verified.

"So? That's no different than what an actual matchmaker does. And besides, it's not like she created your profile. You did that all on your own. And even if she did set me up with you on purpose, she had no control over whether or not anything would come of it, so please don't act like she was this evil wizard orchestrating my life according to her wishes. She might've made moves in my life, but only because I allowed them." I crossed my arms on my chest. "You don't get to flip the script and make this about me."

He threw his hands up. "I was tired of being a puppet in my own life. I just wanted something different."

"And Jade was different?" This time I was the one looking at him with disgust. "Please. Because she didn't grow up and go to the same private schools we all did?" I rocked my head side to side. "Spare me. She went to the same private schools—she just jumped state to state. You act like she's so cultured. What? You don't like the privileged life? Trust fund baby doesn't suit you?"

"None of this suits me." He worked his jaw while he spoke.

"So this is how you decide to become an adult? Have an affair? That's your big breakthrough moment? That's so fuckin' cliché I don't even want to look at you." How dare he make a mockery of me? Everything I'd worked for and done so much for my entire life. "I don't understand. I let you have Kiersten."

I let her have Colin in the same way she let me have Tommy. We never told anyone that we did it, and it only happened once every few years, but it happened. And everyone was on the same page. That's why it worked. That's why we'd never had any problems.

"You let me have her?" He shook his head with disgust at me. "That's exactly what I'm talking about. Like you were so woke. So open minded and liberal letting me sleep with your best friend. Please. The only reason you allowed it is because you controlled every part of it. Just like she did. We both knew that."

"Does Tommy have other women too?" I was horrified. Part of the reason we'd done it was to keep them satisfied. Keep them ours. It was despicable. I wasn't going to deny that. There was a reason we kept it a secret. We should've outgrown it like we'd outgrown so much of our college days. Back when we decided to do it the first time. The first time had been a joke. A triple-double-dog dare while we were drunk from tequila shots. At least I was wasted. I wasn't sure about her. You never could be. They'd painted her as such a damsel in distress. She might've been a damsel, but she was definitely not in distress.

"No, we don't have to do everything the same. We're not like the two of you," he fired back. He looked like he wanted to punch me. In all our twenty years of marriage, I'd never seen him look that angry. "The two of you orchestrated everything in our lives. Down to every single minute detail. Don't even try to tell me you didn't."

Every word felt like another blow to the face, like he was physically assaulting me. Smack. Smack. Smack. How long had this been going on? How many years had it been buried inside him?

All his counselors. They were always searching for his hidden trauma. The big thing. His core issue. You know the one that makes drug addicts have to get high in the first place? People didn't need to run away unless there was something to run away from. What if the thing he'd been running away from all these years was me?

It'd never occurred to me before, and he'd never said it. In all those hours of family groups, counseling, and meetings, he'd never said he was angry with me. Never once. He'd never even raised his voice. But he hated me.

Like he really hated me and the life we'd built.

"You tore our life down faster than I could build it back up, so I'm sorry if I've been a bit distracted and unavailable." How dare he throw this in my face? As if our entire marriage hadn't revolved around and catered to his every single need. That I hadn't given up everything to keep us together and afloat. "Get out!" I pointed at the door. "I can't stand to even look at you."

"I'm not leaving. This is my house too."

"Then I'm leaving, and I'm taking Asher with me. It's just really unfair to him because what did he do to cause this? And now we're going to be living out of hotels and cars? But, hey, go ahead. Kick your wife and baby out on the street." I started going through the house and gathering up things. He followed behind me.

"Oh please, Whit. Stop being so fuckin' dramatic. Guess what?" He grabbed me and flung me around to face him. His breath hot in my face. "You don't get to call the shots anymore. You're done being the boss." He pushed his finger into my chest. "I'll go, but not because you told me to. It's because I can't stand to look at your face either."

CHAPTER THIRTY-NINE

NOW

BROOKE

"It's almost two in the afternoon, and you still haven't gotten back to me. You heard what the judge said, Abby. I get to see Julian every day. That's all I'm trying to do. Arrange a time to see Julian. You have to let me see him. I just want to see my son. Answer your phone." I paced the sidewalk in front of Whitney's gate.

I hit end. I was so tired of begging to see him. A few more messages and her voice mail would be full again. I wasn't being irrational. I was trying to work with her. I'd allowed an hour between each message to give her an opportunity to call back. She just never did. Even though she was supposed to, and it was making me furious. I called Gill next. At least he answered.

"I just left Abby another message, and I've texted like three more times. She's still ghosting me. She can't do that. She has to let me see Julian. The judge said she did," I said before even saying hello.

"I'm sorry, Brooke, but you're just going to have to find a way to get through these next few days. This is all going to be over soon." He'd said the same thing when I called him twenty minutes ago.

"What do you mean? Get through these next few days? She's supposed to let me see him. That's what the judge said. We signed the order. We both signed the order. She knows the rules."

"We did, and the judge isn't going to be happy with her at all when we get back in front of her. I can promise you that." I didn't like his tone. Conceding.

"But you're saying it like there's nothing we can do about it until then." What was the point of making rules if we weren't going to follow them? What was wrong with these people?

"It's Saturday, Brooke. Courts aren't even open on the weekends. Your evaluation is Monday, and we'll be back in court on Tuesday."

"You're making it sound like I might not see him until then?" That couldn't be the case. There was no way I was going another day without holding my baby. It'd been six brutal days since I'd felt his body against mine. Since I'd blown bubbles on his stomach. My breasts were killing me because I was pumping constantly. Poor things didn't know what to do. They were still on his feeding schedule, so every ninety minutes, they engorged and turned into concrete by the end of the hour if they weren't released. I'd filled the entire freezer, but Abby refused to come home and get it, like anything I'd touched was contaminated.

"I'm sorry, Brooke, but that might just be what ends up happening." He sounded tired. I didn't like that. He was my attorney. He was supposed to fight. That's what I paid him for.

"We have to call the police. I'm calling the police," I said.

"Brooke, no. Don't. You can't call the police. They're not going to be able to do anything about this. It's going to be just like it was when you called the last time."

"Then do something." I hit end and kept pacing the sidewalk in front of Whitney's house. Her cul-de-sac was so perfect. I wanted to knock down each perfectly placed basketball hoop. Key all their overpriced luxury cars. Scream at the top of my lungs until someone came outside.

And then suddenly, it came to me. It'd been there all along. I just hadn't seen it. I'd been too blinded with fury and panic to think straight. If Abby could walk into my house and take Julian away from me without getting into trouble, then why couldn't I do the same thing to her?

CHAPTER FORTY

NOW

JADE

Whitney's ring at my front door didn't surprise me at all. Colin had been ghosting me ever since he left the park, and it'd been over three hours. Unless we were sleeping, we hadn't gone more than three hours without communicating since we started texting. That only meant one thing. I'd been waiting for Whitney to figure things out since the night of the party.

I opened the door, and she stormed inside. She shoved me against the wall in the entryway. "How could you, Jade? How could you?" She stabbed her finger into my chest. "Let's not even start with the fact that you're sleeping with my husband, but how about the fact you pretended Lily has cancer? What kind of a sick, twisted person does that?"

"Me," I said. A strange relief coursed through my body. It was finally over. I was so tired of the lies.

She hadn't expected me to admit it. She let go and stumbled backward. "How could you do that? Why? I don't understand. Why?"

"You don't want to know the answer." I shook my head at her.

"Yes, I do, Jade. I want to know everything."

"Trust me, you don't." She looked at me like she was about to attack me again. I put my hands up in defense, but telling her everything would hurt her, and I didn't want to cause her any more pain than I already had. I hated that I'd fallen in love with her husband.

"After everything we've been through, you owe me an explanation. You owe me at least that." Her face was lined with fury. She was breathing hard like she'd just finished working out.

I rubbed my temples and tried to settle my nerves. I couldn't stand not hearing from Colin. This wasn't how it was supposed to happen, and I didn't know how to handle it. We hadn't talked about doing it this way, but I was just going to figure it out and trust my gut. "Do you want to sit down?" I asked, pointing to the living room behind me.

"No, I don't want to sit down," Whitney snapped. "Are you kidding me right now?"

"Okay, okay," I said, trying to hype myself up to get started and secretly hoping Colin would call if I stalled long enough. He'd know exactly what to do, but my phone stayed silent, so I didn't have any other choice except to try explaining things to her. "First, you're not going to really understand my feelings or any of this because we're not anything alike. We might have similar experiences and interests, but we haven't walked through life the same way. Not at all. You've always been the girl everyone wants. The one everyone's vying for their attention and their affection. Probably since elementary school. You're just one of those. I'm not."

She wrinkled her face at me. "What are you talking about? What does that have to do with anything?"

"Listen, I know what I did was terrible, and I hurt you in ways I'm sure you'll never forgive me for, but I want you to know I wouldn't have risked our friendship like that if there hadn't been a really good reason."

Her eyes narrowed to slits. "You didn't risk our friendship, Jade—you ruined it."

I nodded quickly. "Okay, you're right. I'm sorry," I stumbled along. I hadn't planned for any of this. Colin and I were supposed to tell her together after we'd left the country. Explain everything. He planned to focus on their family and frame it in that context, but he wasn't here, so I was just going to have to explain things my way. I wanted her to know why I'd done it. I'd spent a lot of time examining my actions. My behavior was as shocking to me as it was to her. "People are always fighting for your attention. Throwing themselves at you. Men trip over their words talking to you, and they act like idiots trying to get you to notice them. Still. To this day, and we're in our forties. So, whoever you're with? You're always their first choice. They've usually fought hard to get you. You don't know anything different, but up until now, I've never been someone's first choice. I—"

"You're still not making any sense," she interrupted. "You could've had an affair with absolutely anyone you wanted to. Why'd you have to pick my husband?"

She didn't get it. She probably wouldn't, but I tried again. "I was the girl guys took to prom because they needed a date and all the good ones were taken. Or the one they hooked up with to make their girlfriends jealous. The in-between girlfriend. That's my usual gig. You know, the one where you know they're just with you waiting until they meet someone better?" Her face hadn't softened in the least, but I kept going anyway. "Even Ryan. He came to me because I was safe after his fiancée destroyed his heart. She was his true love. He would've done anything for her. Probably even keep a job for her because you do that when you really love someone. Anyway, I'm not saying Ryan doesn't love me. He does. But he loves me like I'm his mom. Not his wife." I let out a long slow breath and tried not to smile, but being in love with Colin might always have that effect on me. "And then I started talking to Colin, and suddenly, for the first time ever, I was someone's first choice. He wanted me more than anyone else." I slowed as I said it because we were talking about her husband and there was no mistaking the implications, but she'd sworn she wanted the truth, and this was it. "Being with him felt so incredible that nothing else mattered, and I couldn't pass up the opportunity to experience that feeling. What if it was the only time it ever happened?"

"Please," she snorted, shaking her head in frustration at me. "I don't care about your stupid love story. What does that have to do with anything? You hurt Lily. Your own daughter. You made her pretend she was sick. What'd you say to her on the car rides over to my house? You had to say something. No way a three-year-old shuts up about what they know. How'd that work?"

"I gave her candy. Promised her ice cream." Whitney stepped back in horror. Like even though she knew I'd done it, she hadn't actually believed it until this moment. "Yes. I told her that adults like to play pretend, too, and that right now you and me are playing 'Mommy takes baby to the doctor.'" I gave her an apologetic shrug. "I'm sorry. I know that's awful. That this is awful. That I'm awful. All of it. But at least you can know the truth, right? Now everything's in the open?"

"Who are you?" She let go of me and stepped back slowly, taking me in with her eyes like she was meeting me for the first time.

"I'm just a super-messed-up individual doing the best I can." I wanted to say *love*. That's why I'd done all of it. Why I was even having this conversation. But that would only make her angrier.

She laughed and took another step backward. "Are you kidding me right now? You're gonna hit me with some Instagram shit? Doing the best you can? God, if this is your best, I'd absolutely hate to see you at your worst. You must be a monster."

"It was his idea."

"Oh, I'm sure it was," she said, her eyes flashing with anger again. "Do you know how much men like to be the hero? To swoop in and save the day? You brought meaning to his miserable failing life. It probably took him two seconds to say yes."

She didn't get it. She still didn't see him for who he was. "Lily's cancer."

"What are you talking about?" Her voice was barely above a whisper. Her face twisted with emotion.

"He came up with the idea. He's broke. Well, you're broke . . . I don't know if you know that, but I'm sorry. There's no money in your accounts. Just like there's none in mine. He's been gambling again. We planned to leave and start over, but neither of us had any money. I never lied to you about Ryan or being broke," I said, hoping that piece might make things a teensy-tiny bit better. "All of that was true. So, I didn't have any money and neither did he. Starting over requires funds."

And she'd given me access to all of them just like Colin said she would. It was amazing how well he knew her. Enough to know she'd never let me in on the business unless there was a good enough reason. That's where the cancer story came in.

"Whitney might be a lot of terrible things, but she's a bleeding heart for anyone that's in trouble," he'd explained. "That's one thing about her. She's going to help you out if she thinks you're in trouble, especially if it's got anything to do with a kid."

He also said she hated paperwork, especially anything having to do with bills, and that she'd gladly turn it over to me to handle. He wasn't wrong about that either. I'd been funneling a portion of all the profits into a fake LLC he'd set up for himself. I'd moved a big chunk of their 401(k) and investments over to that account too. We'd stashed over $300,000.

Whitney stood in front of me grappling with the truth. I could see the wheels spinning in her head. "What about the kids? You were just going to take the kids and rip them away from their homes? From their mothers." She saw the answer written on my face, and she slowly raised her hand to her mouth in stunned surprise. "You weren't going to take the kids, were you?"

That was the worst part. The one I was most ashamed of. He'd been ready to go the moment he came up with the plan, but I'd never been so conflicted. What kind of a mother left their children? I was so incredibly sorry and ashamed, but no one had ever loved me. Really loved me like Colin did, and I was almost forty-two years old. Half my life gone. I kept telling myself that men walked away from their families all the time, but it didn't make me feel any better about it.

"I'm sorry, I know I keep apologizing—and it doesn't make it better—but I am. I just . . ." I shrugged. It was her husband we were talking about, but if it weren't, she'd understand where I was coming from. She might not know what it was like not to be someone's first choice, but she knew all about being a woman. "I've spent almost four decades trying to be someone the world would love and find acceptable. Shifting and shaping myself into whoever I needed to be at the moment, and I was exhausted. Then Colin came along, and I didn't have to pretend. It just felt so good to not have to pretend." I reached out and grabbed hold of her arm. "And the reason I didn't have to pretend was because he was your husband, so he was safe. Off limits. That's why I didn't even try to be anyone but myself. You know how Brooke always says the reason her and Abby were so close was because they were friends first so they never had to be fake or lie about anything? That's what it's like for us. I was just myself. And he fell in love with me. The real me. He wanted me in a way no one ever has, and I know I sound like a naive teenager, but I couldn't let that go. It might never come around again."

"You think he loves you?" Whitney jerked her arm away from me and gave the most bitter laugh. "Ohmigod. You really thought he loved you." She shook her head at me like she felt sorry for me. "You did, didn't you?"

She let go of me and walked inside. I followed after her like she was the one that lived here even though it was my house. She stopped in the living room and turned around. Her eyes were steel.

"When's the last time you heard from Colin?" she asked.

"Just a minute ago," I lied. She didn't need to know our business. She was just hurt. Angry. And I got it. I deserved all her wrath.

"Really?" She raised her eyebrow at me with a smirk. "I'm going to guess you haven't heard from him in a couple of hours, and I'm also going to guess that you have no idea where he is, but I do." She took a step closer to me. "You know why, Jade? Because I'm his wife."

My mouth went dry. It made it hard to swallow.

Don't ever piss off Whitney. That was one of the first things Kiersten told me when I joined the moms' club. *Step on her toe, and she'll break your leg.*

That's how she looked now. Like a wrecking ball intent on destroying every person that'd been a part of this pain. I didn't know what to do. My phone was silent in my pocket. Why wasn't he calling me back? Texting. Something. Where was he? What if she really did know something?

"You're worried, aren't you?" The smile hadn't left her face. She was just hurt, so she was trying to hurt me. But something about the way she said it made my skin crawl. "See, I checked my joint accounts with Colin when I found out about the two of you, but I didn't check my business accounts. I feel really silly saying this because it just makes me look so stupid, but I haven't checked my business accounts in months. Not since you started taking over all of that stuff. And it was a brilliant plan. I'll give you that much. Totally brilliant. Because what am I supposed to do now? Go to the police and tell them that my husband and his girlfriend stole all of the money from my illegal escort business?"

"I'm sorry," I said, and I was, even as messed up as that sounded. I hated doing this to her. Had from the beginning. "I never wanted to hurt you."

"Never meant to hurt me? Oh, Jade, I think that's exactly what you meant to do when you started sleeping with my husband and stealing all my money." She didn't look hurt at all anymore. Just angry. And slightly something else. Something else I didn't recognize. "You know why you haven't heard from him? Why he hasn't called you back or texted for hours?"

"I just talked to him."

She laughed again. That awful bitter laugh. Then she pulled her phone out of her pocket and waved it around in the air. "I'm going to have to call bullshit on that one, honey. And you know why? Because I've got spyware downloaded on Colin's phone, and I can see everything he does. Everyone he talks to. All his texts. The pics he sends. And I know he hasn't said anything to you since he left you at the park. You know why? Know where he went? What he's doing?" She gave me a wicked grin.

"I want you to go," I said, pointing to the door.

"Oh, now you're done? You don't like this part? The part where I tell you the reason you haven't heard from Colin is because he's on an airplane on the way to Costa Rica right now? That all those accounts? Those ones that you were funneling money into all these months? They're empty."

"Get out! That's not true. You're just trying to hurt me." I shook my head. He wouldn't do that to me. No way. He just wasn't calling me because he'd figured out she was tracking his phone. He'd get another one and call me.

"Look"—she stuck her phone out like she was going to hand it to me—"you can see for yourself exactly where he's at. You don't have to believe anything I'm saying."

I snatched her phone instinctively, but once I had it in my hand, I couldn't bring myself to look. My insides twisted. There was no way what she was saying was true. He promised. Said he loved me more than he'd ever loved anyone before—even her. Swore he couldn't go another day if we weren't together. That he needed to fall asleep with me every night and wake up next to me every morning.

"Go on, look," Whitney prodded, interrupting my thoughts. The smug look hadn't left her face.

Everything inside me shrank as I looked down at the phone: his red circle. Pulsing at LAX. Forty-two minutes away. That's what it said at the bottom of her screen. Every muscle in my body went limp. I almost dropped the phone. I handed it back to Whitney like I was in a trance. Suddenly, the door opened behind her, and Ryan stepped through. He was supposed to be at the grocery store with the kids. Where were the kids?

"Ryan? What's going on?" I asked.

CHAPTER FORTY-ONE

NOW

WHITNEY

"Ryan, what's going on?" Jade asked again. Her eyes widened even bigger as Perez followed him into the house. There were two uniformed police officers behind her.

Everything stilled. I tried to make eye contact with Perez, but she was intensely focused on Jade. I quickly looked to Ryan, but he was staring at the floor. His body trembled, and he clung to his sides like he was trying to give himself a hug.

"Hello, Jade. Hello, Whitney," Perez said to us in the most formal voice she'd ever used.

Ryan still refused to look at Jade or anywhere else, but Jade was drilling holes into him. "Where are the kids? What'd you do with the girls?" she asked, completely ignoring Perez and the police officers.

"They're at my parents'," he said sheepishly, like he didn't want to admit it.

Alarm immediately registered on Jade's face. Her kids only stayed with her in-laws when it was an emergency. Her eyes darted around the room. Perez just stared at her with her arms folded across her chest like she was enjoying watching Jade squirm.

"What's going on? What's happening, Ryan?" Jade asked like none of us were in the room.

"Jade, we're here to take you down to the station to talk," Perez said, giving one of the officers an almost imperceptible nod, but I caught it. The officer's eyes were trained on Jade, and he took a few careful steps toward her.

"Okay, well, we'll meet you down there, then." Jade's voice cracked. "What about Whitney?" She gave me a quick furtive glance. "Do you need to speak with her too? Is she coming with us?"

Everyone shifted their focus to me, and my heart felt like it stopped. I didn't have anything to do with this—whatever this was. I just shook my head at them like I wanted them to leave me alone, but I didn't need to. They weren't interested in me. Only her. The officer quickly moved in and grabbed ahold of her right arm. Jade looked panicked, like she'd just been blindsided. Fallen into a trap she didn't even know she was supposed to be watching for.

"Unfortunately, you're going to have to ride with us," the officer said.

She shook her head wildly. "No, no, I'd rather go with Ryan." She turned to him. Her eyes were just as panicked as her voice. "You'll take me down there, right?"

Ryan finally looked up. His eyes were watery and red. "I'm not going anywhere with you." He worked his jaw while he spoke, trying hard not to cry.

I recognized the pain in his face. It was the same soul-sucking pain I'd felt when the first texts between Colin and Jade popped up on my phone after I installed the tracking app. I wanted to run across the room and hug him.

Jade's face went white. "Ryan?"

He pulled his phone out of his pocket. His shoulders drooped with defeat. His Adam's apple bobbed heavy in his throat. Thick tears filled his eyes. "You left me a voice mail that night."

There was no mistaking which night he was referring to. That's the reason we were here.

Ohmigod.

I fumbled for the chair next to me. I had to sit down.

This had nothing to do with my business or Jade's affair with Colin. I stared in stunned amazement at Perez. She'd met privately with every single one of our husbands, hadn't she? Turned them all against us. They'd been the ones driving this entire investigation. Not us.

"What are you talking about? What do you mean?" Jade asked. She sounded like she was going to cry.

"I knew from the very beginning that you had something to do with Kiersten's death. I heard you trying to save her." He glanced at Perez, and she gave him a supportive nod. He cleared his throat and continued, "I've been protecting you this whole time. I—"

Jade cut him off. "Protect me? Protecting me from what? I don't know what you're talking about."

"You still have no idea, do you?" He reached into his back pocket and pulled out his phone. He held it in front of himself. I could barely breathe. Nobody moved. "I heard you trying to save her, Jade. You accidentally called me that night. I didn't pick up, but my voice mail recorded thirty agonizing seconds."

And then he pressed play.

It was hard to hear at first. Lots of rustling. Movement. Muffled noise. Like maybe her phone was still in her pocket. But suddenly there was her voice. Jade's unmistakable voice. Shaking and afraid. I hung on every word.

"Breathe, goddammit, Kiersten. Breathe. Do you hear me?" Jade cried. She was breathing hard. Really hard. Like she'd been running.

A few more seconds of nothing.

More rustling. Static.

And then Jade's panicked voice again: "Don't do this to me, Kiersten. Don't you dare do this. You are not going to die on me, you hear me? Come on, you have to breathe." Her voice was desperate. Terrified. "I don't know what to do. Jesus, what am I supposed to do. I—"

"Turn it off!" Jade shrieked, interrupting herself on the voice mail. "That's spousal privilege!"

Right after she finished screaming, the voice mail ended with her final words to Kiersten. But her final words weren't a scream or even a cry, like she was uttering now. They were a barely audible whisper. "I'm so sorry. I didn't mean to."

Ohmigod. What had she done? I turned to face her.

"That's spousal privilege, right?" She said it again, looking frantically back and forth between Ryan and Perez. All I could do was stare at her. She was the one to hurt Kiersten?

Perez stepped forward. A triumphant grin on her face. "This is the best part of my job," she said, not even trying to pretend like she wasn't enjoying all this. "You're right. We can't really do much with that recording, but we can do something with the trophy he brought down to the station when he let us listen to it."

Jade froze. She blinked. A slow one. Then another.

"What trophy?" I asked, finally finding my voice, while Jade just stood there. How could she just stand there saying nothing? She didn't even try to deny it.

Perez didn't move her gaze from Jade as she answered me. "The trophy used to kill Kiersten."

"The one I found in the back of our laundry room," Ryan added.

"You killed her? You killed Kiersten?" I turned to Jade in horror and disbelief.

But she just stood there. Still. Unmoving. Unspeaking. As if she'd run out of lines for whatever twisted script she was playing by.

Ryan stumbled toward her. Devastation wrecked his face. "You know what's the most messed-up part, Jade?" The tears that had been in his eyes spilled down his cheeks. "I heard the message the next morning, and I scrambled through the entire house to see if you'd left any evidence from the night before. That's when I found it." He shook his head like he was trying to clear it. "I was going to help you, you know that? I was going to keep your secret because it sounded like something bad happened on that phone, and I knew you'd never hurt anybody on purpose. No way." He shook his head again, and I believed him because I felt the same way. Jade had never crossed my mind in all this time. Not once. "I figured there was some kind of an accident, and you'd panicked. I wanted to help you. But then I found out about Colin, and I realized that I didn't know you at all. I have no idea who you are. What you're capable of."

How had he found out about Colin? But then I saw the shift in Perez's face. The hint of a smile pulling at the corner of her mouth when she caught my eye. She was brilliant. Deserving of every one of the accolades lining her wall. None of us had spent a single second on our husbands in this scenario. But she had.

Jade looked stunned. Shell shocked. This was Jade's chance to talk. Maybe the entire reason Perez had set it up this way in the first place, because she didn't do anything without a reason. But Jade just stood there still. Like she'd already pleaded the fifth.

Perez must've told Ryan about Colin, or else how did he find out? She had to be the one. Of course it was her. She probably knew about their affair all along. But she'd never told me. Why hadn't she told me about their affair? She motioned to the officer next to Jade, and he whipped out his handcuffs like he'd been waiting all night for the signal.

"Jade Porter, you're under arrest for the murder of Kiersten McCann. You have the right to remain silent. Anything you say can and will be used against you in the court of law." Perez kept reading Jade her Miranda rights, and all I could do was watch as they led her out the door in handcuffs.

CHAPTER
FORTY-TWO
NOW
JADE

Ryan was silent on the other end of the phone. I wanted to give him his time and his space. Processing something this big was hard. It was a lot to take in, but the other inmates were waiting in line, and each person only got fifteen minutes. I could feel all of them breathing down my neck. I didn't want to find out what happened if you went over your time. So far, jail wasn't that bad, but it'd only been three hours since they booked me.

"I don't know what happened," I told him. They were recording everything, but I didn't care. I'd already told Detective Perez all of it anyway. They knew I did it, so what did it matter? Especially now that Colin was gone. I still couldn't believe he'd betrayed me.

Ryan sounded disgusted. "Which part? The part where you killed one of your best friends or the part where you had an affair with one of your other best friends' husbands?"

He was angry, and he had every right to be angry. Who wouldn't be? But he'd answered the phone. That said something. He took my call. I couldn't make it through this on my own. I wasn't cut out for this. Not any of it. I was going to need him. More than I'd ever needed anyone before.

"I'm so sorry, Ryan," I said, and I meant it. With every fiber of my being. I hadn't meant to destroy our lives. Being in love like that was like being possessed. "Please, you have to forgive me. I'm sorry."

"You're sorry?" he scoffed. "You took away a woman's life. She was a mother. What about Rinley? How could you do that? What kind of a person would do that?"

"This is awful. I look like a monster. I do, but it wasn't like that. It wasn't." I hated the way he spoke. Cut off. Detached. All the love drained from his voice. "You said we could get through anything. That's what you've always said, and we can get through this. We can."

"You killed someone, Jade."

I wished he'd quit saying it like that. It sounded so premeditated. There was nothing premeditated about it. I hadn't intended on hurting Kiersten that night. I'd never hurt anyone before in my life. That wasn't how I operated. I didn't recognize myself any more than he did.

I took a deep breath and tried to stay calm. "But, Ryan, baby, you were willing to hear my side of it before you knew about Colin, right? You were. That's what you said earlier today. You were trying to help me because you knew I'd never hurt anyone on purpose. You said that. You're only doing this to punish me. This isn't about Kiersten. It's about Colin. You know I'm not a murderer, Ryan. You know that. That's why you were running around the house looking for evidence to get rid of. You were going to help me. You still can. The only thing that's changed is that I screwed up. I made a really big mistake, but you can forgive me. You have to forgive me. We have a family. Think about the girls."

He was silent, and I tapped my feet together, waiting for him to speak. We were literally on a ticking clock.

"What happened?" he asked when he finally spoke.

"With Colin? That's over." Whitney wasn't lying. He was on a plane to Costa Rica. It'd probably landed by now. I heard it over the police scanner when they were transporting me to booking. I was still so shocked. He'd screwed her over as much as he'd screwed me over.

"That's not what I'm talking about. What happened with Kiersten?"

I didn't want to go into all those details again, but I was going to have to if I had any chance at salvaging my marriage. "She was going to tell everyone about me and Colin," I admitted quietly.

She'd walked in on me FaceTiming him in the maid's quarters. The private suite next to the kitchen. The one closest to the pool. I tried to lie, but she heard his voice. Swiped the phone from me before I could hang up and saw his face.

"So, you killed her?"

"Stop saying that!" I yelled, then quickly lowered my voice. "Stop saying that." I repeated myself. "I wasn't thinking, okay? I just reacted. I kept trying to get her to stay in the room with me. I just wanted her to talk to me about it, but she wouldn't. She just kept screaming at me and telling me what a terrible person I was. Saying she was going to find Whitney and tell her everything she'd overheard." He was silent again. I couldn't stand it, so I kept explaining, hoping it'd get him to soften. "I've replayed the moment a thousand times since it happened. It was so quick. Half a second. Not even. She turned around, and I just grabbed the trophy she'd set on the desk and smacked her on the back of the head. I didn't mean to hurt her. I definitely never meant to kill her. I just wanted her to stop, but she wouldn't. She dropped to the floor immediately. I thought she'd just passed out, but I couldn't get her to wake up. I kept smacking her on the face. I dumped my water on her." I remembered every second in great detail. Like time had slowed down. "I didn't know I'd killed her, Ryan. I swear I had no idea she was dead. She might not have been at the time. I don't know. I just wanted to get her outside. Get her some fresh air."

I was sure she was going to wake up. There wasn't a part of me that thought it was permanent. Her being dead never crossed my mind while I dragged her outside. All I could think about was what I'd tell her when she woke up. I was secretly hoping she wouldn't remember anything. All the incident gone, including what led up to it. I was just going to tell her that she'd tripped and fallen. Or even that she passed out from the gummies.

"How did you get her outside? You would've had to carry her." He asked it like he didn't believe me. Like I was leaving something out of the story, but I wasn't. I had no idea how I'd pulled her out there. It hadn't seemed hard at the time. Almost effortless.

"I guess the adrenaline fueled me? People do unbelievable things in life-threatening situations, and I thought I was saving her life. I was trying to save her life. I really was." I'd told the same thing to Detective Perez, but I wasn't sure Ryan believed me any more than she did. But I was telling the truth. Somehow, I half dragged, half carried Kiersten out of the house. I kept thinking someone was going to see me, but nobody did. I was drenched in sweat by the time we got to the backyard.

But that's when I noticed she wasn't breathing. Up until that point, it had never occurred to me that she was anything but passed out.

I'd laid her down flat on the concrete right next to the pool. I had no idea what I was doing, and I was so nervous that I threw up in the middle of it. It wasn't Kiersten's vomit on her lips. It was mine. "I'd never given anyone CPR before, and I don't know if I even did it right. But I tried. I tried, Ryan. I did. But she was gone. She was gone when I got her out there."

Silence. It went on so long, I thought he'd hung up.

"You could've run back into the house and called 911. They might've been able to save her," he said when he finally spoke. The person standing next to me in line had to give up their spot. My time was almost over.

I burst into tears. "I know, baby. I know. Believe me, I've replayed it all, and I should've called 911. I know I should've, but I just panicked. I totally panicked. You have no idea how you'll react when something like that happens. None. All I could think about was how it would look. What people would think. How they'd interpret it. Everyone was going to think I killed her, so I just shoved her into the pool. I know that doesn't make any sense. It doesn't make any sense to me now that I'm in my right mind, either, but I just reacted. That's all I can say. And from a completely panicked state. Please, I'm not a monster. I'm not."

"You know what, Jade? If that was just it, that story. That you lost it in anger. Didn't know what you'd done and then you panicked? It's a big stretch. A huge stretch, but I might've been able to find a way to look at the situation and understand how things could've played out like that. But here's the deal—you never said a word to me. You kept everything a secret."

"But, baby, you have to understand, I couldn't tell you because I was protecting you. I didn't want you to get involved. I wasn't in my right mind at the time. I made a horrible mistake, but I've taken accountability for my actions. I told Detective Perez every single thing that I'm telling you. I—"

He cut me off. "No, I'm not finished. You destroyed my life, and you destroyed our girls' lives. They're the victims. Not you. People like you are sociopaths. You've learned the right language so you can look like a good fake human, but you can't do what you did and carry on the way you did afterward and have any real empathy inside you. None. You are a monster. I don't want you anywhere near our children. I'm going to—"

The line went dead. At first, I thought he'd hung up on me. Then I realized it was because it automatically cut off because it was on a timer. I returned the receiver slowly. He never got to finish. I never got to say *I love you.* What if he didn't take another call? Things couldn't end this way with him. I wouldn't let them. We could work this out. We had to.

"Hurry up, girl," the woman with the swollen left eye shouted at me. We'd been fingerprinted at the same time. I quickly hurried away before anyone else could say something to me.

I headed toward the common area thinking about Colin. I couldn't feel him anymore. That's how you knew when the love was gone. Sometimes it died slowly like a battery draining over time, and other times it happened in an instant. He'd unplugged himself from me. Probably the moment he heard the news. I felt his absence as hard as if we'd been together for ten years instead of ten weeks.

I had no explanation for my actions except the oldest cliché in the book—love. The moment I thought I'd lose the most beautiful feeling that I'd ever experienced, I went primal. Protection at all costs. I never would've believed I was capable of something like that, but I'd never been in love the way I was with Colin either. Maybe the people that didn't understand losing control over love were the ones who'd never felt it.

I'd spoken with my attorney at the police station. She said she understood exactly how something like that might happen. Called it a crime of passion, which I always thought meant you had to be caught in the middle of having sex, but I guess not. She also said if I just pleaded guilty to manslaughter, I might only do seven years. In the grand scheme of things, that's not all that long. The girls would still be in elementary school when I get out. I'll get to be there for all the really hard stuff. Middle school. And, ohmigod, high school. They'll really need me for that.

My life didn't have to be over because of this. I'd made a huge mistake. A really big one. But I'd taken responsibility for it, and I'd make sure everyone got their apology. Life didn't have to end from one mistake. It didn't, and I wouldn't let it.

CHAPTER FORTY-THREE

NOW

WHITNEY

What would I say to Brooke the next time I saw her? *I'm sorry that I thought you were a murderer?* She was never going to forgive me. I wouldn't forgive myself either. I was still shell shocked from everything that had happened. Ryan and I had sat in their living room for over twenty minutes after they arrested Jade. Neither of us speaking. Just reeling.

My husband was on a plane headed out of the country, and his mistress—one of my closest friends—was in jail for murdering my best friend. It was the only thought that rolled through over and over again because I just couldn't get past it. Things like this happened in Lifetime movies. Not to me. My life was shattered. How would I ever pick up the pieces?

I still hadn't heard from Colin. Did he know Jade killed Kiersten? Was that why he'd gotten on the plane by himself? Was the original plan for Jade to be with him? Or had he been playing us both from the beginning?

And what about Abby? Somebody must've told her by now. At least she'd get some relief from this awfulness. I'd texted her on my way home, but she still hadn't responded. It wouldn't be long before word got out to her, though. How was that going to affect things with her court case? Poor Brooke. They'd put her through the wringer, and she'd been right all along. I actually really felt sorry for her.

"Abby?" I called out, stepping into the foyer. Her car was still in the driveway, so she was probably here. Unless someone picked her up. Liza picked her up last night. There was no response. "Abby?" I called again.

The diaper bag sat by the door right where we'd left it last night when we came home from dinner. Everything slowed. The twinge in my gut. The slight nudge.

"Abby?" I called out louder and started walking faster through the house. "Abby!" I screamed her name this time. I couldn't shake the sense of impending doom.

She wasn't anywhere. Not in the living room. The family room or the movie room. The kitchen sat as spotless as I'd left it. I raced upstairs, taking the steps two at a time. Something was wrong. Something was terribly wrong. The walls of the house pulsed with it.

She'd been sleeping in the guest room at the end of the south wing. My favorite suite. That's where I slept when I needed to get away from Colin. I raced down the hallway and flung open the door.

And froze.

Blood splattered the walls behind the bed.

A lump lay on the bed unmoving.

Red seeping out from underneath it. Dripping onto the floor.

Stillness.

"Abby?" My voice was a raspy whisper, barely audible.

Nothing.

"Nononono. Please, God. No," I cried, bringing my hands to my mouth. "Please no. Please no." I pulled my phone out of my pocket and dialed 911 while I took a few tentative steps toward the bed. My heart hammered in my chest.

"911. What is your emergency?"

"I just got home, and my friend is hurt. She's hurt really bad. Really bad. There's blood everywhere." My eyes swept the room. I'd forgotten about Julian. "And she has a baby. Ohmigod, he's not here. He's gone. The baby. He's gone too."

"Is there anyone in the house? Are you safe?"

I twirled around. My eyes racing to take in everything. "I mean, I think so. I've been gone. I've just gotten home. The alarm was set, and nothing went off. I would've gotten notified if someone broke in. Nobody broke in. Ohmigod. Ohmigod."

"No one's been in the house?"

"Not that I know of." I twirled around again. Scanning. Listening. Searching.

"Okay, ma'am. Can you see if the baby is with the person on the bed? Do you feel safe?"

My insides heaved. I'd never been so scared in my life. I didn't want to look, but I didn't have any choice. "I'm going to look." I took another slow, measured step.

"I don't want you to do anything if you feel like your life is in danger. First responders are on their way there. You can wait for them."

I shook my head. "I'm not. I can't. What if she needs help? She might need help." Just because she was lying there like that didn't mean she was dead. But the blood. There was so much blood on the wall. I stood over the body. The coverlet was sliced. There were feathers floating in the air like snow.

I held my breath while I slowly peeled back the covers. Abby lay on the bed faceup. Her arms flopped to her sides. Her chest was splayed open wide. Meat spilled from her insides. Her face. Her arms. There were slices everywhere.

"She's dead," I said into the phone as I heard the sound of sirens coming down the streets. And that's when I heard the moans. Slow, deep moans coming from the bathroom. Someone was in there.

"Someone's in the bathroom," I whispered to the dispatcher.

"Ma'am, are you safe? Don't go into the bathroom. Can you find yourself a safe place and wait for the paramedics to arrive? They're almost there."

But I was already opening the door.

Red splattered the alabaster-tiled floors in the same way as the bedroom. Brooke was sitting in the huge concrete tub. Naked and white. She held Julian against her chest. There was blood all over the sink. The walls. The tub. Like someone had finger painted but with blood.

I put my hand up to my mouth. "Ohmigod, Brooke. What have you done? What have you done?"

I stood frozen. I didn't want to move. What if I spooked her? She clung to Julian's body. His face buried in her chest. His lips latched on to her breast.

Please let him be okay. Please let him be okay. I silently prayed to every god in the universe. I stared at his back, but I couldn't tell if he was breathing.

"Brooke?" I said with the most nonthreatening voice possible. Kind. Loving. I forced it to be calm, but it still wavered with fear.

That's when I noticed the knife. The chef's knife from my kitchen downstairs. It lay at her feet. Next to an empty bottle of whiskey. Blood circled and pooled around her. Was she bleeding? It was hard to tell.

"Brooke?" I said it again, and she slowly lifted her head. My insides recoiled. She'd never looked so pale. Eyes washed out and hollow. Her dark hair stringy.

She shrugged like she was moving in slow motion and wobbled her head around while she spoke. "Look at Julian, Whitney. He's eating. He's finally getting to eat."

And then she smiled at me.

There was blood on her teeth. How'd she get blood on her teeth?

"Jesus, Brooke. What did you do?"

"She said I could visit my baby. She said I could." All her words slurred.

Who said she could? What was she talking about? I wanted to ask her the questions, but I couldn't speak. My words were suddenly frozen too. Just like my body. Shocked.

"Ma'am, are you okay? Who are you talking to?" the dispatcher cut in, grounding me. Keeping me steady.

"It's my friend Brooke."

"Is she okay? Does she look like she's been harmed?"

She looked like she'd been to war. That's what she looked like. And she was one of its biggest casualties.

"She said I could visit my baby, Whitney. That's what the judge said. She told her that. It's all I wanted to do. I just wanted to visit my baby. See my baby." Her lower lip quivered. I'd never seen her cry. Not once through all this. Even on her social media rants. Something about her on the verge of tears made it more disturbing.

"What happened, Brooke?" I asked again. It came out a whisper.

She shook her head. Big tears filled her eyes. Slowly rolled down her cheeks. "I don't know, Whitney. I don't know. I just . . . I just came over to see him. All I wanted to do was see my baby. I just missed him so much. But she wouldn't let me. She had no right not to let me. No right." She worked her jaw while she spoke, doing her best not to lose it. I held my breath. Not wanting to push her. Not wanting to do anything to set her off. But I wanted that baby to be okay. I needed that baby to be okay.

Brooke struggled to go on. The dispatcher was silent on the other end of the phone. Wasn't she supposed to be giving me instructions? Telling me what to do?

"What happened, Brooke?" I repeated myself.

"I came over to see him. I just wanted to see him. Hold him. Feed him. You know? You know what it's like when you're away from them, Whitney. Right? You know how that feels." Her eyes pleaded with mine for understanding, and I nodded at her because I wanted to keep her talking. "She wouldn't answer any of my calls or texts. I don't know how we're supposed to communicate or set anything up when she has me blocked. So, I came over here, and I buzzed at the gate. I didn't come over here to hurt her, Whitney, I swear I didn't." She let out a strangled sob. "Nobody answered, but I knew she was in there. So, I hopped the security gate, and she got really mad about that. She was so mad that I jumped the gate." She paused like she was seeing it play out in front of herself. Her pupils moved quickly but her blinks were slow. "She got so mad that I'd climbed the fence. But what else was I supposed to do? I didn't know what else to do. What else can you do? I just . . . I just . . . what if, how come I—"

I had to stop her. "Brooke, sweetie, honey"—I said just like I was talking to a little girl—"is Julian okay?"

She snapped back. "I'd never hurt my baby. That's what you don't understand. That's what nobody understands. I just wanted him back. You can't take him. You can't take him from me."

"Can I see him?" I asked gently. "I'd just like to see him, okay? Just know that he's okay."

"He's fine," she said. Still angry. But I didn't believe her. Not for a second. I wanted to pray. This was when people with faith prayed. I had nothing. Nothing except a cold ball of fear in my gut.

"I'm going to set my phone on the sink, okay?" I said, moving while I talked. What was taking the paramedics so long? I raised my hands in the air like I was being arrested, but I wanted her to see how serious I was. That I'd surrendered. I just wanted to know if Julian was okay. Something good had to come out of this day. This couldn't end in complete annihilation. "Please, will you show me him? I'd feel better if you showed him to me."

She finally relented. She moved painfully slowly, like she didn't want him away from her. She peeled him back gradually. His big brown eyes blinked back at me, and I let out a small cry of relief.

"I told you I'd never hurt him."

"What'd you do to Abby?" I asked to the sound of sirens in the background.

"Ms. Gilmore"—the dispatcher's voice interrupted my question—"the first responders are on the site now. You've done a great job. They're going to be there to help her soon. Help everybody. You've done a great job."

CHAPTER FORTY-FOUR

NOW

WHITNEY

I sat on the edge of the couch after the police and paramedics had left the house. Shattered. Natasha was on her way to get me. I couldn't stay in this house. Not tonight. Maybe not ever again. I'd told Grace to stay at the park with Asher and not to come home. We'd pick him up on the way. I felt like a shell. All the life energy had been sucked out of me. How had my life blown up overnight?

Or had it all slowly unraveled the moment I started lying to Kiersten about Colin's gambling? Was that when this all started? When I inserted the first piece of dishonesty into my life? Can you live a dishonest life and still have good things happen to you? Or was it karmic punishment for not holding up your part of the bargain? Like God gave me this beautiful person to have a relationship with—someone tailor made specifically for me—and I screwed all that up by lying to her. The lie had set in motion all the other lies, until eventually it all became a house of cards.

God, I missed her. Colin hadn't been right about a lot of things, but he'd been right about one: she was my person. And I didn't know what I was going to do without her.

My phone vibrated with a call from Tommy. It was only a matter of time before he heard the news.

"Ohmigod, Whit, I don't know what to do," he said as soon as I answered.

"I know. It's unbelievable. I can't believe he'd do something like that."

"So, you knew?"

"No." I shook my head even though he couldn't see me. "I had no clue they were having an affair."

"Who?"

"Wait? What are you talking about?" He had to know about the affair. He was Colin's best friend.

"The baby's DNA test."

My stomach rolled. Just the way he said it, the heaviness in his voice let me know this day was going to keep getting worse. I sank into the couch. "The results are back in? Already? Thought they weren't supposed to be here for another two weeks."

"That's what they said, but for whatever reason, we got them. Remember when we were kids and there used to be the Jerry Springer show, where everyone was trying to figure out the baby's father?" He didn't wait for me to answer. "That's what this is. Some sick, twisted talk show joke." His voice cracked. "I'm not Rinley's biological father."

"What?" That was impossible. No way. Kiersten wouldn't have had an affair, and if by some remote possibility she had, I would've been the first person she told.

"You heard that right—Rinley's not my biological daughter."

"I'm so sorry, Tommy," I said, feeling the crushing weight of his pain through the phone. I was so numb from today. Or maybe I was just in shock. This was too much. Why didn't she tell me? Somewhere out there, Kiersten had a baby daddy. Did he know about the baby? That she was dead? How long had it been going on? But that didn't make any sense. How could she have gotten so upset with Jade for cheating if she was having an affair? And family meant everything to her. It's why we never talked about what I did. She loved me, but she hated what I did.

"Oh, it gets even more messed up than that," he said before my thoughts spiraled any further.

"What are you talking about?" Things couldn't get any worse.

"The baby wasn't hers either." He let out the most disturbed laugh.

"Have you been drinking?" Another laugh. Or maybe it was a cry. I couldn't tell.

"You heard that exactly right. I said the baby wasn't hers."

"That's not possible. She was pregnant." I shook my head.

"Yep, I had to have Perez walk me through it like five different times. Over and over again before it actually registered in my brain. She used somebody else's embryo."

"That makes no sense. Where did she get an embryo? Why wouldn't she tell us about it? Did she think you'd say no? That you wouldn't let her? And if that's the case, then fine. I get it, but why wouldn't she tell me? Even if she didn't tell you, she'd tell me," I thought out loud. My questions tumbling on top of each other faster than I could keep up.

"I don't know, Whitney. I don't know who the hell she was or what she was doing. That's what I'm trying to tell you."

I held the phone out in front of myself and tried to make sense of everything that had happened in the last twenty-four hours. Had everything and everyone in my life just been a lie? And for how long?

"I have to go," I said softly. I had no more breath. No air. No words.

I hit end and let my phone fall to the couch. The only person I wanted to call was gone. The one I'd processed every single major event in my life with since I was six years old. I never thought I'd be processing her. Did she have a secret life I knew nothing about? How could I have been so wrong about the people closest to me?

I shook my head. I refused to believe Kiersten had some secret double life. I knew her to her core. And I might be bad, but she was one of the few people who were good to their soul. Whatever she'd done, she had a reason. That much I was sure of because she was my best friend, and if you couldn't trust your best friend, could you really trust anyone?

CHAPTER
FORTY-FIVE
THEN
KIERSTEN

I hurried to the receptionist's desk and breathed an immediate sigh of relief that it was Josie. She'd been here the first time Whitney let me come with her to one of her treatments. Mrs. Fancy Pants Women's Clinic.

Code for: we can get people pregnant nobody else can.

And they did.

One of the few places in the city that offered at-home embryo transfers. They came at a price only a select few could afford to pay, but doing it in such a relaxed and comfortable atmosphere increased the likelihood of implantation by 12 percent.

That's why I was here.

"Hi, Josie," I said, going straight to her desk without wasting any time. She looked up, recognizing me immediately.

"Hi, Mrs. McCann."

"How's school? Did you pull off physics?" She was a premed student working as a medical receptionist part time to pay for it. She always looked tired.

"Oh my gosh, you remembered," she said, surprised. "That was like months ago."

Seven weeks exactly. The first time Whitney came back to start her first round of treatment for baby number two. Baby number two was proving to be even harder for her than baby number one.

"Of course I remembered. I remember how hard college was, especially those sciences." I batted my hand at her. Batted my eyelashes even harder. "I took astronomy my sophomore year because I thought it was going to be an easy science"—I gave her a dramatic look—"and girl, it ended up being one of the hardest classes I ever took. So much math. I don't know about you, but I absolutely hate math. I'm terrible at it. Anyway"—I continued without giving her a chance to interject or say anything—"I'm here to pick up Whitney's package. She really wanted to be able to pick it up herself, but she's not feeling well today. You know how those hormones affect her sometimes. She can't even get off the toilet. She just wants to do it at home with her midwife."

She raised her eyebrows at me. "The midwife is going to do the transfer at home?"

I nodded quickly so she didn't get hung up on that fact. "She's done it that way a few times before. They've got all the proper equipment set up. Do you want to call her?" I dug my phone out of my purse and pretended like I was pulling up her number.

Josie waved me off. "No, that's fine. I understand the doctor sees private clients."

I gave her a smile and waited as she pulled up the file in her computer. It'd been so easy to schedule the appointment. Just like I did before with Rinley.

Whit and I did everything together, so of course, we'd started trying to get pregnant at the same time too. We'd been planning our lives together since kindergarten. None of them included a version where we had trouble getting pregnant, but both of us did. That's why we ended up at the fertility clinic. Both of us patients. She's the one that got us on the list. One of her clients had a connection.

We had all the same tests. Needle jabs. Blood draws. Scans. Charted our cycles, all of it. Answered endless questions. But that's where our similarities ended.

Whitney was going to be able to get pregnant just fine, she was just going to need a little help.

My problem was a bit bigger. Way bigger. I could easily carry a baby. My uterus was in perfect shape. I just didn't have any eggs to put in it. All mine were dead. My periods were fake. It's why they'd always been so light. Who knew you could get fake periods?

I never meant to lie. I wasn't a liar. It just got away from me, and then once it did, it grew out of my hands, took on a life of its own. It all started with Tommy.

"Shouldn't you have had your fertility test results back?" he'd asked while we cleaned up after dinner.

It'd been exactly eight hours since the doctor called me and told me it was impossible for me to have biological children. My options were using a donor egg or adoption. He'd spelled it all out very clinically. And all I could think while he kept going over things was *I don't accept that.*

Maybe that's why the lie popped out so easily that night.

"Oh my gosh. I can't believe I forgot to tell you, but I got them yesterday. I'm good. For some reason, it's just taking me longer to get pregnant, but the doctor said not to worry about it," I told Tommy. He wrapped his arms around me and danced me around the kitchen. I'd never seen him so happy. He was practically beaming.

I spent the entire night telling myself to tell him the truth. Let him know what I'd found out. It's not like there weren't options. There were so many choices available to women that we didn't have before, but I just couldn't tell him. I couldn't say it. I just wanted things to be perfect. That's all.

Whitney was distraught over how tough it was going to be for her. Unlike me, her uterus was the problem. She had plenty of eggs, but her uterus wanted them dead. Between the two of us, we were a perfect pair. She with the healthy eggs and I with a good uterus.

I could've asked her to do it, and there wasn't a doubt in my mind that she'd say yes. Whitney would give her kidney if it meant helping me. We could've kept it a secret. We had lots of them. Nobody would've known unless we told them, but I didn't want anyone to know. Not even her. I gave people reason to believe everything was going to be okay. She was the best friend anyone could ever have. But it would've felt weird. Too weird. We were together almost every day, and would we ever forget that technically, my baby was half hers? And what if the two of them bonded? Then what would happen?

When she'd come to visit Rinley and me in the hospital after she'd been born, all my heart monitors went off because my blood pressure skyrocketed. All the nurses had rushed into the room to see what was the matter. They all thought it was related to the drops that happened postpartum, but I'd just handed my baby off to her biological mother and was terrified of what would happen. How deeply were our genetics for our parents embedded in our DNA? Would she recognize her?

But Rinley barely stirred. She was only a few hours old. You know how some people have kids that are a carbon copy of themselves? That's what I was afraid was going to happen. What if she looked identical to Whit? What would I do then?

She didn't. There were times that I saw it, though, even though she was only a few months old. She was just starting to give us her smiles, and something about her toothless grin had Whitney written all over it.

The receptionist grabbed the brown paper bag and handed it to me. I knew the drill. Forty-eight hours. I thanked her and hurried to my car.

Could I do this? A second time? Was I pushing the envelope? Asking too much?

But we wanted two. Two perfect kids in our perfect house to complete our perfect family. I set the bag on the seat next to me, placing it delicately in the small cooler. I seat belted the package in like it was a child. Once unfrozen, they had forty-eight hours before they went bad. An expiration date like milk.

Tommy was leaving at five, and he'd be gone all weekend. He was going with Colin to a music festival to see bands I'd never heard of. I'd gotten him the tickets for his birthday with the specific dates in mind. I'd already dropped Rinley off with my parents for the night. The midwife should be waiting for me when I got home.

And then I'd take a nice long hot bath. Just like I'd done before. Get nice and relaxed. Prepare myself.

Baby number two.

Fingers crossed. Here we go.

ACKNOWLEDGMENTS

Huge thanks to my publishing team at Thomas & Mercer and my agent, Christina Hogrebe. I appreciate all of you, and I'm so grateful we got to bring another book into the world. And to all my readers—new and old. I'd still write stories even if there was nobody to tell them to, but I'm glad you like them and enjoy being traumatized. Thanks for going with me on this wild ride.

ABOUT THE AUTHOR

Photo © 2020 Jocelyn Snowdon

Dr. Lucinda Berry is a former psychologist and leading researcher in childhood trauma. Now she writes full time, using her clinical experience to blur the line between fiction and nonfiction. She enjoys taking her readers on a journey through the dark recesses of the human psyche. Her work has been optioned for film and translated into multiple languages.

If Dr. Berry isn't chasing after her son, you can find her running through Los Angeles, prepping for her next marathon. To hear about her upcoming releases and other fun news, visit her on TikTok or sign up for her newsletter at https://lucindaberry.com.